From Barcelona

Stories Behind The City: Second Edition

Jeremy Holland

Dedicated to the people of Barcelona, both Catalans and Spanish. You deserve better leaders.

Acknowledgements

If you're reading this, thank you.

This book would not be possible without the support of Jo Parfitt and everybody at Summertime Publishing who have given me a chance to revisit some old stories and add new tales. A special thanks also to Debbie Jenkins for publishing the original volume and Ira Shull for helping me hone my craft.

To my wife, Guillermina. Thank you for your endless patience and support. Hopefully, it will not be in vain.

More than any one person, however, I would like to thank the people of Barcelona, past and present, who have made the city it is. *Moltes gràcies / muchísimas gracias* for providing the inspiration behind these stories. If I tease, it's only with love, mixed with a bit of sadness. I will never forget my eight years there and hold Catalunya close to my heart.

Un petó molt gran per tot / un beso enorme por todo.

Jeremy Holland
June 2012

Praise

Foreword

Barcelona is a city that, since its 'rejuvenation' for the 1992 Olympic Games and the advent of cheap flights and weekend city breaks, has become one of the tourist 'hot spots' of Europe. Gaudí, Las Ramblas, the Barri Gòtic and pickpockets loom large in the minds of most foreigners along with Catalan nationalism and Barça's sublime football.

But the nature of city breaks is that you do not get under the skin of a city, any city. Barcelona is steeped in history and culture as well as being a modern and cosmopolitan city which has, until recent times, been the cultural and economic powerhouse of Spain, even before Spain was united under Isabel and Ferdinand.

Both my parents are Spanish, though they moved to England in the 1950s, and I have now lived permanently in Spain for 10 years myself. This series of short stories not only captures the essence of modern Barcelona from the perspective of the Catalans themselves and foreigners living and working there but also provides valuable historical lessons.

Each modern day story demonstrates the strengths, weaknesses and realities of living in a modern city as well as the difficulty of living and working in Spain, as a Spaniard or foreigner. For example, *One Step Forward, Three Steps Back* highlights the frustrations of dealing with local bureaucracy in an entertaining, but realistic, manner. Likewise, *Mónica & Juan* shows the economic difficulties faced by normal working Spaniards following the recent economic boom and bust, while there are also stories about love (*A Book for a Rose*) and crime (*CSI Barcelona*). The collection also brings together many threads of the Spanish character, from the harshness of the spoken word, to the hard working Catalans versus their perception that those from the south of Spain are only interested in flamenco, sangria and siesta.

The historical stories provide colour and context, for example *Senyor Jordi i el Drac* (*George and the Dragon*), St George being Catalunya's patron saint (and the donkey its national animal!) and *Gaudí's Crypt* both inform and entertain. The latter covers important aspects of late 19th century Barcelona in addition to Gaudí's nationalism and religious fervour.

But these are not 'heavy' stories, they are entertaining and well written as well as being insightful and informative – a rare combination.

When asked to write this foreword I had no intention of reading every story but soon found myself drawn in by Jeremy Holland's writing and insight into Barcelona, its people and the valuable lessons each story offers. I cannot recommend the book highly enough.

Rod Younger
www.Books4Spain.com

Contents

Just Landed

Every guidebook about Barcelona said, "The first place you should visit is the city's historical heart, Las Ramblas and the Gothic Quarter." These oracles of local knowledge also suggested the metro as a more economic and authentic alternative to a taxi. They must know. They're the experts, right? Me? I hadn't a clue how to get around. It was my first time in Spain. My choice of Barcelona over Madrid had come down to which one was closest to a beach.

I wondered whether I could walk to the Mediterranean Sea from the bottom of Las Ramblas as I sat down on a bench in the middle of an empty platform. The overhead lighting was blinding, the type you'd expect in a police interrogation room. The air trapped in the underground tunnels had condensed into a searing mist that burned the skin and heated the metal seat under me. None of the guidebooks I had read compared taking the public transit to visiting the seventh circle of Dante's Inferno and I began to think travel-writers were nothing but paid hacks who only highlighted the positives of their assigned locations.

Over my left shoulder, a black screen hung from the low ceiling. I used my bicep to wipe the sweat stinging my eyes and looked up to see what the yellow letters and numbers had to say.

Proper Tren 3:04min.

My mind puzzled over a linguistic mystery to distract

me from the suffocating heat. High school Spanish had taught me that *próximo* was the word for "next" while *propio* meant "own." What type of train was set to arrive in three minutes, four seconds? I decided it must be a "proper one," which stopped at all of the stations, unlike say, the express services in New York or London. A perfectly logical theory for a Spanish city, right?

The familiar sound of flip-flops echoed off the white walls, reflecting the harsh overhead light. I squinted and peered across the train tracks to see a raven-haired girl in a loose white dress sit down on the metal bench directly opposite me. Even in the murky yellow haze of the metro inferno, she cut a cool and angelic figure, making her far more attractive than the airbrushed model on the poster next to her.

Maybe the guidebooks had been right after all. Maybe using the public transit wasn't such a bad idea. How many novels, movies and anecdotes have starred lovers who were once strangers before crossing eyes at a train station? It was almost enough to be classified as cliché.

The girl's sultry gaze sliced through the searing mist and popped the bubble that always surrounded me when I got lost in my thoughts. I could've been suffering hallucinations from heatstroke, but I swore she even smirked at me. Her dark features exuded Spanish sensuality, like a flamenco dancer, and hope clapped an uplifting song in my head.

A gust of wind blew away the four-step beat, drying the sweat pouring from my hairline. My ears cringed from the squeal of metal wheels grinding to a stop on metal rails. Sparks from the friction flew under the sleek carriages until they parked and blocked my view. The clangor of high-pitched beeps, sliding doors and hurried footsteps, shook the dense air and I glanced at the clock above my shoulder to see how long until I could expect such commotion.

Proper Tren 1:08min.

I looked back across the tracks. The train jerked and rose on its wheels. The string of polished white carriages then sped toward the next station, leaving the metal bench across from me empty, the girl but a visceral memory.

More flip-flops slapped against the stone ground. Locals descended the stairs on either side of the platform where I sat. Most spoke Spanish with a severe lisp. Others seemed to communicate in a hybrid language, some sort of Spanish, French and Italian mix. I couldn't be sure what it was. I wasn't a linguist and all the books I had read about Barcelona were in English, written by so-called city experts who had failed to warn me to avoid the broiling metro in summer, at all cost.

The sighting of the girl in the white dress did stimulate the single male in me, though. The lonely guy who had come to Spain to get over an ex-girlfriend and an all around bad relationship. Men no longer appeared in my line of vision. Nor did affectionate couples or leathery women old enough to be my former high-school Spanish teacher.

Only more brown skinned, dark haired girls, in colorful short-shorts and tank-tops, manifested before my eyes. They were all petite and curvy, with a sexy swish to their strut. Not one was as attractive as *la señorita* in the white dress, though. And I sighed, breathing in steam, as if I stood over a whistling kettle.

Another refreshing blast of wind rumbled down the tunnel. I cast a quick glance at my old friend the clock to confirm this was my "proper" train.

ENTRA, it said.

My eyes swung to see the box-shaped engine whiz by. A chain of five rectangular carriages raced behind it before screeching to an abrupt stop. Rapid-fire, high-pitched beeps shot a sense of urgency into me. I jumped off my bench and jogged to the metro doors. The metal handles turned up. People flooded out, shoving me to the side, as if I were the one outside of their line of sight, making me wonder whether it was bad karma to ogle at pretty girls.

A boy in Bermuda shorts was the last to leave and at his exit, I stepped into a dirty-white carriage illuminated by flickering strip-bulbs. A rickety air-conditioner wheezed warm air on standing passengers. The breeze stirred the fog of cologne and body odor that was thick enough to clog my nose. I reached for a life-line. A strap. A rail. Anything to hold on to, to keep my head above the foul bog of local commuters and fellow tourists. Grooves in the metal ceiling were deep and wide enough for my finger tips. I felt the dull edges dig into my skin as the carriage jerked and swerved down a dark tunnel.

At a luminous Plaça Catalunya, everyone stampeded out. I followed the crowd down the platform, up wide stairs and through shoulder-high sliding doors. A short passageway led to the circular heart of the metro station, where music filled the dusky air and a domed ceiling, colored green by sparkling mosaics, sat atop charcoal-colored walls.

My head turned toward the source of the scratchy falsetto. A guy in camouflage cargo-pants strummed Radiohead on an acoustic guitar. He lacked Thom Yorke's tune and range, but the harried commuters rewarded the performer's sincerity by tossing coins into a dusty cap at his feet.

I looked for an exit but saw only more frazzled faces as people scurried up and down stairs, toward the metro entrance or into a bright bar with a glass windowpane. The chaotic scene spun my head to an acoustic rendition of the song *Karma Police* until my eyes latched onto a bronze sign that said, "Las Ramblas."

As an escalator took me above ground, sunlight moved from my hand to my forearm, resting on the moving handrail. The jolt that preceded a grand entrance pulsed through my veins when the murky subterranean light lifted in its entirety. A steady stream of conversations in different foreign languages grew from a murmur to a cacophony. By the time I reached street level and stepped off the mechanical stairs, I couldn't even hear the deep breath I took. But I could still see and my neck craned as I gazed at elegant stone buildings with black iron balconies, glistening in the late morning sun.

The glare stung my eyes. I blinked and lowered my sights. Camouflage-colored tree trunks with spindly branches and green leaves shaded a pedestrian promenade. One-way streets on either side buzzed as if they were avenues from the volume of scooters, buses and cars. The sandy pavement beneath my feet was solid, but gave the optical illusion of walking on waves, which was appropriate, because it was the only word to describe the situation.

The first wave of tourists crashed into my shoulders on their way to the metro station's escalators and steps. Other visitors knocked into my back as they rushed to join the sea of people, stretching as far as the horizon. Unable to get my bearings, I felt the undertow of the crowd sweep me away, taking my flailing body down one of the 100-places you had to visit before you died, according to a popular Facebook app.

The drowning sensation ebbed and I caught my first breath as I passed a man covered in thick white paint. He sat completely motionless on a toilet atop a wooden box. The humidity leaked through my clothes and latched to my skin, like droplet-sized leeches which fed on life energy, not blood. How the hell was he not sweating enough for his costume to melt?

I had no time to stop and ponder whether the locals might have a heat resistant gene. A new tide of people carried me forward. Chirps and whistles from the blue stands selling caged animals pierced the blend of babbling conversations and stop-and-go traffic. My nose wiggled to sooth an itch from the pollen of blooming flowers on florists' shelves while my eyes glanced at artists, sketching cartoon faces and celebrity portraits.

Amid this medley of sights, smells and sounds, I spotted a familiar image. In the window of a red kiosk was a poster of a black and white donkey. I wondered whether the animal's popularity had anything to do with the locals preferring Democrats to Republicans. The more I thought about it the more I didn't like that theory. Why would Barcelona's residents publicly support a US political party? They had their own, right? There had to be another reason behind the ass's importance to the Spanish.

I needed to pause and slow my overstimulated, jet-lagged mind. I stood on my toes to see where Las Ramblas ended. It didn't. There was nothing but wavy lines of tourists, vendor stands, human statues and trees, for what seemed like miles into the distance. To my left, past the one-way street flanking the promenade, I spied a sign in a restaurant window, pitching typical Spanish food and air-conditioning.

The place had the lighting and charm of a hospital

cafeteria. There were plenty of free tables available in the main dining section, but I had always found it less lonely to eat at the bar when dining for one. All of the stools along the wood-trimmed counter were available so I pulled one out and sat in front of glass case that covered plates of small fish, chopped meat, and diced potatoes, along with a couple of fat flies.

Like many restaurants in the US, the waiting staff seemed to be non local, although from China and Pakistan, rather than Central America.

"What have you got for breakfast?" I asked the Chinese waiter, hoping his answer was scrambled eggs, bacon and French toast, not the food on display.

He pointed to a single croissant and a pack of doughnuts under another glass case, this one by an old-style cash register.

I wanted something more substantial before my big day sight-seeing. "Any eggs?" I asked.

He nodded.

I prodded, "And bacon?"

"*Plato combinado* number fou'." The Chinese waiter thumbed over his shoulder at a large black board high on the wall. He hadn't pointed it out earlier so I figured the neatly written chalk letters gave the different lunch, not breakfast, specials. The fourth from the top read: *ous fregits, beicon i patates fregides / huevos fritos, beicon y patatas fritas.*

I told him, "One of those."

"To drink?" he asked.

"Orange juice and coffee when you get a chance."

"You want coffee *now*?" The Chinese waiter's incredulous tone provoked his Pakistani colleague to shoot me a concerned look at my mental well-being.

I felt like I was back on the steamy metro platform

again from all of the unwanted attention. I gulped and nodded before checking out the other customers to see what *faux pas* I had committed.

A family spoke in German over baguettes and soda bottles at a table with a view of the sidewalk. Near them two women chatted loudly in lispy Spanish over small cups of coffee and empty plates. They caught me staring and smiled. The women were old enough to be my former Spanish teacher, but things like this didn't happen to me at home. I smiled back, sensing a warm vibe in the air, despite the arctic blast from an overhead vent, drying my sweat-soaked hair.

"You wan' *thoomo natural* or *bo'ella*?"

The Chinese waiter's accented English interrupted the moment. I turned away from *las señoras* and said, "*Natural por favor,*" feeling proud at how much Spanish was coming back after a ten year hiatus.

Five minutes later, my waiter returned with the complete order and a scowl. "Here you go," he said, setting down a plate with two fried eggs, two strips of bacon and a handful of French fries. The coffee wasn't the watery drip variety, but espresso with milk served in a teacup rather than a soup bowl, like in the US. The freshly squeezed orange juice, meanwhile, came in a champagne glass, with a pack of sugar and small spoon, on a saucer.

I sipped the drink to make sure my waiter hadn't accidentally brought me a mimosa and tasted nothing but sour pulp.

"Ketchup?" he asked.

"No, thanks," I said, beginning to saw at the tough bacon. "Just pepper."

Another befuddled look at my request before the Chinese waiter disappeared into the kitchen.

The meal was greasy and had little flavor or spice, but left my stomach full and satisfied. I called for the check and did a quick conversion from euros to dollars. Spain wasn't Mexico cheap, but the American in me made sure that I left a 15 per cent tip, regardless of the less than chipper service.

I stepped from the air-conditioned restaurant, into an air that felt even hotter and muggier than before. From this perspective, the world famous Las Ramblas seemed to consist solely of the backs of vendor stands and human statues, spaced between camouflage-colored trunks of leafy trees. The thousands of tourists were less individuals than a single moving organism that swallowed everything in its path as spectators looked down from the ornate balconies and windows of hotels, tattoo parlors and language schools.

I stuck to the less congested sidewalk. Large windowpanes displayed *I heart Barcelona* t-shirts, Mexican sombreros and Barça Football Club jerseys. A revolving wooden door tossed out a confused guest from a five-star hotel located between two restaurants where Pakistani waiters stood outside, chanting: "Paella, tapas and sangría."

After an arched arcade, I walked down a short set of stairs that led to a narrow cobblestone street. The four-story buildings on either side seemed as tall as towers and blocked out the overhead sun. More shop windows, with decorative fans, elaborate scarves and the finest Spanish swords and leather, populated the shaded ground level. The wooden shutters belonging to the apartments above were closed. The only sign of life was a random potted plant, bicycle or clothes rack behind the black railings of a two-foot wide balcony.

A quick check of the guidebook I kept in my back

pocket confirmed that I had now entered Barcelona's legendary Gothic Quarter, which dated back to Roman times, but came of age during the 14th century. There just weren't neighborhoods this old back in the US, except for Indian burial grounds. I felt the telluric forces radiating from the blackened stones. The stories embedded in the bricks and mortar seeped into my muscles and bones. The name of a tavern written in golden letters caught my eye. I stopped and wondered whether I was at the doorstep of an old haunt of past Barcelona residents, like Picasso, Orwell and Hemingway.

In need of answers, I took out the guidebook again, flipped through the pages and stopped at the "Eating Out" section, to see that I had circled the location during my pre-vacation research.

Irati was a popular place whose specialty was food from the Basque region. There was no mention of famous patrons, but the menu was classified as affordable, with the house cider receiving a special mention.

Apples were one of my favorite fruits while no front wall offered a clear perspective of the diners. They were squashed between the bar and the wall, eating and drinking, with their arms tucked in like chicken wings. The cramped situation looked like my stomach felt—uncomfortable.

I realized when the reviewer wrote, "popular," he or she meant, "packed." I slipped the guidebook back in my pocket and opted to rely on my instincts from now on.

I dipped down the first alley to escape tourists who bought souvenirs. An approaching group of Italians in designer sunglasses forced me to take another right, then a left to avoid some precarious scaffolding.

As I journeyed deeper into the Gothic Quarter, the air grew murkier and the temperature dropped. The distance between soot stained walls was barely wider than a corridor and there were no windows at ground level — only closed metal shutters and doors, with piles of trash and discarded furniture out front.

Midway down an alley, I looked up to see a tarp with a picture of a urinating stick-figure crossed-out. The sign was big enough to span the alley, but I knew such an image wouldn't be in the guidebook. I pulled it out anyway, hoping the maps inside might help me figure out where the hell I was.

At the end of Gothic Quarter section was a plan with the main streets and nothing more. Even if it had been detailed, it wouldn't have mattered — the alley I was on didn't have a name for a reference point. I slipped the guidebook back in my pocket. My ears perked to listen for someone to ask directions on how to get back to the comforting chaos of Las Ramblas.

The only noises I heard were my increasingly panicked breaths and footsteps as I passed the same nondescript buildings and marched down the same narrow alleys that turned and dead ended. I was about to say, "Fuck it," and sit down and wait for someone to find my lost self, when a flash of light stung my eyes.

It was a miracle. A smudged window under a raised shutter caught rays of a sun I still couldn't see above the rooftops. I pushed open the creaky door and ducked my head to avoid the low clearance. The first step down felt like a steep drop. My right knee buckled from the surprise when my foot hit the stone floor and I stumbled into a room full of ancient leather treatises and used paperbacks crammed into ceiling-high bookshelves.

A cough sent ripples through an air that was only a few degrees cooler and slightly less dense than in the metro. I turned toward the sound and saw a wiry man emerge from a dark backroom, into an ashen light, the same color as his skin. He wore his loose shirt unbuttoned to reveal a smooth chest, his gray hair wild on the sides of an otherwise bald head.

"J-es?" he asked. His cloudy blue eyes narrowed, causing round glasses to slip down a pronounced Roman nose.

I smiled politely and said, "Just looking around. You got a lot of interesting books here," feeling elated to be conversing with a human being who spoke accented English, instead of my increasingly hysterical thoughts as I searched for a way out of the labyrinthine Gothic Quarter.

"Yes, this is a bookstore." The man's gruff tone called me an idiot for stating the obvious. "But only in Spanish and Catalan. Do you know Catalan?"

I had come across something about it in the guidebooks, but preferred to spend my pre-vacation time, investigating the best places in Barcelona to eat tapas, hear flamenco music and pick up women. "Um, no," I muttered, feeling embarrassed by the shallowness of my recent life choices.

The bookseller's stare bordered on contempt at my admission of ignorance. He stormed around the desk and picked a random book from the shelf.

"*This* is Catalan," he declared, pointing at the leather cover and embroidered golden letters that read—*El Senyor Jordi i el Drac.*

"Is it about Dracula?" I blurted the first theory that came to mind because my teachers had always said, "There's no such thing as a stupid question."

The bookseller yelped in astonishment at my suggestion, shaking his head in frustration. "No! This title is *in* Catalan. It's the language of *Catalunya*. That is where you are!"

"Thought I was in Spain."

His eyes darkened and squinted at what seemed to be a serious cultural error on my end.

"What's the book about?" I asked, hoping to ease the tension.

"Saint George and the dragon. He's our patron saint."

I felt pleased. I had heard of him before. "Isn't that the same saint as England?"

"Yes, and the country of Georgia." The bookseller dug something from his long nose, which he then flicked to the ground before he sneered, "You must be American."

"What makes you say that?" I asked, wondering what had tipped him off. I wore no white socks, no baseball cap, no Hawaiian shirt, just cargo shorts, flip-flops and a baby-blue polo.

"You have no sense of history." The bookseller's voice rose with the exacerbation. "No one in the United States knows about *Catalunya*. We were once a great nation. We sailed the Mediterranean and conquered Sardinia!"

"That's part of Italy now, right?" I thought my question showed I knew a little something about European geography until I watched the man's upper lip curl in disgust again.

My entire body heated at the realization I was re-enforcing the ugly American stereotype.

"What happened?" I asked, looking to win the offended bookseller over by showing interest in this apparently very important topic of *Catalunya*. "Did Spain conquer you guys?"

He shook his head and said, "The King of *Aragón* married the Queen of *Castilla* in 1469, uniting the Iberian Peninsula. There was a famous opera about them." He stopped and studied the blank expression my face assumed whenever I was about to receive a history lesson.

"Did you know September 11th is our National Day?" he asked, not pausing long enough for me to answer, because he probably knew my reply would be *no*. "It's when we celebrate losing the Spanish War of Succession in 1714." The bookseller sighed a heavy sigh and his pale eyes misted before he added, "It's a tragic date, no?"

I nodded and grinned to hide the sadness I felt in my molars when I thought about how much had changed since that sunny day in New York.

"Do you know Barcelona?" the bookseller asked.

"Not well," I told him, feeling relieved we had moved on to a lighter topic of conversation. "It's my first day."

He stopped and hummed before he suggested, "There's a good Catalan restaurant near here. You must try it."

I wanted to show him that I wasn't a total ignoramus and asked if the place served those famous Spanish tapas I had read about. "You know the ones," I added, gesturing with my thumb and index finger. "The little pieces of bread with fish and toothpicks."

The bookseller's aged face crinkled as he tried to place my animated description. "No," he said, his leery expression hinting at the possibility of second thoughts when it came to taking me somewhere to eat. "Those are *pintxos* from the Basque country. Follow me. I will show you what Catalan food is."

I was glad this gruff old man hadn't changed his mind. This was starting to feel like an adventure and he ushered me outside the bookshop to find cobblestones bathed in light as the orange sun appeared in the blue sky for the first time since I had entered Barcelona's medieval Gothic Quarter.

The bookseller turned the sign in the window to *Tancat*, locked the door and pulled the shutter half-way down. "Come on," he commanded, clutching my wrist.

He walked at a quick pace that explained his trim figure. I struggled to keep my shins from tangling as he dragged me through twisting and meandering streets and alleys, with the confidence of someone who had grown up there. When he finally let go of my sore wrist bone, I was even more disoriented than before. I caught a glimpse of an intergalactic mural spray-painted on a closed shutter and picturesque flowers draped over balcony railings, but my bewildered mind lacked the cognitive ability to appreciate the scenery.

The bookseller stopped at an open door. "Here we are," he announced, with a welcoming smile and wave.

I glanced at a dust-caked window. All of my cerebral processes were up and functioning again, but the burst of exercise had shaken loose my stomach contents and I asked, "Where's the restroom?" while tightening my Glutei Maximi.

The bookseller looked confused by my word choice. "Eh?"

I started to bounce from the building pressure in my colon. "*El baño*," I snapped, remembering the Spanish word for bathroom.

"Oh, *el lavabo*," he corrected, pointing through the open door. "At the far back."

The restaurant was dank and the humid mist of cooking oil seeped through my clothes. I sprinted under wooden ceiling beams that brushed my scalp toward a sink with no mirror. On either side was a door. One was labeled *Homes*, the other *Dones*. Each looked more like the entrance to a walk-in closet than a bathroom stall.

The non-Spanish vocabulary presented another

linguistic puzzle. The restless noises in my intestinal tract sped up my thought processes:

Dones is to "Dame," what *Homes* is to *"Homie."*

I pushed that door. It banged against a toilet bowl. The space to enter was narrower than my thigh. A sense of urgency burbled in my midsection. I twisted my body sideways. First my shoulders, then my torso, finally my head, squeezed through a crack that led to pitch-blackness, except for a glowing orange button.

I pressed it. A bright light shined; a ticking began. Stone walls brushed my shoulders as I turned around in tight confines to put down a plastic seat, which wasn't there. My bowels now shook from the blob of eggs, fries, bacon, juice and coffee, that pounded and growled to burst out of my rectum and into my boxers. I snatched some stiff toilet paper to wipe the brown spotted porcelain. The jingle from the euro coins in my pocket bounced off the encroaching walls. I unbuckled my belt, dropped my shorts and squatted, just as the ticking stopped; the timed light cut.

There were no towels in the rusted dispenser above the sink so I dried my washed hands on my polo shirt. The bookseller sat at the end of the bar, near the dusty window. He caught sight of me and burst into laughter, as if I had just returned from running into a bully who had given me a swirly.

I wondered whether lack of tact was a Catalan or Spanish trait and snapped, "What is it?" sitting down next to him.

"I have seen that green look many times," the bookseller said it like a boast. "You aren't used to so much oil when you cook food."

"What do you mean?" I was curious to know if my

current funny tummy had a story behind it, like Mexico's Montezuma's Revenge.

"In the United States you cook everything with butter," the bookseller stated this with absolute certainty. "That's why you are all so fat."

"Think that's the English who love butter," I told him, no one I knew used it to cook. "We sometimes use lard, but mostly we use this spray called *Pam* to grease pans."

The bookseller gave me the same dumb look he received after mentioning *Catalunya* for the first time. "Anyway," he said, "this isn't South America or Morocco. You won't have the shits for more than one day."

The direction of our conversation didn't help my delicate situation. "Okay," I smiled to cover up a wince, "but can we talk about something else?"

The bookseller smacked the bar counter and laughed at me again. "What?" he shouted, his voice full of feigned insult, as he shoved my shoulder in jest. "You don't like talking about shit?"

"Not where I eat."

Another hearty chuckle at my response. "*Escatological* humor is part of Catalan culture, like Gaudí and *butifarra*." He waved at the thick blood sausages, hanging from the ceiling. They ranged in color from white to sepia to black and were the size of well-fed pythons, but smaller than the severed pig's leg, which dangled by the hoof from a nearby wooden beam.

I took a deep breath of hot air and tasted a hint of salt, along with the cooking oil responsible for my stomach's shaky status. I really wished there had been better guidebooks, ones which had explained that there had once been a Kingdom of *Aragón*, now known as *Catalunya*, and its people liked to talk about defecating, even in restaurants with more raw meat than butcher shops.

"Do you know *El Caganer?*" The bookseller's voice broke my concentration as I searched for something to add to the toilet-centric conversation.

I shook my head to admit my ignorance again and saw a warm smile on the elderly man's face rather than his usual disgusted frown. "He's a figurine of someone shitting we hide in the Nativity Scene. If you find him, you'll have good luck next year."

"Seriously?" I couldn't resist the pun, "You're shitting me?"

Silence following a joke that had fallen flat in translation.

"What do you want to eat?" The bookseller's question ended another awkward moment between us and he nodded at the gaunt bartender who watched a TV in the corner of the bar.

I wasn't hungry before the trip to the bathroom and certainly not after learning there were people in this world who celebrated human waste during the Christmas holidays. "Actually, just had breakfast," I said, worried the truth might offend this proud Catalan patriot.

"You want a beer?" His tone chirped with anxiousness that bordered on eagerness. "We, Catalans, have a reputation for being cheap, like the Jews, but not all of us are."

The man might have worn his shirt unbuttoned like a young stud, but he dropped politically incorrect stereotypes with the same ease as my redneck grandfather.

I smirked at the bookseller's lack of tact and said, "Sure. Why not?"

He barked at the bartender who glowered at being

called away from his TV program.

"*¿Qué?*"

"*Dues cerveses, si us plau.*"

That must mean, "two beers, please," in Catalan, I thought, repeating the phrase in my head until the bartender gave me an amber lager in a perspiring snifter-shaped glass.

The beer had more body and bite than the watery mass-market brews sold in the US and lubricated my unsettled stomach. I asked the bookseller if he lived nearby and got laughed at again for asking another apparently stupid question.

"Only immigrants and *guiris* live in *Barri Gòtic*," he said. "I live outside Barcelona and away from the noise and stress."

I wondered whether *guiri* was Spain's version of "gringo," but didn't want to get mocked for not knowing again so I shut up and sipped my beer.

"Listen." The bookseller's expression grew serious as he tossed change onto the counter. "I must get home for lunch or my wife will kill me. Then back to work." He glanced at the disinterested bartender. "Jordi will take good care of you. Enjoy your stay."

I was going to miss this old man, rough edges and all. Twenty minutes with him had taught me more about Barcelona than any of the guidebooks I had read. I picked up the chilled glass between my middle and ring finger. "Here's to you and *Catalunya*," I toasted. "Thanks for showing me this side of the city."

"How do you say *de nada* in English?" he asked.

I was surprised the bookseller didn't know the simple phrase but left that unsaid. "You're welcome."

"In Catalan it's *de res.*"

"How do you say 'goodbye' in Catalan?" I wanted to

continue our language exchange.

"*Adéu,*" the bookseller belted, with a final stately wave, leaving his barely touched beer and me with a bartender who could have played the butler in a Catalan version of a TV series set in a Gothic mansion.

I finished my drink in three swallows, burped and left the bar. It was time to meet some fellow tourists or better yet, a *Barcelonian,* like the girl in the white dress whom I could impress with my new-found knowledge of the area. Left lurked the tangled knot of tiny streets known locally as *Barri Gòtic.* To my right, a wall of light marked the end of the dark alley.

I emerged from the cool shadows to feel the heat of a fiery sun, beating down on a square tucked in the middle of buildings. The only shade was provided by a church whose imposing stone walls towered above the one spindly tree. There was little in the way of engraved decoration, making the monument to God almost utilitarian, especially compared to the intricate designs of the *Sagrada Família,* on the cover of the guidebook, I pulled out.

Continuing the negative trend, none of the sections listed the church or offered much on the square. After the encounter with the bookseller, I realized I didn't want to be the typical ugly American anymore. This vacation wasn't just about chasing skirts in an attempt to overcome heartache, but also getting some culture, discovering a world that didn't exist in the US. There was so much to learn about Barcelona, *Catalunya* and Spain. Why not take a moment to experience its history? Maybe, despite all evidence to the contrary, God did exist. Maybe He'd even reward my enlightened decision and lead me to a girl who looked like the one in the white dress?

I didn't really believe any of that or in the Holy

Trinity, but I respected the buildings religion had inspired ordinary people to create. The silent church made me feel like a gurgling infant under its vaulted ceilings. Beams of light sprayed through the rose stained-glass window above the main entrance, the colored rays guiding my eyes to the wooden statues hidden in the dark recesses of the walls.

The air felt thicker as I approached carved figures of Jesus and the Virgin Mary, adorned with enough gold leaf, to shimmer in the dusky light. The detail of their painted expressions conveyed the hope of a new mother and the serene suffering of a martyr with artistic precision and dedication. In front of each display candles burned in red cases on metal stands. The number of flames varied, as if they were votes, with the bloodiest and most gut-wrenching Passion Scene, receiving the most light.

The painstaking craftsmanship moved me to donate a euro for a candle. I chose to pay my respects to the mythological being, known as Our Lord, at the Nativity Scene, hoping the one joyous moment in the medieval church would bring me a bit of romantic luck before the end of my week trip to Barcelona.

The image of the crucifixion everywhere made me realize that it was time for a less solemn atmosphere and I headed toward a small door within an imposing arched door. The blistering sun singed my corneas, forcing my eyes to shut, when I stepped onto the top of stairs that led to the square below. The brouhaha from English tourists, singing and slamming jugs of beer, jarred my ears. I squinted and watched as other customers, under white umbrellas, cringed and fled the inebriated celebration.

I walked down the steps, full of patriotic pride.

Americans might have a reputation for being ignorant and obtuse, but at least we weren't thought of as drunken palookas.

A summery breeze blew a leaf across the ground, but I shivered from the chill. I turned to face the source of the disturbance and watched a door open and shut beneath a glistening forest green sign with wooden trim. Time for the guidebook again. If it actually broke out its slump and provided me with something useful, I might change my religious affiliation from atheist to agnostic.

Not only was the locale in the "Eating Out" section, but I had circled it and put a star.

Bar del Pi dated back to the eighteenth century and was famous for exhibiting art from Barcelona's bohemian heyday.

Inside, the front bar was small, but airy. At the back, five steps led to a tiny sunken saloon, with tables and a small piano. A steep metal ladder offered views from a loft with more seating. There were few customers, but the noise level of their conversation made the bar seem bustling.

I turned to see bottles on wooden and mirrored shelves vanish into a bright light. In my sights was the girl in the white dress, now wearing a typical black and white server's uniform.

Well, I'll be damned. It seemed that there really was a higher being who controlled everything and His, or Her, intervention was to lead to a Hollywood ending, not even half way through my first day in Barcelona. A big smile lifted my cheeks as I pulled out a stool to sit down at the bar counter.

The girl's full lips smirked, suggesting she might remember me, too. Time to impress her with my knowledge of the local lingo. "*Una cervesa, si us plau,*" I ordered, giving equal emphasis to each word.

"*¿Qué?*"

Was it the pronunciation or did I say the phrase incorrectly? Play it safe, I decided. Stick to English. "Beer, please."

I felt her dark eyes studying me while she filled a large jug to the brim. Images of girls, dancing in bright floral dresses to the rhythm of Spanish guitars, played in my mind before I spotted another sign of divine intervention—a sticker of the same black and white donkey I had seen in the kiosk's window.

"I have a question," I said, looking to chat the girl up, with a little light banter.

"What?" Her grin offset her harsh tone as she set a frothy jug of beer on a coaster.

"What's the deal with the donkey?" I pointed at the sticker on the old-style cash register for a visual aid.

"It's the national animal of *Catalunya.*"

"Are you Catalan?"

The girl's expression twisted and darkened, like the bookseller's when I mentioned Barcelona being in Spain. "Argentinian," she hissed before her features softened again. "Sorry. I speak very little English. Do you speak Spanish?"

"*Un poco,*" I replied, hoping my most charming smile soothed her ruffled feathers.

I got her to smirk again, but not in the way I had wanted. Her taut lips were the equivalent of a blow-off kiss and a wave. The only thing missing when she walked away was the "wa wa waaaa" game shows blared before expelling their losing contestants. Not that I could have heard the mocking harmony over the disquiet in my belly as breakfast made rumblings about a second act.

Senyor Jordi i el Drac

On April 23rd, 303 AD, a knight and his teenage squire rode their horses to the click, clack of hooves, moseying down a barren and windswept mountain. They had been traveling to this lulling beat for weeks and the squire began to nod off when a woman's shriek pierced his eardrums, jolting him awake.

"Wha... what was... what was that, *Senyor* Jordi?" the squire stammered, feeling the blood drain from his cheeks, as he stroked the mane of his braying horse, Nano.

"There is only one cry powerful enough to reach us up here, my dear Jaume," the knight said. "And that is the cry of a mother who has lost her child."

Senyor Jordi took off his dented galea helmet, fitting the red crest on top under his arm. His large brown eyes squinted as he peered down his hook nose. Over the top of a black forest stood a walled village on a small hill. Montblanc was his childhood home and the knight's return marked the end of an odyssey that had taken him, from the front lines of war to prison, on the same Emperor's orders in whose name he had fought.

"Come on," *Senyor* Jordi said, with a heavy sigh, wanting to rest and heal, not fight whatever terrorized his village. "Let's see what's going on."

"Are you sure?" Jaume asked. "Why don't we go north to Barcelona instead?"

"Of course, I'm sure," the knight snapped. "I have not

speared men with my sword and watched life leave their eyes to then turn around and do nothing when I hear such suffering."

"Yes, I know..." Jaume paused to collect his thoughts. His teeth ached from the unease he felt, "but something tells me you shouldn't go home."

"Boy, how many times have I told you that one must fight for what one wants?" *Senyor* Jordi huffed and placed the crested helmet on his head before taking the reins of his white stallion. "Come on, Anici," he ordered, signaling an end to the discussion. "Let's go."

Jaume moaned and followed his master down a path no wider than a horse's shoulders. The trail snaked down the treacherous mountain face, making it seem as if they went mostly sideways. The squire dared not breathe, fearing the slightest disturbance might send him off the cliff, which seemed to be constantly on one side.

It wasn't until the slope straightened and flattened that Jaume spoke again. "*Senyor* Jordi," he yelled, as they approached the first row of dead trees of what had once been a lush forest.

"What?" His master didn't bother to turn around.

"Should we not rest here for a bit?"

"Jaume, if you wish to go back, by all means, go ahead. Tilt at a few windmills along the way while you're at it. I will be marching forward."

The squire decided he had had enough. He, like the knight, had witnessed his fair share of suffering and wanted no more. He yanked his horse's reins to turn around. But Nano had other ideas and didn't to budge. Jaume glared as he tried to steer his steed. And again, Nano refused. As the squire stared into his horse's brown eyes, he realized that the animal's loyalty rested with his master, not him.

"Fine, Nano, you win," Jaume hissed, kicking the horse's ribs with spite to spur them into a dense fog, which swallowed the desolate landscape and blocked out the sun. The squire listened for any sound of life – a bird chirping, an insect clicking, a rodent rustling. He heard nothing but dead leaves, twigs and an unfamiliar snap of what might have been bones, being crushed under his horses' heavy hooves.

Could the remains be human? Jaume shivered at the dark turn his thoughts had taken. "*Senyor* Jordi," he yelled, listening to his shaky voice fade as his master disappeared into the vast grayness, to the same crunching noises that so terrified the teenage boy.

Jaume tapped Nano to follow, cursing his father for sending him with this crazy knight. All he wanted to do was return to *his* home in the city of Nicromedia. Life had been easy before his father had rescued *Senyor* Jordi and used all of their family's money to heal a man who had been lashed into unconsciousness. A world free of suffering was what Jaume wanted, not one which made mothers scream to the mountaintops, after the death of their children.

A whiff of smoke in the mist dried a sniffling nose. The squire lifted his eyes from the reins in his trembling hands. A blurry orange speck flickered in the distance. The idea of a fire warmed the teenage boy's frightened and weary soul. He pointed and shouted, "Do you see the light, *Senyor* Jordi?"

"What?"

"The light, the light! Do you see it?"

The knight's thin lips pursed in concentration and the thousands of lines etched in his face deepened. "I don't see anything," *Senyor* Jordi eventually said. "Then again, my eyes aren't what they once were." He turned and smiled at his squire. "I trust you, boy. Let's pay them a visit, shall we?"

For the first time since they had heard the woman's shriek atop the windswept mountain, Jaume didn't complain about his master's decision. They tracked the orange speck until it grew into the light behind the thin windows of a small farmhouse. The building was the shape of a box, with a red-tiled roof and walls constructed from stone and mortar. But its sturdy construction did little to ease the queasiness Jaume felt from the foul stench of rot that overpowered the smoke billowing from a chimney.

"*Senyor* Jordi," he gagged.

"Almost there, boy." The knight slowed his white stallion with a gentle pull of the reins. He covered his mouth and suppressed a cough as he sat up erect. "Ready to see what this is all about?"

Jaume didn't think he had much choice. "Yes, *Senyor*," he grumbled, hopping off Nano to tether the horse to a brittle wooden post.

He turned around to see his master struggling to dismount. His hands gripped the saddle's horn and his stick arms shook from the strain of lifting his body weight. The breastplate under a white tunic rattled as *Senyor* Jordi swung his left leg, brushing Anici's rump.

Jaume ran forward to catch his master in case he lost his balance.

"Back off, boy," the knight growled, one hand on the horn, the other on the back of the saddle. He took a deep breath. His body relaxed. He pushed off his horse, landing with a thud. "Jaume," he sneered, rising from his crouch to face the squire. "My body might have been ravaged by war and torture, but I have been dismounting horses by myself since before your parents were betrothed to each other and I will continue doing so. Is that understood?"

The chastised teenager gulped and nodded.

"Good." His master turned to his horse and brushed its silver mane as he spoke softly into its ear. "You never doubt me, do you?"

Anici replied with a neigh, a spit and shake of the head.

"Right," the knight barked, strolling to his stallion's side. He grabbed the dyed-green hilt and unsheathed his trusted *spatha* sword, Ascalon, from its wooden scabbard. The long glistening metal blade sliced through the air, catching the light from the house's small windows. A fiery beam soared toward the heavens as the knight stood there in his threadbare white tunic, crossing red lines on the front and back, his weapon raised high above a crested helmet.

"Let's go," he commanded, sheathing Ascalon in the scabbard tied to his belt. The uniform grayness, which had shrouded them since entering the forest, returned.

"Yes, *Senyor*." Jaume shivered and followed his master up a set of crumbling steps to a door. The knight pounded it with his fist. A few seconds passed before the hinges swung in and a blast of the warm blew past the squire's exposed knees.

"What do you want?" snarled a scowling woman, in a dress as black as the few wisps of long hair on her head.

El Senyor Jordi gave his name and claimed Montblanc as his home, sounding chipper despite the woman's harsh tone and appearance. "And this is my trusted squire, Jaume" he added, patting the teenage boy on the back.

"Who?" the woman snapped.

Senyor Jordi repeated his name and asked, "How

could you not have heard of me? I became the Emperor's most trusted and valued knight until he asked me to renounce my beliefs and kill my men."

"Who is in favor with his Highness the Emperor and who is not means little to us." The woman pointed a scabby finger at empty pens where oinking pigs had once rolled in their own filth. "As you can see, we are facing a fate worse than any edict he could order."

"Yes, *Senyora*." A visibly concerned knight nodded. "Please, tell me, what has brought such misery upon my village?"

"A dragon," she deadpanned.

"A dragon!"

"Yes." The woman paused and eyed *Senyor* Jordi with suspicion after his shocked reaction. He was obviously wealthy enough to have a squire. She had met other country gentlemen who had claimed to be knights, but the only beasts they battled were the dragons in their minds. "It lives in the lake from where we draw our water," the woman continued, her wary expression unchanged. "At first, it only charged us a sheep and then a pig, but it soon grew bored of our animals' taste." She cast her glistening eyes to the ground and her voice dropped to a hush, "Then it ordered us to bring our daughters."

"Please, tell me you didn't," the knight blurted.

"Of course we didn't," the woman snapped. "But our refusals only angered the beast and it rose from the lake to roar such a roar that all the birds and bees left, never to return."

"Does the dragon breathe fire?" Jaume inquired.

"No. Worse. It breathes pestilence and death, killing all of our crops and flowers." The woman's eyes welled again and she sniffled. "When we still refused the beast's orders, it slayed all our livestock, leaving us only their rotten remains on which to feed."

"The cry we heard?" asked the knight.

"That was the queen." The woman explained how the dragon had told the king his privileged status didn't exempt him from the suffering and ordered the princess next to be sacrificed.

"It's got a point," Jaume quipped.

"Nonsense," the knight belted. "No one should have to sacrifice a child to eat and drink." He turned to the old woman and put a gloved hand on her shoulder. "*Senyora*, I promise to rid you of this ghastly beast."

"Please, don't try." She shrugged off his reassuring gesture. "I do not want to imagine what the dragon will do to us when you fail."

The knight stepped back in surprise at her defeatist attitude. "*Senyora*, one must have faith," he said. "What can be worse than this?"

"Death," she declared, slamming the door.

Senyor Jordi turned from the house and gazed at his powerful stallion, gnawing on the dirt ground. This was his third Anici. Each one had been the son of the one before him. They all shared a strength and courage stronger than most men he had known. But each horse had its own distinct personality. The first was as stubborn and hard-headed as an old donkey, but the strongest and most valiant. This one carried with it a quiet confidence and strength.

"This is how it is to end—us against the dragon?" the knight postulated, with a glint in his eye.

"*Senyor* Jordi, you don't have to do this." Jaume didn't know if the woman's story was true or a legend, but he had no desire to find out.

"You're right. I don't," his master admitted. "Then

again, I've never had to do most things in life, have I?"

"Why have you done the things you've done, *Senyor*?"

"Well, I suppose at first it was to please my father." The knight's sheathed sword began to swing with his strides as he started down the steps. "Like him, I joined the military, but became a soldier where he was more of a politician."

"And not just any soldier. But one of the Emperor's finest, correct?"

"Don't know about all that, boy." *Senyor* Jordi sighed and his stare grew distant as they stopped at their awaiting horses. "Let's just say a soldier who succeeded at staying alive."

The squire wanted to hear more. "But then his Highness had you imprisoned and tortured, right?"

"You've heard this story before, haven't you, Jaume?"

The knight strolled to Anici's side and returned his sword to the wooden scabbard attached to the saddle. He lifted his boot into the stirrup, turned to the young boy and said, "Lad, give a tired man a hand, would you?"

"Yes, *Senyor*." The squire dashed to his master and lifted his foot over a horse which stood so still that it could have been a marble statue outside a general's mausoleum.

"Must conserve one's energy before a fight." The knight winked as he settled into the worn saddle and took the reigns.

Jaume looked up with pleading eyes. "*Senyor*, about this dragon… is it wise? At least let me try."

"That is very brave of you, boy. But you are not ready for such a beast and this is my home. I must be the one who defends it." The knight patted Anici's shoulders to calm the spitting horse. "Now, no more talk," he ordered. "Mount up and let's go. There is a princess to save!"

thrusting his arm in the air.

A braying stallion lifted its front legs and kicked in excitement at the news. Jaume's stomach sunk from the recurring disappointment he'd felt since his father had ordered him to accompany the crazy knight on his long journey home.

As the squire rode behind his master, he stared at the shrunken man in a frayed and stained tunic, sitting with his head up, back straight, as if he expected a party to honor his return. Jaume remembered the day his father had brought the bloodied knight into their home. As the story went, after fighting for Rome against Persia, *Senyor* Jordi returned to the empire a changed man. Instead of retiring into a comfortable life or politics, like most decorated soldiers, he gave away his wealth and spoke out against the Emperor and his edicts.

Jaume once asked his father, "Why?" and he responded:

"Living through war changes a person."

He was the only one who offered this rationale. Most subscribed to the theory that *Senyor* Jordi had converted to some barbaric foreign religion. Eventually even his old friend, the Emperor, turned on his most loyal and valiant knight, ordering him to be lashed on a wheel of swords outside Nicromedia city's walls.

When Jaume asked *Senyor* Jordi the reason behind his transformation he replied, "Anyone can change. It's just a matter of choosing to or not choosing to and I chose to," before switching the topic from himself to the weather almanac he now kept.

"Jaume, look at this place." The knight's sonorous voice brought the squire back from the world of his memories into the present. Forlorn men in tattered brown robes pushed wheel-barrows stacked with bruised corpses down streets, both narrow and wide. In the main square, women's filthy visages were dotted red from sores. Their listless eyes flickered with the last scintilla of life as they looked right, then left, with their bony children hidden under shredded cloaks.

"Now, do you see why we must try and do something?" the knight asked, as he rode next to his squire.

"It is truly horrible, *Senyor*. But why us? Can't someone else do it?"

"Why not us?"

"Because we can't!"

"Perhaps not if we try, Jaume. But for sure if we don't."

"But *Senyor* Jordi, you will die."

"So will you one day." The knight slowed his horse and glared at his squire. "How you can look around at all this misery and not be moved to do something other than complain is beyond me." *Senyor* Jordi took a deep breath and raised his finger as he declared, "I, for one, cannot and will not sit idly by."

"But to battle a dragon?" Jaume's voice squeaked with disbelief that was the enemy they were about to face. "Is there not something else we can do?"

A man's desperate pleas cut their conversation short. *Senyor* Jordi turned from his squire and looked at the village's back wall where a gate swung in. "The time is upon us," he belted, spurring his horse into a gallop.

Jaume kicked Nano to follow. The wind smacked his face as the vibrations from hooves hitting cobblestones shook his skull. Nano jumped and landed on the ground in perfect stride, but the teenage boy no longer felt his horse's movements. Nor did he see the rag-tag group at the bottom of a hill near a round lake, with water as black as tar. He imagined a different present, where he rode from Nicromedia toward an oasis, with his neighbor's daughter's arms wrapped around his waist.

"What's going on here?" *Senyor* Jordi beckoned, his commanding voice slaying the fantasy that played in Jaume's mind.

"They want to sacrifice my beautiful daughter," a father cried. "Please, don't let the dragon eat my Elisenda. She's the only child we have."

"It's the only way! It's the only way!" screamed the crowd.

A fat man with a thick brown beard and gold embroidered tunic pushed his way to the front of the skeletal villagers. His eyes widened and quivered as he stammered, "Jor... Jordi, is... is tha... that you?"

He recognized the king as the one time scrawny prince who had been third in-line to the throne. The knight wondered what palace intrigue had taken place during his long absence, if the elder brothers had died of natural causes, fighting in a war or under suspicious circumstances. He decided now was not the time to ponder such questions.

"Bring me your daughter," *Senyor* Jordi commanded and the villagers parted to reveal a young woman chained to a stake at the edge of the lake.

The king had not been blinded by fatherly pride. Princess Elisenda was truly a stunning beauty, with long brown locks and twinkling hazelnut eyes. The girdle of a pearl and lace wedding dress boosted her ample bosom and hugged round curves.

Senyor Jordi noticed his squire's jaw drop. "You'd fight a dragon for that, wouldn't you, boy?" he teased, pulling Anici alongside Nano.

Jaume blushed. "Um, er..."

The knight didn't need to hear an answer to know what he had said had been true and turned his attention to the princess. "What's this I hear about you being fed to a dragon?"

Her trembling voice strained to be firm as she spoke. "Please, I understand you are a knight and it is your nature to be brave, but leave us be. The beast has promised to leave the lake and our land if my father sacrifices me."

The knight shook his head. "Nonsense," he said. "There will be no more death!"

A guttural hiss erupted from the bowels of the black lake. The ground shook as a growl grew from a roar into a deafening splash. Water cascaded down like a flurry of arrows. In the gray sky, a red scaled beast with webbed bat wings and a serpentine head stretched arms and legs of loosely connected bones before looking down at those it blanketed with its shadow.

The villagers fled up the hill toward the safety of stone walls. The king ducked behind a large boulder. *Senyor* Jordi cast a worried glance at the dripping princess chained to a stake.

"This girl is not to be sacrificed and you are to give the land back to my village," the knight commanded, drawing his glistening sword, as he stared at his enemy, hovering high above a still black lake.

The beast made a noise that was more a wheezing laugh than a roar of anger. It flapped its wings to thunderous claps as it soared higher and higher into the air. A red speck in an overcast sky accompanied a moment of silence before a ferocious howl parted the heavens and cracked the village's walls.

"Hold," *Senyor* Jordi ordered, his round shield up, his shimmering sword steady on his hip.

The dragon dove with such speed that it shrieked through the mist. Jaume trembled at his master's side and watched as the beast unfurled its wings to slow its descent. Like the bat from which they took their shape, the wings fluttered in every direction and angle, giving the movements a hypnotic quality, which held the knight and his squire in a trance.

The back of a bony hand slammed Jaume's helmet. His body felt weightless before a judder shot from his shoulder, up and down his spine, when he slammed into the hard ground.

The dragon snickered through clenched fangs and darted into the air, disappearing from sight. Silence before another feral yowl and ear-piercing attack.

Senyor Jordi did not hold, but turned and spurred Anici into a desperate sprint toward the cover of the dead forest. The dragon closed in, spreading its black forelimbs like a cape. The knight felt the beast's dripping drool on the back of his neck and yanked the reins of his galloping horse. Anici's hooves slid and skidded with such violence that the stallion's legs almost snapped from the sharpness of the turn. The dragon yelped with surprise at the sudden change of direction. Its webbed wings flailed to slow its momentum, its snake-like body twisting sideways, as it crashed into a row of trees.

"Your breath is really quite rank," *Senyor* Jordi taunted, steadying his proud, neighing horse.

No sound came from the dragon's steaming nose. It rolled onto its stomach and used its skeletal arms to push itself up until it stood taller than any tower. Then it made the faintest of snorting noises as it smiled an evil smile and curled a talon-like finger at *Senyor* Jordi, daring him to make the next move.

The knight traced the red lines across his tunic, cocked

his sword back and spurred his horse's ribs. Its hooves pounded the ground louder than a cavalry charge. The dragon hissed in excitement. It flung its viperous head back to strike. Anici leapt in the air, bringing the knight's crested helmet beneath salivating jaws. *Senyor* Jordi lunged and stabbed the long blade of his *spatha* sword into scaly skin. A shriek erupted, piercing the sun behind the clouds, shrouding the world in darkness, but not silence.

***

The ringing between Jaume's ears had dulled to the point he could peel open his eyes to see a world that was again a murky gray. Dazed as if he had just gone a round with a gladiator, he pushed himself up to one knee.

The earth still seemed to tremble as he stood on his feet and swayed. The blurry image of a thin man, approaching with a shining smile and a galea helmet under his arm, numbed the pulsating sensation that tenderized the squire's body and he screamed, "*Senyor* Jordi, you're alive!"

"Of course, I am, boy. Not going to lose to an animal, no matter how big it is." The knight tapped his bald head to re-enforce the lesson he was about to deliver, "The number one rule of a soldier is pick one's battles wisely. Dragons are a predictable lot. Fly up, swoop down and bite."

"Is it dead?" Jaume asked.

"No. Dust yourself off and come with me. I want to show you something." *Senyor* Jordi threw an arm around his squire's throbbing shoulder. "You were very brave not running like the rest, Jaume."

He grimaced but didn't pull away from his master's embrace. "Thanks, *Senyor*. But I failed to see it swing at me and got knocked off my horse."

"I have to admit I didn't expect that either." The knight called the beast arrogant, suggesting that it had wanted to prove its mettle by killing him, not a squire. "Had the animal been a rational being," *Senyor* Jordi continued, "it would've used the element of surprise to attack me, leaving it one-on-one with you."

Jaume didn't know how to take that comment. He shrugged off his master's arm and turned away to find Nano and Anici, munching on shoots of green grass, in the crimson blood splattered on the dirt ground.

Cries of joy rang in the air and the squire turned to see a jubilant Princess Elisenda run up and kiss *Senyor* Jordi over and over again. "Thank you, thank you," she repeated between pecks.

Even the white whiskers on the knight's sunken cheeks turned pink. "That's alright," he muttered, eying his muddied boots. "Had to do something."

The princess kissed him again. "You are the bravest knight I have ever met!"

A grinning *Senyor* Jordi nodded at Jaume. "According to my squire—a stupid one, right?"

"Um, er..." The teenage boy covered his mouth and coughed to clear his throat, "never called you stupid."

"So Jordi," the king said, with a clap. "What do we do with the dragon?" his booming voice conveying a restored sense of power and authority.

"Princess Elisenda." The knight bowed with a courteous wave of his hand. "Would you do me a favor and take off your girdle?"

Her hazelnut eyes flashed in surprise. "You want me to do what?"

"Please, I want to show you something." *Senyor* Jordi walked to the young girl's back and clumsily undid the first knot of string.

As *Senyor* Jordi worked on removing the princess's wedding dress in the most unromantic way, Jaume tried to picture her body underneath, the location of her freckles, the shape of her bellybutton. Drool formed in the corner of his mouth and dribbled down his chin. The king's firm hand on his shoulder was a reminder that he was not alone.

"You see..." *Senyor* Jordi slipped the princess's girdle over the serpentine head of a beast, which no longer seemed so towering and menacing, more like an animal kept at the Emperor's zoo, "completely meek and compliant."

"Are we supposed to keep it around as a pet?" the king snickered.

"No." The knight paused and watched as the whispering villagers gathered around.

"Why isn't it dead? Why isn't it dead?" they demanded to know.

"I will slay it on one condition," *Senyor* Jordi told them.

"What? What? What?"

"That you never return to the life you had before the dragon. A life where a few individuals were strong, but the village was weak. A life where a monster can come, take your lake and make you sacrifice your own children, just to live on the rotten remains of all that you once had. For if you don't do this, this will not be the last dragon to visit your land!"

The king squirmed after *Senyor* Jordi's speech and the people chanted:

"We swear! We swear! We swear!"

The knight raised his blood soaked *spatha* sword into the gray sky. A hush fell over the land. Spots of exposed metal attracted faint rays of sunlight and the long blade flashed before coming down across the dragon's neck.

The crowd erupted into cheers and claps.

"A blood thirsty lot," Jaume muttered.

His comment did not go unnoticed and Princess Elisenda cut him a smirk in agreement.

"Thank you, thank you," the king said, his bearded face beaming. "Jordi, your return has been a gift from the heavens! We will erect monuments and anoint a holiday in your honor."

"Please don't. Just try and heed my words." The knight didn't want to put a damper on the festive mood by telling the villagers that he refused to serve a king he didn't respect. "I don't think I'm ready to retire just yet," he told them instead, which was also true. He explained how the battle with the dragon had reinvigorated his thirst for adventure so he wasn't going to stick around to protect them.

"Come on, boy," *Senyor* Jordi ordered, stroking his neighing horse's silver mane.

"One moment, sir." The squire held up his hand and sprinted to where a rose bush grew in a pool of blood near the dragon's severed head. He cut the thorny stem with the knife his father had given him for the journey and dashed to the princess. "This is for you," he announced.

"Bu... but..." she stammered, smelling the petals as the whistles and hoots of returning birds filled the buzzing air, "but I don't have anything for you."

"You have given me a story to tell," Jaume said, mimicking his master's chivalrous bow. "And for me there is no better gift."

A Book for a Rose

Johnny woke up to the taste of stale beer and the sensation of his inflamed brain pressing against his skull. He needed lots of liquids and sleep to rehydrate and recuperate, physically, from a night out on the town. Recovering emotionally from the news that had caused him to get hammered on a week day would take much longer, probably days, maybe even weeks.

He slapped a cluttered bedside table for his cellphone to check the time. 6:45am. 20 minutes before he usually woke up for work, groggy, but not craving morphine-based pain-killers, like he did now. He debated canceling his first Business English class, claiming bad kebab as the reason. His grandmother's favorite expression, "There's no rest for the wicked," said in her soft-spoken yet stern Midwestern accent, looped in his pulsating head, as a reminder of his responsibilities.

Johnny turned off the alarm on his phone before it blared at him to get up and rolled out of bed. It was stuffy to the point of muggy in his pitch-dark room. The yellow-tinged glow from the display of a bulky, old school Nokia cellphone illuminated the way to a closed door which he opened to a gust of cool air.

It was still dark outside, not that he could see the pre-dawn sky. The communal area, shared with two other flatmates, was no bigger than a storage closet, with a small window that looked onto the adjacent building's wall. After the living room was a narrow hallway where sputtering snores, seeping from under a flatmate's closed door, disturbed the peace and quiet.

The blue tiled bathroom continued the miniature theme of flats in Spain. Johnny slipped off his boxer shorts before stepping over a toilet bowl in order to enter a shower barely wider than his hips. Steaming hot water sprayed his closed eyes and rinsed the stale taste of last night from his open mouth. The tension in his head eased and his mind soon drifted to the reason he had drowned his sorrows on a Monday night.

Elena Sánchez was her name. She was a student of his and the quintessential Spanish beauty, with silky black hair and dark vivid eyes that were prone to spark with a smile. She spoke English, not with the harshness of most of his female students, but with the charming intonation of a European actress in a Hollywood production. For eighty-five minutes, it seemed as if Johnny's childhood dream of coming to Spain and meeting a beautiful *señorita* was about to be realized, leaving only the house on the beach to be achieved.

"I have a boyfriend," Elena said, dropping the news at the end of their first lesson. She described her significant other as man who was fifteen years her senior, with two children from a previous marriage. His Christmas gift to her that year had been a thoroughbred horse and he liked to sail his yacht to the Balearic Islands in summer.

Johnny understood the situation and was ready to file his comely student's image away for those lonely nights at home when his boss called, not two minutes after class. Elena had requested Johnny to be her permanent teacher, rather than a one-off substitute, as had been the original plan. From that point on, they met twice a week, every week, unlike 90 per cent of his other students, who blew off class on a regular basis.

After the long shower, Johnny felt a sense of urgency speed up his movements. He slipped on a pair of wrinkled slacks and buttoned up a plaid shirt. He grabbed a backpack, turned a key to unlock the double cylinder deadbolt and stopped. His front door had no knob or handle, just the sturdy lock, a peephole and coat hook. He pinched the latter and pulled to the high-pitched whine of rusty hinges.

The first rays of daylight lightened the sky outside, but the large window on the other side of the stairwell was caked with decades of dust. The narrow landing Johnny stood on was a shade brighter than his room. He pushed the glowing button to start the timed light so that he could see the keyhole to lock his door, as well as his feet, as he gingerly headed down four flights of stairs.

He lived in the Poble Sec District of Barcelona which had begun life as a shantytown outside the medieval city walls. Once those came down, the area transformed into a dense, unregulated neighborhood of tiny streets, small squares and plain buildings, at the base of Montjuïc Mountain. Johnny's flat had to be at least a few hundred years old and the stone steps were slick and uneven from centuries of wear.

He slipped. He clutched the wooden banister to stop from falling. His backpack came off his shoulder. He caught the strap in and stumbled onto the second floor landing, where old widow Teresa cut out newspaper articles, as she sat on a stool in front of an open door.

The timed light cut, leaving them in the dim glow from the bulb in her entryway ceiling. "Hello, sweetheart." Teresa said in creaky Spanish, as she put down a pair of scissors and stood to greet her neighbor. "Are you going to work?"

"*Bon dia*, Teresa." After five years in Barcelona, Johnny spoke conversational Spanish, with some Catalan thrown in. "Yes, and running late as usual."

He glanced at the illuminated wall. Corruption at the municipal and regional offices, along with proposed cuts in social services, were the day's highlighted headlines.

"You look a little sad." Teresa's thick glasses magnified the concern in her eyes as bony fingers wrapped around Johnny's hand.

He forced a smile at her cold touch. "I'm fine."

"Do you know what today is?" An old widow nodded her head in encouragement.

Johnny's brain lacked the fluids to run the necessary thought processes to determine the date and he mumbled, "Um, er, no."

"*Sant Jordi.*"

An image of Elena flashed in his mind at the news. "That's right!" Johnny projected fake enthusiasm, after hearing it was Catalunya's version of St. Valentine's Day. "Forgot all about it. *Bon Sant Jordi*, Teresa."

The ticking light switched on to the sound of barreling footsteps. Johnny pulled his hand from Teresa's icy grip and watched as Paco (the stereotypical 35 year-old Catalan and Spanish man who still lived with his mother) sprinted down the treacherous stairs, without any fear of slipping and breaking his neck.

"*Adéu*," he blurted, with a dismissive wave.

Teresa's stare followed the pudgy neighbor down the next flight of steps. "He's a strange and rude boy," she stated, looking up at Johnny for confirmation.

"Probably just in a rush." He pressed the timed light again to make sure it didn't cut before he reached the safety of the ground floor. "Alright, Teresa," Johnny told her. "Gotta go."

"Wait," she ordered, going into her moldy apartment to get a book from a shelf in the entryway. "As is the tradition today."

Teresa handed Johnny a used paperback written in Catalan about the city's most famous architect, Antoni Gaudí. *"Moltes gràcies,"* Johnny said, bending down to kiss an old woman on each cheek. "Owe you a rose now."

The first class of the day started at 8:30am with the Financial Director of the same German multinational where Elena worked as Human Resources Director. The offices were in a tall copper building near Plaça Espanya, a fifteen minute stroll from Johnny's flat if he took it slow.

Those mornings were rarer than a week with no hangover. Despite waking up early, he was running late and hoisted a heavy backpack over both shoulders. He pumped his arms and took long strides. Pedestrians came at him in waves. He zipped around possible collisions, arriving at sliding glass-doors, in under ten minutes.

Johnny's cellphone rang. *"Sí,"* he answered, feeling his chest heave, but trying not to wheeze, after the near run.

"Hola, Yonni." She switched to English. "It's Mónica."

"Hey, Mónica."

"Sorry for the late notice. There's a note on my desk from Manel, saying it's impossible to attend class this morning."

The Spanish and Catalans both loved to claim the impossibility of making a class when it was possible, if they just made an effort. Some advance notice would have also been nice, although Johnny couldn't complain.

He got paid whether his students showed up or not. His next lesson wasn't until lunch, giving him plenty of time to go home, rehydrate and recover from his late night out.

"Um, okay." Johnny feigned annoyance to hide his joy at the good news. "No problem. Tell Manel to call me the next time he cancels, though. He needs to practice his phone English."

"You know how he is," Mónica told him. "See you Wednesday." She hung up and Johnny made a u-turn to leave the copper building's courtyard. Professionally attired men and women brushed past him on their way to fingerprint scanners in the lobby before reaching the elevators to take them to different floors. He lifted his head and looked for Elena, but she was not a worker-bee who arrived at the hive at a set time.

Johnny knew where to go to "accidentally" bump into his student. She was probably having a coffee at the same bar where they met twice a week. Their classes included lessons on English grammar, presentation language and business vocabulary, but mostly they chatted about each other's lives, with the ease and openness of...

"close friends" wasn't the right phrase, even though it was the best match to describe their relationship. But friends weren't supposed to get jealous, right? Especially ones who were already spoken for. Yet whenever Johnny mentioned the crazy nature of the women he dated, Elena's normally serene black eyes flashed green with envy. "You can do better," she would then quip, and he tried not to grin at the emotion the subject of his love life provoked.

Johnny snickered as he pictured Elena's face. The sense of victory was always short lived. Her red lips would spread into a sly smile before she spoke openly of her belief in friends with benefits, her love of sex in the kitchen and her affinity toward men, with clear blue eyes, like Johnny.

What was she implying? Did she want me to talk dirty? Tell her to ditch the old geezer and get with "a modern guy. Of course, I've had in the ear before," to quote Iggy Pop. Maybe I should ask her if she was into role-playing, crotchless panties and a little light bondage? Johnny always blushed when such thoughts crossed his mind, his tongue too limp to articulate his erotic desires in a smooth, playboy manner, whenever in front of his student.

Yesterday's news answered his musings with an emphatic, "Negative, mister!" so he decided not to hunt down his childhood dream personified and returned to his flat for a nap.

The 20 minute march to and from work sweated out last night's toxins and released enough endorphins to make Johnny feel as if he'd just polished off his third espresso and a glass of freshly squeezed orange juice on an empty stomach. He plopped down on a chair at his desk and turned on his laptop to surf the Net until his mind and body settled down enough to rest.

Off his right shoulder was an open window the size of his closet doors, with a view of antennae on flat rooftops and a dreary sky. The spring had been unusually wet this year, although he thought the same thing every March and April. Still, as he rubbed the temples of his still throbbing head, Johnny wondered whether it would be the first *Sant Jordi* in memory that the sun didn't shine.

The chime of a computer booting up rang in his ears and he focused on a laptop screen. A personalized homepage had the day's headlines in English and an inbox full of bold new messages. Most were job postings from the employment websites Johnny had registered with last week. The emails announced openings in London, with decent monthly salaries, working in his pre-Spain field of technology. A few had a personal note from a recruiter, stating that he would have a better chance of finding gainful employment, if he moved to England.

Mixed in with these offerings were rejection letters from agents regarding his latest novel based on a drug made from human DNA. Finally, there was an email from Elena asking if he was interested in a position that had recently opened up at her company.

Johnny didn't feel like answering any of his messages and logged out of his inbox.

He checked his online bank account to see his balance. The company he worked for was an agency that offered English courses to businesses and individuals at exorbitant rates. He got paid once a month, receiving a 50 per cent cut for every class he taught that fell on a weekday, even if the students canceled a week in advance or, like Manel, never came. (Johnny's boss said to tell anyone who complained that it was like a gym membership.) The gig, however, didn't offer any benefits in the way of healthcare, vacation or sick days. Nor did he earn a wage when class fell on any of the fourteen public holidays, during the three month summer break, or the three weeks at Christmas.

As a whole, though, compared to the litany of other jobs Johnny had done, teaching English wasn't that much of a soul-killer. He got to meet and befriend the locals while enjoying the craziness of Barcelona on the weekends, with enough money left over to travel Europe, without the need of credit cards. A cubicle wasn't his workspace and twenty hours a week was a full load, giving him plenty of free time to work on his craft.

His heart and head no longer pumped from the burst of exercise. Somnolence crept over him like a winter fog, rolling in from the Mediterranean Sea. Eyelids drew down to blink but lacked the will to lift back up. His head continued to need sleep to stop the low frequency ringing between his ears. Eyes still closed, Johnny jumped from a swivel chair to a bed that creaked as he crawled under the comforter and hugged a pillow.

A wheezing drill bored through the vast depths of unconsciousness. The racket stopped after Johnny's eyes popped open. He heard muffled voices on the other side of his bedroom wall and got up to face the rude, noisy world.

In the cramped living room, his half-Portuguese, half-African flatmate lay on a red two-seater couch, pillows propped against wooden arms, in an attempt to do the impossible: make lounging on a piece of IKEA furniture comfortable.

"Hey, Johnny," Germano said, his eyes fixed on a TV screen smaller than what was found on a standard laptop.

"*Hombre.*" Johnny rubbed his eyes and yawned. "*¿Qué pasa?*"

"*Nada.*" They had originally agreed to speak only in Spanish, but with Germano near fluent and Johnny merely conversational, they ended up communicating in the one language they both spoke equally well, English. "Just watching the local news." Germano translated what he was hearing, "Guess a guy got five years for attacking a civil servant."

Johnny glanced at the TV to see a picture of a mousy man with a bad comb-over. Homicidal rage was a common emotion expressed after dealing with the infamous local bureaucracy. He had never heard of anyone acting on their violent rhetoric, though. What had driven the poor sap over the edge?

"What are you doing home so early?" Johnny asked, not looking to enter into a conversation on the topic of the causes of human rage.

"My work contract ended last week," Germano's eyes were still glued to the small screen, "and decided not to renew it."

"Gonna look for another job?" Johnny sat down on a straight-back chair and felt the springy wooden frame.

"No." Germano paused and swung his feet from the wooden arm of the couch to the stone floor. He sat up, put a pillow on his lap and made eye contact before he spoke again. "Gonna use my severance and unemployment benefits to travel Spain until the end of summer, then go back to the UK and study for a masters."

"You're not staying here?" Johnny's voice scratched from surprise.

Germano smiled in appreciation at the emotion his leaving caused. "Barcelona's a great city," he said, "and *so much* fun. But there's not much work with good pay, you know?"

Yes I do, Johnny thought, with a chuckle to hide his disappointment. He had grown fond of his young flatmate and hoped to discourage the move, despite halfheartedly contemplating it himself. "But it rains all the time in England," he gave one of the reasons he didn't want to live there.

"Yeah, I know." Germano shrugged as if to say, *What are you going to do?* "But it hasn't stopped raining here for the last two months."

Johnny laughed again, this time in agreement, before

he made a pitch for his friend to stay, "Why don't you teach? Your English is excellent. I can get you a job. Pays better than a call-center."

"Not really my thing," Germano told him. "Wanna go into import-export with my family after getting my masters."

Johnny no longer tried too hard to change people's minds. The average stay of transplants was two years as people left the adult fun time of Barcelona in search of stable opportunities elsewhere to settle down.

"Good luck to you." Johnny glanced at the weather girl predicting more showers on the small TV. "When are you leaving?"

"At the end of next month." Germano studied Johnny's bloodshot eyes. "Do you think you'll ever go back to the US?"

"When I can buy a beach house in Malibu and have a driver."

Germano roared with laughter at the chances of that happening.

Johnny smiled, taking no offense to boisterous reaction. "Doubt it," he added, not needing to pause to think of the reasons why. "Got a five-year gap on my resumé, stacks of unpaid credit card bills and I really, really hate driving."

Johnny looked at the round clock on the wall. The time was 12:20pm.

"Shit, running late again," he blurted, jumping up from the springy seat to wash the sleep from his eyes before his next class, in the Maria Cristina District of Barcelona, near Camp Nou Football Stadium.

The building Johnny approached was famous for the lush plants hanging from its windows and patios. Inside, he passed the security desk for the main offices of a media conglomerate that owned a TV station, the most popular newspapers for both Spanish and Catalan Nationalists, as well as publishing houses in Spain and South America.

The class itself took place in a windowless meeting room with no vegetation. Johnny pulled a seat from a round table and sat down. Nobody had arrived yet so he took a book from his backpack and continued reading a story about a married man who searched for his wife's missing cat, with the aid of a psychic prostitute.

"Hi *Yonni*," a male voice said fifteen pages later.

"Hey, Enric," Johnny replied, putting *The Wind-Up Bird Chronicle* back in his bag. He glanced at his cellphone on the table to see that it was already twenty minutes into the one and a half hour class.

"Sorry, I'm late." Enric patted his flat stomach and gave the reason, "Had to eat something," as he took the seat with the best view of the white board on the wall.

"No problem." Johnny stood from his chair. He rolled his shoulders and cracked his neck to get into teacher mode. "How's everything?" he asked, with a final torso twist.

"Good. My boss said he'd give me a year sabbatical if I found an internship with a newspaper in the UK or US."

Enric was one of the few motivated students Johnny taught and he offered to help with the applications.

"Hi, teacher," two female voices of different pitches filled the room.

"Hey, Núria. Hey, Mireia."

"Sorry we're late," they said in unison, as they sat two seats away from Enric.

"No problem." Johnny strutted to the white board, ready to inspire his students to learn a foreign language, which they hardly ever used.

He opened the lesson with a simple question, "How's everyone today?"

"Great!" Núria's heavily madeup eyes flashed with excitement behind thick librarian glasses. "I went out on a date this weekend."

"That's fantastic." Johnny gave a thumbs up before turning to the younger of the two ladies. "And what about you, Mireia?"

She finished checking her face in the compact and looked up with blue eyes and a pout that oozed indifference. "It was fun. Carlos and I went to *Danzatoria* and partied until six."

"Been there," Johnny told her, trying to relate to his student. "Bit posh, isn't it?"

"My boyfriend gets free passes."

What do you say to someone you have nothing in common with? "I see," Johnny said.

Núria took out a small notebook. "No grammar or listening exercises today, right? They're so boring! And work's been really stressful lately."

Johnny shook his head and saw all smiles. "Thought we'd do conversation and correction," he announced, picking up a marker from the metal railing at the bottom of the whiteboard. He stood and scribbled the lesson's main points as he spoke. "With it being *Sant Jordi*, the topic is books."

He wrote: "What was the last novel you read? Do you prefer fiction or nonfiction?" and eight more questions that mixed the tenses, vocabulary and grammar points, he'd taught so far that year. The answers generated a lively discussion. It was the same lesson plan he did every April 23rd since he'd started teaching English shortly after arriving in Barcelona. His three students all had advance levels and managed to get through the exercise without committing any major errors, making his job feel too easy, almost pointless even, at times.

Class finished, leaving three-and-a-half hours until the next one. Johnny didn't feel like heading home. He wasn't in the mood to write, listen to music or connect to the Net. He knew what the headlines on his homepage would say, "The world is going to shit faster than we realize."

As he walked out the lobby, his mood lifted at the sight of two fellow teachers, smoking after class cigarettes next to the revolving door of the plant draped building.

"Hey, Brad," Johnny said, shaking the hand and patting the back of a tall ex surfer.

"Hey, Johnny. Haven't seen you around in a while. How are things?"

"Drank too much last night."

"Any reason?"

"Usual shit—life, women." Johnny turned away from the knowing grin of a fellow booze-hound and looked down at a puffy face that seemed to get sunburned even when it was cloudy. "How's everything, Tim?"

"All right, old chap," he said, with the intonation and pronunciation of English royalty. "I wanted to do a *bah* and conv*ah*sation class again because the Spanish and Catalans need to speak and listen to English more." Tim paused to take a long pull from a cigarette. His red face darkened and he hissed, "But as always is the fucking case. That cunt Ester complained. She wanted to study bloody fucking grammar again."

"Dude," Johnny blurted, still shocked at prison language being spoken with such a refined accent, despite hearing Tim's profane rant every time they ran into each other. "Why not just do grammar the first half of class and convo the second?"

"Because she wants to know the difference between *can* and *to be able to* when she can't even use the fucking *simple past* correctly."

Brad chimed in, "Don't even know the difference between them," stubbing out his cigarette in a stand-alone ashtray.

"Hell," Johnny added. "Had no clue what the *simple past* was until I became a teacher." He paused and looked at two men who could have played the roles of opposites on the kids show his young niece liked to watch, after they had retired and spent all of their earnings on cheap whiskey.

Johnny wondered what failed, "Where are they now?" TV character he reminded people of as he watched Brad sling a backpack over his shoulder.

"Gonna grab lunch," the fellow American said. "Wanna join?"

"*Menú del Dia?*" Johnny's voice cracked with hope.

"No better value in town unless you're vegetarian."

A shared laugh at Brad's joke as they set off under a darkening sky and passed rotund gypsy women with long black ponytails. They sat on stools behind fold-out tables, a bucket of flowers within arm's reach. "Don't forget your mother," the women barked in Spanish, waving individually wrapped roses at the three grungy teachers and the suited passers-by who carried bags of books on their way back to work, after a two-hour lunch break.

"What book did your wife get you for *Sant Jordi*, Brad?" Johnny asked, as they waited at an intersection to cross the bustling Avinguda Diagonal.

"Something called *The Secret.*"

Tim's round face bulged with disgust. "That new-age

bollocks!"

"Yeah." Brad's visage was as gloomy as his tone as the three teachers passed the black tower of *La Caixa* Bank. "She says my perception of life is too negative and that's why I'm so unhappy." The former surfer and Ibiza bartender paused and his hollow blue eyes sunk to new depths. "It has nothing to do with the fact that I don't love her and hate Spain, but don't want to leave my son."

"Wow, man. That's heavy." Johnny didn't know what else to say to a man in such dire straits as they stopped at the green awning of a restaurant.

On the other side of a glass pane, businessmen and women sat at all of the tables, sipping their after meal coffees. An overcast sky meant that the two aluminum tables outside were empty. Johnny didn't taste rain in the air so he dropped his backpack and took a seat.

"Other than not liking the wife and Spain," he opened, hoping for a little lighter topic with their meal. "How's life, Brad?"

"Alright." His monotone said different as he sat and huffed, not out of resignation, but desperation. "Really, really need to find something else to do. Just not a teacher, you know?"

Johnny laughed at the ground-hog day nature of their conversation. "We say the same thing every time we see each other. Been looking for work in London myself."

Tim pounded the metal table and squinted with contempt at the mention of his hometown. "Why on God's green earth would you fucking want to go there, mate? It's bloody miserable. Why do you think an Englishman's dream is to live in Spain?"

"Teaching's like restaurant work but with better hours." Johnny used the best analogy he could think of, to describe a career that offered the same nowhere future.

"Your Spanish is good enough," Tim told him. "Why not work for a company here?"

"Dude..." Johnny stopped and sighed before launching into a rant, "after teaching the Spanish, I can't work for them. All they like to do is have three-hour meetings and argue about subjects that have nothing to do with the main topic."

Brad's glum expression brightened. "What about your writing?"

Johnny remained stone-faced, but the question stabbed at his chest. "Got a lot of hits on the query and synopsis," he said, leaving out the many more rejection letters he had received. "A few agents asked for the complete manuscript. Haven't heard anything back, though."

Tim looked into the restaurant's open front door and waved for the waiter. "Being a writer isn't an easy thing, old chap."

"Yeah, I know." Johnny felt the need to pour out his bottled up emotions to men who weren't colleagues or friends, but fellow transplants who knew what life was like in a place, where you would always be a stranger, even when you called it home.

He shared how writing was the only activity that kept his inner William Burroughs at bay and his arm puncture free. "Maybe I'm just not good enough," Johnny conceded, not seeing any reaction on their faces at his predicament. "But if I can't make money as a writer... then what? I have no skills. But I feel this need to find a career in something respectable and stable."

Brad nodded in agreement. "Welcome to my world. Think it's the American in us."

"You two depress me." Tim tutted and shook his head in disappointment before talking up the virtues of

Barcelona.

The locals could be warm and hospitable. You could drink outside in October or stroll through *Parc Cuitadella* on the way to the beach in January. Nearby mountains offered the chance to climb, hike or snowboard. Then there was the city itself, with architecture out of a Gothic fairy tale and the chance of something random or absurd happening down the next blind alley.

Johnny wanted to say, "Sometimes life needs more than good weather and an enchanting atmosphere—it needs a purpose." But the waiter arrived, stopping him from pouring water on Tim's pep talk.

The three teachers looked at a standing chalkboard, with the set menu of the day written in neat Spanish and Catalan. For a first dish, there was one of three choices: macaroni in a Bolognese sauce, a salad with all the usual suspects (lettuce, tomato, onion, hard boiled egg, plus canned tuna) or a dish of paella. For seconds: either roasted chicken with fries, grilled Catalan blood sausage with peas or baked hake with boiled carrots. A drink (beer, wine or cola) and a dessert were included, at a price that was less than a plate of tapas on Las Ramblas.

Johnny didn't mention Elena as they ate lunch. She had always been his little secret, one which he believed would cease to exist if he shared it. Instead of tales of heartache, he told his fellow transplants about a wild weekend, with a group of Flemish tourists.

Tim laughed and Brad wished he were still single. Their tones changed from friendly to whimsical as they remembered their former lives and plans, family and friends, with a bittersweet longing of a world that no longer existed. And when the check came, they split it three ways and went to their separate metro stations, with no set plans to meet again.

As Johnny sat on an empty metro carriage, he picked up a free newspaper from the seat next to him. A young Londoner faced murder charges for an incident at *Port Olímpic* while another British man (this one with a gray Hitler mustache) looked at five years in prison for attacking the muggers of *El Raval* and *Barri Gòtic* last summer.

A homicide was a once a year occurrence in Barcelona. Johnny had yet to meet a person (tourist, immigrant or transplant) who didn't have a story about falling victim to the city's infamous pickpocket mafias.

The Nokia ringtone snapped Johnny out of his thoughts as the train rolled into a turn. He set down the paper and answered his phone, "*Sí.*"

"*Hola* Johnny."

Elena's soft voice floated up his ears and tickled his sluggish brain. "Hey," he said, trying to keep his composure as he lied, "Sorry haven't gotten back to you yet. Been a bit busy today."

"Do you have time to meet for a coffee?" Elena's tone hinted at concern that the answer might be no. "I'm leaving work now to walk around the city-center."

"I'd love to," Johnny told her. "But gotta plan for my next class."

"It's *Sant Jordi*!" Oh, how he loved the passion in her voice. "I'm sure they'll cancel." Elena paused and he felt her mood sooth on the other end of the line. "It'll only be a few minutes. I have something for you."

"You didn't have to get me anything," Johnny grumbled.

"I wanted to!" Again, with passion. "I'd like to see you."

That expression, the slight neediness to the tone. How could he deny her? "Okay," Johnny said. "Send me a text where you wanna meet," getting off the metro at the next stop.

Rambla Catalunya started a few blocks from Plaça Catalunya and the more famous Las Ramblas below it. The same leafy sycamore trees shaded an intimate promenade, which gently sloped upward toward the foothills. The buildings on either side hailed from the city's golden age, *La Renaixença,* when Gaudí and other architects blended Art Nouveau and Modernist styles into edifices rivaling, sometimes even surpassing, those found in Paris. The only image more magnificent than the architecture was Elena in a black pant-suit as she emerged from the sea of people before they blurred into nothingness.

"*Hola,* Johnny," she said, as they exchanged pecks on each cheek, a whiff of her fresh perfume conjuring up a fantasy in his mind, of the two of them in the mountain cabin his company used, on a week-long intensive English class, alone. "*Bon Sant Jordi.*"

"*Hola,* Elena." Johnny paused before finishing that day's standard salutation. He turned away from an easy smile and stared at the dense clouds above the church atop Tibidabo Mountain. The uniform grayness began to tear, revealing patches of blue sky and the first signs of sunlight in a month. The breeze, rustling the trees, would soon clear the gloom. But the change in weather didn't cheer Johnny up.

"*Bon Sant Jordi,*" he eventually mumbled, unable to help himself from using his limited Catalan to widen his student's grin.

Born in Castile-La Mancha, Central Spain, Elena was actually *Castellano* through and through, although she publicly claimed to be Catalan because of a closer affinity to the serious, hard-working locals, rather than her fun-loving Spanish ancestors.

Johnny had never understood how someone could disavow their heritage or the Catalan Nationalist Movement behind such sentiments of self-loathing. "Catalunya is not Spain." What a load of bollocks. Just like comparing the Catalan plight under Franco to that of the Jews in 1930s Germany and the current situation to Gaza. As with any other delusional jingoist movement, true believers in the separatist cause were a small minority, but evangelical in their beliefs and masters at generating enough noise to browbeat and bully the more passive majority into silence.

The truth was, for a neutral outsider, there were far more similarities than differences between the various peoples of Spain. Everybody worked to live, rather than lived to work. They loved their weekly family gatherings and a good party, their local bar and cuisine. No one spoke quietly, got irony or saw any reason to ever leave their hometown. These characteristics were shared by the majority of Catalans, Basques and *Castellanos* alike. This was to be expected, if you think about it, after 500 years as a country under one crown, including a golden century when each region played a role in the rise and fall of the great Spanish Empire.

Elena's charming smile was the kind that made Johnny willing to renounce his personal convictions, though. He'd ignore the fact that most locals had at least one parent who had been born outside the region, making Spanish the most spoken language on Barcelona's streets, and shout to the rooftops, "Long live a free and independent Catalunya! No more fascist Madrid plundering our resources! No more occupation and linguistic genocide!" if he believed those were the magic words to win Elena over. But he knew she already heard such statements enough at home.

"Got a present for you," she said, handing him a white paper bag.

Johnny reached in and pulled out a paperback with the title: *My Christina and Other Stories* by Mercè Rodoreda. "It's in English," he blurted, touched by the gesture.

"Ordered it especially for you." Elena explained that the author was a famous Catalan writer during modernist times.

Johnny looked into smoldering eyes and saw not a Catalan, nor a Spaniard, just a beautiful, kind woman. "Thank you, " he said, giving her a kiss on the cheek. "Owe you a rose now."

"Don't worry about it." Elena linked their arms together and her velvet hair brushed his neck as her head rested on his shoulder. "Let's take a walk," she suggested.

Sant Jordi wasn't a public holiday, but the thousands of people, clogging the sidewalks and promenades, made it seem as though no one was at work. The book for a rose tradition was unique to Catalunya and celebrated with patriotic pride. The region's mustard and crimson colors were everywhere, from the thin striped flags hanging over balconies and out of windows, to the decoration of the cellophane around roses, to the pattern of the cloths draped over long tables with stacks of books in front of white tents.

"How's everything going?" Johnny asked, after a long period of comfortable silence.

"Okay." Elena lifted her head from his shoulder. "Andreu's taking his sons sailing this weekend if the weather's good." She paused and Johnny felt her studying his profile. "How are you? You look a bit sad."

"Same ol', same ol'. In a rut."

"In a what?"

Sometimes Johnny forgot his student wasn't fluent in English and rephrased his current state, "Just don't know what to do with myself anymore."

"What about the position at my company?" Elena's voiced sang at the prospect. "We could work together."

Johnny stared into unblinking and sincere eyes. "That's very kind," he said, with a weak smile. "But I don't think I'm cut out for office work anymore. The years living here have made me a bit lazy."

Elena laughed and Johnny didn't feel like a slacker, chasing an impossible dream. "What is it you'd like to do then?" she asked, stroking his stubbly cheek.

"Write." He expected to hear mocking laughter at his chances after his answer.

"You'd like to be the next Dan Brown?" Elena's even tone made it sound as if such a thing were possible, not as remote as winning the Oscar.

"Maybe not as famous," Johnny quipped, "but hopefully a better writer."

He had read *The Da Vinci Code*. An Albino for an evil henchman? A little clichéd, wasn't it? What about an androgynous dwarf, with an eye-patch? Or a more realistic scenario, such as a pedophile priest who whipped himself to stop his Satanic lust toward prepubescent children?

Johnny sighed and watched as thousands of people bought books as if they were still in vogue, not going the way of poetry. He didn't think he was a literary great, but neither was Dan Brown, nor most other well-known authors, such transcendental talent being rarer than a rose with perfectly symmetrical petals. "I'd be happy with one per cent of his success," Johnny confessed, "just enough to live on, you know?"

Elena took his hands and stood before him. "You're such a brave man coming here and chasing a dream," she said, pausing to make eye contact, as if they were about to exchange vows. "It's a shame you can't meet a woman to support you. If only I were single, that's what I'd do."

Johnny wanted to cry at such a beautiful thought. He snickered at the absurdity, knowing it was never going to happen.

"What?" Elena snapped and let go of his hands.

Johnny chuckled to ease the tension. "Nothing, babe. Just thinking about something that happened the other day."

Silence as Elena tried to process what he really meant, if it was true or a lie. Her eyes sparked. "I have an idea," she announced, with a matching electric smile. She explained that the contract with Johnny's company ended next month. "I'll tell your boss we're going in a different direction and hire you as the in-house English teacher," she added. "I'll pay you what we pay them so you can work half the hours."

Johnny felt air catch in his throat. He gulped to breathe. "Wow," he mumbled, massaging the back of his neck. "Don't know what to say."

"Don't say anything. Just use the free time to write."

Johnny's spirits lifted into a partly sunny sky at finally finding a person who believed in him. "And when I publish something," he promised, "you'll be the first person I thank."

"That would be very nice."

Their stares latched again. Elena's pupils pulsated as she bit her swelling bottom lip. Johnny recognized the look of mutual carnal attraction, although he preferred to think of it as the possibility of sharing a romantic dream, even if just for one night.

Elena's eyes clouded and dulled. "I told my boss about my pregnancy," her words slaying the moment between them.

Johnny's facial muscles hardened in an attempt to mask the sting the supposed good news still brought. A deep breath, and he swallowed the bitter disappointment, stomaching it like he did every time a rejection letter arrived in his inbox.

"How'd he take it?" he asked, forcing a half-smile to hide the discomfort of heartburn.

"He was a bit angry." Elena's neutral tone suggested such behavior was the norm. "Carla just got back from maternity leave and Sonia only got back from Russia with her little boy last December."

"It's a regular baby boom at the office," Johnny chuckled again so that Elena got he was trying to be witty.

"I suppose." She still didn't seem to find his comment funny.

"You'll make a great mother, Elena." Johnny thought a compliment was a good way to break the uneasy silence after a joke that had bombed.

"Hope so, *cariño*." She cut him a smile, but it didn't shine. It was the kind someone gave to feign excitement before embarking on an unplanned future. "Andreu never wanted more kids until recently," she explained, checking the time on her dangling gold watch. Her usually soft features hardened and she blurted, "Better go. Have a meeting in an hour and still need to get Andreu's book."

A fresh fragrance scented the air as Elena leaned in to kiss Johnny's cheeks. "We'll see each other next week," she whispered, letting him linger over her smell and warm breath before pulling away.

He grinned to pretend he was looking forward to it and watched as his student slunk away and disappeared into a haze of books and roses. The possibility that Elena was *la señorita* from his childhood dream was gone, like his life back home, leaving the same bittersweet aftertaste of, "What if?" Although, as with the splitting headache from this morning's hangover, the emotional hurt wasn't as strong. In its place was a sensation similar to freshman year when Johnny had to read *Great Expectations* by Dickens. The story of a Victorian orphan had caused an American teenager to spend the rest of his life wondering, what it would be like to have a benefactor. Now, nearly twenty years later, he had one, kind of, and she was much better looking than that witch of a woman, Miss Havisham.

CSI Barcelona

A mass of a man stormed into a smoky discotheque at *Port Olímpic*. The strobe-light flashed on his crazed, twitching face. His fiery eyes didn't blink as they peered over the heads of party-goers, grooving to a Latin beat. The man snorted and ground his teeth. His sights locked onto a statuesque blonde, flanked by two men. Both faces were familiar. Both provoked the urge to smash. Steam rose off a shaved head. The man snarled in a cockney accent, "Get outta my way, cunt," shoving a boy with braids and baggy jeans to the side.

He crashed into a group of similar looking kids who dropped their drinks. "*¡Joder! ¿Qué te pasa, tío?*" the scrawny boy cursed, bird chest puffed out, looking for a fight.

"Speak English, cunt." The brute smashed his head into the bridge of soft nose.

A yelp, and the boy clutched his face as he staggered back, slipped on an ice cube and fell to the ground.

"Anyone else got a problem?" The barmy Englishman growled at a group of trembling onlookers who picked up their bloodied friend and parted to a series of mumbled Spanish insults.

Luckily for them, he had no idea what they said, that they shat on his whore of a mother (who he adored) and in her milk. He refocused on the blonde, chatting with two men he wanted to pulverize. An oft-broken nose flared in concert with blood-shot eyes. The bull of a man dropped his shoulder and charged.

Revelers bounced off swinging arms to the spray of cocktails and the crash of glasses. Two bouncers, big enough to be professional wrestlers, rushed in and tackled the rampaging beast to the wet dance-floor.

"Get the fuck off me," the Englishman cursed, as the juiced-up bouncers dragged him, kicking and jerking, through the parting sea of stunned party-goers, out the front door and across a sidewalk before dumping him at the edge of a parking lot, during a late spring storm.

The mass of a man rose to his feet, face still twitching and crazed. Rain bounced off his shiny chrome dome as he dusted the shards of glass and gravel off his palms. The two bouncers stood in the murky glow of the discotheque's entrance, their comically large arms folded across inflated chests. Smoke steamed out of the brute's flaring nostrils. He stomped a fresh puddle and readied for another charge.

"Hey, Jared," a familiar voice shouted from above.

He stepped back and looked up into the stormy night sky. Rain drops glistened in the city's lights; a black speck grew in size. The large Englishman turned to hightail it, but before he took a step, a piece of jagged concrete scraped the back of his head and slammed into his shoulders.

***

The flashing blue lights atop navy and white police cars melted with the orange lights on yellow ambulances, to color the crime scene in a gas-light green. Outside the shuttered discotheques of *Port Olímpic*, club-goers with smudged makeup and soaked shirts waited around to give statements to the uniformed officers who set up a tent to keep their notes dry.

Away from this scene, a solitary man marched through the driving rain with the hood of his black anorak up, a capped long lens camera with a flash, swinging from his neck.

"Grissom!" belted a young male officer, in the fluorescent-yellow and dark-blue uniform, of the *Guàrdia Urbana*, or city police.

Dr Josep Caldet (the most senior, but not highest ranked, Field Agent for the Scientific Police Division) cringed and ignored the annoying comparison to a character on a TV show most of his colleagues loved, but he made a point never to watch.

He addressed a thin female officer, in the navy and crimson colors, of the *Mossos d'Esquadra* who, like him, worked for the Catalan Regional Authority. "What happened?"

"Looks like a piece of concrete fell on our victim from the boardwalk above."

Caldet peered through square glasses, popular with pseudo-intellectuals and hipsters, to see a hulk of a man, lying face down in a puddle of blood and muddy rainwater.

The forensic scientist spoke to the female officer again. "Do we know who the victim is?"

She shook her head. "No ID on him. The bouncers think he's English. He picked a fight with some South Americans."

"Where's the coroner?"

"Finishing his coffee," a tall man, in a dark military-looking uniform, representing *la Policía Nacional,* or the Spanish National Police, answered the question.

Caldet stared at the three officers of the different law enforcement departments he had to keep in the loop during the forensics investigation. They all had the expressions of passive students, waiting for the professor to speak.

He felt his neck strain as he turned and looked at the MAPFRE Insurance Tower, standing tall and dark, on the upper boardwalk behind him. The falling rain pelted the thick lenses of his black-rimmed glasses and salt-and-pepper beard. "Do you know why in England they say, 'It's raining cats and dogs'?" A dripping Caldet faced the three police officers, standing at attention, in their different colored uniforms, as they awaited his answer. "Because in the past, pets slept on the roofs and when it rained, they fell off."

Silence at the urban legend.

"That's interesting, sir," the female officer eventually said.

"Yes. Thought so, too." Caldet took off his glasses and wiped the lenses on damp slacks. The young woman was still blurry as he adjusted the black frames on his uneven ears. "Although, tonight," the forensic scientist added, with a well-practiced smile, "we must amend the phrase to, 'It's raining concrete slabs'." He paused but his grin held firm. "And please, call me 'Josep', 'Pep' or 'Pepito'. Anything but *Grissom*."

There was no patter of falling rain in the basement of the Bellvitge hospital. Overhead strip-lights shined with the intensity of solar lamps and reflected off steel slabs, countertops and sinks, common in most morgues. But the glare did little to brighten the grayish blue paint on aged stone walls that amplified the echo of footsteps.

"Well, well, well," a mustachioed man muttered, looking up from a corpse on a metal gurney to greet his visitor. "If it isn't Grissom."

Caldet focused on the trunk of a nose in the middle of

a long leathery face and grinned. "Good morning, Quincy."

"Who the fuck is that?"

"Do you remember that American TV comedy *The Odd Couple*?" The forensic scientist went for the most popular of Jack Klugman's work to explain the joke. "Think it was also a play."

The coroner shook his head. Caldet realized his daughters were right—he was a *friki*. He had met only a few people (his wife being a convert) who shared his love of classic TV comedies, especially British, but some American ones, too. The coroner, Francisco 'Paco' López, obviously had no idea who Quincy M.E. was, rendering Caldet's comeback as limp as a man's penis after a vasectomy.

The forensic scientist opened the leather folder he carried under his arm. "What can you tell me about the victim?" he inquired, hoping at least the awkwardness of the moment would stop the Grissom comparisons.

"The police report was right," the coroner told him. "Time of death was 2:30am. Although, blunt force trauma wasn't the cause of this man's demise."

Caldet hadn't expected that answer and stroked his well-groomed salt-and-pepper beard, encouraging Dr López to elaborate:

"He drowned in his own blood and rainwater."

"How long would that take?" Caldet jotted down some notes before glancing at the shattered nose and eye sockets of the cleaned-up victim.

"A few minutes," the coroner said.

The forensic scientist needed some clarification, "Nobody came to check if he was alright?"

"Appears not."

Caldet, a father of two girls, thought of the poor boy's

parents. How would they react when they learned no one had bothered to help their son as he died?

"Do we know who he is?" the coroner asked. "He's obviously not Spanish. I'd say: English or German."

"English. And not yet."

"Figures." Dr López snapped off his latex gloves, signaling an end to the autopsy. "All the English like to do is come to Spain, get drunk and fight."

"I wouldn't say *all*," Caldet sneered, feeling irrationally defensive of a people he mostly knew through their entertainment. "Have you ever been to England?"

"No." The coroner shuddered at the suggestion. "Who would want to? Terrible food and weather. Plus the people are strange. They lack life. Spain is much better."

"That's a bit of a generalization, isn't it?" Pep chuckled. "Like all Spanish take siestas."

"That's true of the people down south." The coroner did not seem amused. "In Catalunya, we work too hard to sleep siestas."

"Except for weekends and holidays, right?" Caldet winked.

Dr López's leathery, mustachioed face slanted with confusion, at the insinuation that there wasn't much difference between northerners and southerners when it came to the love of post lunch naps, only the opportunity to take them. "Anyway," a skeptic coroner said before his expression relaxed and he described the victim's blood alcohol level as, "five times the legal limit, with enough cocaine in his system to have killed most men and a few bulls, too."

Caldet wondered if the incident at the discotheque was the cause or the catalyst of death. "Had he not drowned, would he have OD'ed?"

"Doubt it." Dr López explained that when he had worked at Hospital del Mar he had treated Englishmen with three times those drug and alcohol levels. "They seem," the coroner spoke as if he were about to present his opinion to a trial judge, "genetically predisposed to drinking and drugging."

Caldet remembered a forensics conference he attended in Manchester two years ago. Girls in short dresses stumbled into wintry night streets as boys ran around twirling their blazers above their heads. "On that point, Paco..." Caldet paused mid-sentence to finish writing notes and close his folder, "I would have to agree with you."

Caldet's seniority got him a fifth-floor office at the Scientific Police Division's Head Quarters in the city of Sabadell, located on the other side of Barcelona's foothills. The morning sunlight poured through open blinds as he sat at a cluttered desk, reviewing the autopsy report, crime scene photos and case notes.

Knuckles rapping on a hollow door broke his concentration. "Come in," Caldet said in Spanish, rising from an ergonomic chair to welcome his visitor.

It was the young female *Mosso* from earlier, dressed in a pale-blue shirt and dark slacks, that swallowed her slim figure.

"Hello, doctor." She spoke in Catalan and gave her rank as Sergeant and name as Montserrat Llobet.

With a Catalan father and Spanish mother, Caldet had no problems switching between the two official languages of the region. "It's nice to see you again, Sergeant," he replied in *Català*. "Take a seat."

"Thank you for seeing me and call me: Montse." She sat down and noticed the framed picture of the doctor, his wife and two daughters on a messy desk. "You have a beautiful family."

Caldet smiled and nodded in appreciation. "I am very lucky. Although right now my girls are at university and all they do is ask for money." He went on a riff about one daughter being in Australia for a year, the other in London, both under the pretense of improving their English. The father of two princesses confessed to spoiling his children, saying that was what happened when you grew up in post Civil War Spain.

The young female police officer sighed and rolled her eyes at the mention of the tragic past.

Caldet stopped speaking and grinned. "Forgive me. I tend to digress. What can you tell me about the victim?"

Montse matched him an apologetic smile. "That's alright," she told him. "My father does the same thing," giving the victim's name as Jared Stewart. A drunken American girl had ID'ed him at the scene. Apparently, she was the victim's ex-girlfriend and he was at the club, hunting her down.

"Is she a suspect?" Caldet inquired.

"Everyone's a suspect right now, doctor." Montse's sharp features hardened behind square glasses that, like her uniform, were too big for her avian face, except for her Toucan nose.

Caldet took off his glasses. He pinched the nasal bone between closed eyes to collect his thoughts before he spoke. He didn't understand his sudden infatuation with the olfactory organ because the one characteristic that bound the various people of Spain was their large schnozzes. Only the shape seemed to differ, depending on the region. Seeing a corpse with a smashed-in face *must be influencing my thinking on a subliminal level,* Caldet decided, trying not to laugh at the surreal detour his mind took sometimes.

"No need to be formal and use titles like *doctor*," he said, with a little smile, as he set black-rimmed glasses on uneven ears. "My wife and daughters call me 'Pep.' And I think we can rule the American girl out."

"Why do you say that?" Montse eyed him with askance after his long pause, as if she had read his thoughts and knew he had compared her nose to one of the biggest bills in the animal kingdom.

"The piece of concrete was too big for one person to lift." Caldet widened his smile to ease the tension. "Besides, the nearest construction debris was by the beach." He opened his folder to a rough sketch of how he imagined the crime taking place and continued, "Based on the time-line, Jared died shortly after being kicked out, which means the killers were waiting for him here."

Caldet used his mechanical pencil as a pointer to show Montse a group of tiny black figures he had doodled at the base of the MAPFRE Tower.

"You're positive the brick was thrown and didn't simply fall?" she asked.

"Yes. Look." Caldet pointed at the other side of the folder and a meticulously sketched, scaled-down crime scene. A curve traced the trajectory of the concrete as it fell from the upper promenade to Jared's shoulders. "He was too far from the edge for it to be an accident," the forensic scientist stated. "Someone had to have thrown the heavy piece of concrete over."

"You're quite the artist."

Montse had been the first person to have ever commented positively on the precision of Caldet's sketches. Most gave them cursory glances; others asked if all of the attention to detail was really necessary.

"Thank you." Caldet caught himself before he went on

a tangent about the frustrated painter inside him. He stuck to the case, explaining how the rain had corrupted most physical evidence, such as cigarette butts, but he had found some skin samples on the concrete.

"Could it have been a random attack?" Montse inquired.

"Could be." Caldet shrugged to admit anything was possible. "But such incidences are rare. As you know, most violence here is domestic in nature. *Machismo* is still unfortunately strong in Catalunya, as in the rest of Spain. Things are changing of course." The forensic scientist stopped and smiled. "Sorry. Digressing again, aren't I? What do we know about Jared?"

Montse wore the same patient smirk as Caldet's wife and daughters when his mind branched out into other topics, taking his flapping gums with it. "The British consulate was quick to call back," the female sergeant said. "Guess the vic is the son of a well-to-do family."

"Perhaps Scotland Yard will get involved?" Caldet had always wanted to work with the world-renowned British Police Force.

"Doubt it." Montse was quick to shoot down the possibility. "The victim isn't a cute blue-eyed toddler. Also, his ex-girlfriend called Jared a 'spanker' who had a long list of enemies."

Caldet had never heard of such an occupation. "A what?"

"*A spanker.*" Montse repeated the English word, describing the American girl as "not very forthcoming" about Jared's work. She did, however, provide the names of English and Irish pubs he had frequented. Montse took this information to her captain who ruled the material irrelevant. The most obvious culprits, according to him, were the South Americans that the victim had fought with.

"Why does your captain believe that?" Caldet asked.

"He thinks the perps are Latin Kings, but he says that about all young South Americans."

"What's your opinion?" The forensic scientist was surprised by Montse's independent streak, not because she was a woman, but because of the conformist nature of the Spanish and Catalan people, himself included.

"My hunch tells me to investigate Jared Stewart more." The female sergeant flashed a cheeky smile. "Like they say on *CSI*—'follow the victim,' right?"

Behind her square glasses, dark eyes flickered, gauging Caldet's reaction to her comment. He let the irksome pop culture reference pass. At least Montse hadn't called him Grissom. "Why don't you do that?" he suggested.

"My captain doesn't like to be disobeyed."

"At least check out the bars," Caldet told her. "Say it was my idea if he asks why you did it. There's an international forensics conference in Edinburgh next week and I want to practice my English before going."

That was a boldface lie, but there was something about this young Catalan woman Caldet admired. She didn't have the typical *funcionario* mentality of shirking responsibility. She was willing to put in the work to nab the real culprits, rather than pin the crime on somebody who was probably guilty of being an illegal immigrant, drug dealer or pickpocket, but not a murderer.

The day after a storm, Barcelona's buildings glistened, as if their engraved stone façades had been waxed and polished. The layer of smog often trapped between the foothills and the sea vanished, ushering in a lucid blue sky. Even Sergeant Montserrat Llobet's navy and white hatchback SEAT [say-aht] seemed to sparkle as if it had been hand-washed, not rinsed by the previous night's rain.

"There hasn't been a kidnapping," Caldet hissed, pinned back in the passenger seat, eyes squeezed shut, to quell the motion sickness he felt as the car weaved through traffic on Grand Via, sirens blaring, lights flashing.

"Sorry." Montse eased off the accelerator and switched off the dissonant noise before pulling behind a black and yellow taxi that braked. "Just anxious to solve this case, you know?"

Caldet rocked forward and back from the abrupt stop. "Patience my dear," he said, looking at her profile, which was all glasses and nose, framed by stringy raven hair pulled tight into a pony-tail. The female sergeant was only a few years older than his daughters, but had a toughness to her that the forensics scientist usually only found in products of broken or abusive homes.

The SEAT parked in front of a small domed sand-colored church. Dread-locked Caucasian teenagers jumped off nearby benches and snatched their backpacks as Montse got out of the car.

"This is the third place on the list," she complained, slamming the door.

The sweet odor of the hashish the kids had been smoking still scented the air when Pep got out. "Third time's a charm," he said, as he turned his attention to an Irish Bar across the narrow street.

Green wood paneling framed the doorway of a beige building and a stand-alone chalkboard displayed the dates and times of upcoming football matches. The inside was dim, the smell of cooking oil rife in the steamy air. The decor on the walls celebrated the Irish. Street signs pointed to Dublin and Limerick while framed posters showed a Toucan in a tuxedo, flying a fixed-wing plane or on a bicycle, with an enormous front wheel, serving a pint of Guinness.

Caldet and Montse took a seat at the top of the bar near the kitchen entrance.

"Whakin aye gitcha ya two?" mumbled a pale bartender, sporting a patchy beard.

Caldet drew a deep breath and tried to muster the courage to speak to a native English speaker. "One pint of Guinness please, mate," he ordered, using the colloquial phrase his English teacher had taught him many years ago before a family trip to London during Holy Week (Easter).

"Doctor!" Montse reprimanded him in Catalan, "We're on duty."

Caldet felt his hairy chest swell in pride at how much English he still remembered. He didn't use it much now, but for most of his career, he had been the only one in the Science Division who spoke the language well-enough to attend international forensic conferences.

"A Guinness clears the head," the English idiom came out with ease, as if Caldet had said his favorite Catalan tongue-twister, *Setze jutges d'un jutjat mengen fetge d'un penjat*, (Sixteen court judges eat the liver of one hanged.) "You should try one."

"Anything for me." Montse spoke to the bartender in Spanglish. "*J-ou espeak espanish?*"

"Not yet," he replied, as he topped off the pint of stout, which he set down in front of Caldet.

Montse sighed to signal her annoyance and asked, " *J-ou* know *Yea-rad* Stewar'?" barking each word.

The boy's scruffy face crinkled as he tried to decipher the question. "Jared Stewart?" he confirmed the name a few seconds later. "Yeah. I know 'im. What's he done?"

The kid spoke as if he had a mouth full of sunflower seeds. Montse looked to Caldet and asked in Catalan, "Have you understood him?"

"More or less." He stayed in English and sipped the creamy beer before changing the subject, "I love Guinness. This reminds me of when my family and I went to Ireland."

"Pep," Montse snapped.

"Sorry." He flashed an apologetic smile and looked at the pasty boy, with long shaggy brown hair a shade lighter than what sprouted from his cheeks and chin. "Can you tell me how long Jared be coming here?"

"He's *been* coming since before I started and that was over a year ago."

Caldet was used to being corrected when he spoke English. "Sorry. Could you repeat, please?" he asked. "And a little more slowly," gesturing with his hands so that the boy who looked like an anorexic Neanderthal got the point.

He seemed annoyed by his customers' lack of English fluency. "One second," he grumbled. "The owner's Spanish. Lemme get 'im."

Montse watched the gangly boy lope into the kitchen before she turned to Pep. "I don't understand," she whispered, her voice dropping out of an irrational fear that the English bartender, who didn't speak Spanish, could understand Catalan. "How can you come to this country, live and work, and not bother to learn the language? Maybe not *Català*, if you are only here a short while, but at least *Castellano*."

Caldet chuckled and spoke Catalan in his normal tone. "I imagine when you come to a foreign country, you tend to stick together."

"That's no excuse," Montse snapped, cutting a

withering look at the glass shelves and brick wall behind which was the kitchen where the focus of her anger stood. "If I lived in London, I would have to learn English."

"Yes, of course you're right." Caldet raised his palms to show agreement with her argument. "I was just explaining why they don't."

Montse gave him the same judgmental glare she had given the kitchen, saying that she didn't buy the forensic scientist's reasoning.

Caldet sipped his Guinness and changed the subject again, "Are you sure you don't want to try some?"

"Positive. Look. Here comes the owner."

He was a mountain of a man, with the swollen face and heavy eyelids of a former boxer. "How can I help you?"

Pep picked up on his Spanish accent that dropped the -r at the end of *ayudar* the -s in *ustedes*. "From Andalucía?"

"Born in Jaén, but grew up in Madrid. Understand you're here about Jared Stewart?"

Caldet readied to tell stories about his last visit to both places, but Montse cut him off:

"What can you tell us about the English boy?"

"He started coming almost two years ago. Believe he's from London. A real hard case, but he's always well-behaved when he comes." The bar owner was bigger than the bouncers at *Port Olímpic* and ground a large fist into his palm. "*I* make sure of it," before cracking his knuckles.

"What's a *spanker*?" Caldet inserted himself into the conversation to satisfy his curiosity about the new English vocabulary.

"You really don't know?" The burly bar owner's

gravelly voice cracked with surprise as he ran gnarled fingers through curly gray hair. "I mean—there are only a few things English speakers do in Barcelona: teach, work at a bar, on boats or as a spanker."

"That's great to know," Montse quipped, snatching off her square glasses to unleash the full fury of her black eyes. "Now tell us what exactly *spanking* is."

The bar owner jumped back and looked away from Montse's dark stare, down the empty stools, then at the closed front door behind her. "Okay," he huffed, facing a glowering Montse again. "But keep my name out of the investigation."

"Can't promise that." She squinted and continued in an even tone, "But if you don't tell me, there will be an inspection tomorrow to make sure all of your employees are legal and paying their taxes."

"Alright, alright!" The bar owner threw his arms in the air and shook his hands at the heavens. "I'll tell you what I know."

His voice dropped to a hush as he leaned over the bar counter and detailed the shady world of fraudulent telesales, otherwise known as *spanking*.

The boiler-rooms were mostly run by British men (English, Scots and Welsh), with a sprinkling of Irish (North and South), Americans (Canadians and US), South Africans, Ozzies and Kiwis thrown in. The bosses, like Jared, were long time veterans of different operations that had fled the UK after authorities cracked down on their illicit activities at the start of the 1990s.

Barcelona was the perfect location to set up a spank shop. There had been a legal loophole which allowed boiler-rooms to operate with impunity, even if the only thing sold was false hope to the senile, lonely and naive.

The law was eventually changed, but the locals' lack of language skills meant that the criminals could continue to conduct their illegal business, with little fear of the Spanish or Catalan authorities understanding the shady nature of *spanking*. Add in a sunny climate and a beach for a recruiting tool, plus cheap rents thanks to the euro-pound conversion, and you had all the ingredients necessary to become "The Spanking Capital of Europe."

"I don't believe you," Montse snorted, placing her glasses back on a nose, the same shape and size as the Guinness bird. "We would've heard about these *spankers* if they still worked out of Barcelona."

"Really?" The bar owner yelped, tilting his trunk of a neck, like a confused bulldog when confronted by a yappy terrier. "Sit in my bar for one night," he challenged the female officer. "They make up 20 per cent of my clientèle, but 60 per cent of my profits."

"Why do they call them *spankers*?" Caldet spoke in Spanish, but used the English word because he had yet to think of a good translation.

"Because of their ability on the phones." The bar owner's hooded eyes lifted with relief at not having to talk to Montse. "A regular of mine said..." the former boxer pretended to have somebody bent over his thick thigh and slapped the air to convey the meaning, "they verbally spank the person on the phone until they agree to buy a fake stock."

"How could anyone fall for such a scam?" Montse's visage smoothed as she leaned forward to show interest.

"All of these guys have the gift of gab and zero conscience." The bar owner' tone rose with a hint of admiration as he explained how first time investors always got a great return. "Then they put their whole savings in the scheme and lose everything."

"Tragic," Caldet muttered, finishing his Guinness. "How do these criminals get people's numbers?"

"Just like any other telesales business—they buy leads from multinational banks."

"Why haven't you called and told us about them?" Montse demanded to know.

The bar owner raised his hands above his head to plead his innocence. "They don't break the law when they come here."

"Did he have friends?" Montse continued her interrogation.

"Look to your left. Do you see that picture?"

Caldet and Montse swiveled on their stools to see a photo collage of inebriated customers plastered to a wall. A sun-burned Jared Stewart stood in the middle of a group of equally prawn-red friends. "That's his crew from last year," the bar owner explained, pointing a crooked finger at the picture. "Some are still here, but most have gone. Jared seems to have new people working for him every month."

Montse faced the bar owner again. "Do they come in often?"

"They'll probably be in for the Champions League match tonight. They're all Chelsea fanatics."

"Great!" Montse jerked her arm in celebration and thumbed at the wall. "Can we take that picture?"

"Sure." The bar owner grinned as if he expected to hear some gossip. "Is Jared in some kind of trouble?"

"Jared's dead."

A swollen face deflated at the abrupt delivery of the shocking news. "You think his friends did it?"

"We don't know," Montse told him. "But if they come in tonight act normal, okay?" She pushed away from the bar and turned to Caldet. "Come on. Let's go."

Her strength and character left him docile and obedient. Police work was obviously her life and the forensic scientist envied that. He had never wanted to go into medicine. His father had pushed him to become a doctor, claiming that there was no pay for an artist. He wasn't going to rebel against a man who had lost so much during the Civil War, a man who had worked two jobs so that his children could get the best education, including an English tutor when every one else learned French. And while Caldet took a professional pride in his vocation, he felt no passion for solving crimes, unlike the assured female officer he followed out the door.

They returned to the crime scene as the sun began its gradual descent toward Barcelona's foothills. The black MAPFRE Tower cast a cool shadow on the boardwalk where Caldet stood, peering through his thick glasses.

He looked beyond the shimmering forest of masts, belonging to the yachts and sailboats docked in the marina, to see the horizon where an azure sky met a turquoise sea. Barges trolled the waters, dredging up sand to spray the man-made beaches. Breakwaters made from reused rubble stretched away from the coast, like a series of *T's*, in a futile attempt to stop the erosion from the lapping tide.

Caldet remembered the time when none of this district existed. The area north of the old fisherman neighborhood of Barcenoleta had been a derelict industrial zone left to gypsies and vagrants until the Olympic Games in 1992. It was that year the bronze lattice fish sculpted by the famed architect, Frank Gehry, arrived and assumed its iconic position in front of the white exoskeleton of the five-star Hotel Arts.

Caldet stopped zoning out on the vast horizon and his memories. He opened his leather folder to sketch Montserrat Llobet who stood near a pile of construction debris, less than a meter from the shore. He thought it was better to leave the investigation to professionals who weren't prone to distracting tangents. As the female sergeant conducted interviews with the employees of the surrounding discotheques and restaurants, a frustrated artist tried to put her animated gestures down on paper.

Montse stopped talking and spotted Caldet on the upper boardwalk. She waved in the air for him to join her. He slipped a mechanical pencil into his inside jacket pocket and closed his folder, tucking it securely under his arm before proceeding down the steps.

"Any luck?" Caldet asked, as they met at the spot where Jared drowned in a puddle of rainwater and his own blood.

"Yes," a beaming Montse shouted, punching Caldet in the shoulder, hard enough for knuckles to touch bone. "Three people remember hearing a group of Englishmen by the beach before the concrete fell." Montse's smiling lips pursed with annoyance as she continued, "I told my captain when we first arrived that we should canvass the boardwalk to see if there were any witnesses, but he said it was an accident and went to have a coffee."

"That's the easy way to do it." Caldet grinned as he rubbed the tender spot where Montse had hit him.

"It seems only idiots become bosses," she said.

He nodded in agreement and told her, "That's why the world is the way it is," feeling his capricious mind take control of his mouth. "What are you going to do? It is what it is, like people calling me Grissom. Do you know some of my colleagues actually think I can solve any crime by investigating the bugs at the scene? I used to get irritated and scream: 'I hate fucking insects and have arachnophobia'. Still, everyone calls me fucking Grissom and yells at me about not closing cold cases."

Caldet scowled at the luxury yachts and waved his arms at a calm sea. "'This isn't America," he roared. "We don't have fancy computers. This is Spain. I have a five year-old piece of shit that freezes if I open more than two programs and I spend most of my time writing duplicate reports for three different police departments."

Caldet's heart poked his chest bone, like two stiff fingers, reminding him to calm down. He took a deep breath of salty sea air and turned to Montse. "Now I try and let the comparison go," he flashed his usual apologetic smile as he concluded his rant, "because anger is destructive and I value my health."

The female sergeant replied with a bemused look. "I see, I think," she added, putting a slender hand on his shoulder. "The good news is," her voice lifted with optimism, "we have enough to bring in Jared's friends tonight."

Caldet nodded in agreement again, but kept his answer short. "Yes. That is good news. When you bring them in, call me. I can match their DNA sample to the skin trace we found on the piece of concrete."

"Wouldn't you like to come along?" Montse had expected the forensic scientist to suggest that himself. "It's your investigation after all," she reminded him. "You've also got a forensic conference in Edinburgh coming up. Great chance to practice your English, right?"

Caldet had forgotten about his lie. He pondered the offer out loud to distract from the guilt he felt at his duplicity, "There hasn't been another crime that needs my attention and I can't close my report until I match the DNA sample." The forensic scientist paused and announced his decision, "I'd love to. Thank you."

The *Mossos d'Esquadra* police station assigned to the Port Olímpic District was just below the Glòries Roundabout, where Barcelona's four main avenues intersected and crossed, like the lines of the Union Jack. The walls and linoleum floor inside the building were the same pale-blue shade as the short-sleeved shirts Montse and the other police officers wore.

The only female in the room, her arrival didn't provoke hoots or double-takes from the men who stood at wooden desks. Instead, they drank coffee in plastic cups and shouted over each other in Spanish about that night's Champions League football match, between *Barça* and Chelsea.

Caldet chimed in, "It all depends if Messi is healthy or not."

"Grissom, you like football?"

Caldet saw the high-pitched voice belonged to a fresh faced recruit, looking to impress the more seasoned officers. "Yes," the forensic scientist said. "I enjoy a good match or when *Espanyol* play."

"You're a *perico*, Grissom? But they're fascists."

Caldet thought about quoting Godwin's Law which ruled, whoever used the terms like "Nazi" or "fascist" first, lost the argument. "Are they?" he asked, keeping his tone light, to avoid the conversation getting too political and heated. It was just football after all.

"Yes," the young officer confirmed, switching from Spanish to Catalan. "Everyone knows *Espanyol* is the team of Spanish fascists. Barça is the true team of Catalunya. It's more than a club!"

"They may play sublime football," Caldet admitted in the same language. "But why do you, *culés,* only shout and applaud when Barça win, but whine and whistle when they lose?"

The recruit's boyish features wrinkled as he tried to think of something to say. Caldet didn't let up. He brought up an interview with a current player who spoke longingly of the support English teams received. "He said Barça would've won twice as much if only they had such passionate backing."

The recruit's expression darkened as he continued to search for a comeback and Caldet closed his argument, "They say the quietest place in Spain is Camp Nou when Barça is trailing nil-one, which I believe was the result last year when we beat you!"

The red-faced recruit cursed, "Son of a whore," in Spanish and stormed away.

"You put him in his place, *Grissom*," Montse needled, as they walked into her captain's office.

Xavier Fernández rose from behind his wooden desk at their entrance. He had the dark coloring of someone found in the deepest regions of Spain, but was much taller than any Spaniard or Catalan. The bald spot on the back of his head almost touched the ceiling as his eyes narrowed into slits.

"How can I help you, Sergeant?" he growled in *Castellano*, his tobacco and coffee flavored breath reaching their noses.

"We've been following up on some leads regarding the Jared Stewart case," Montse replied in the same language, as she looked up from a broad chest and stared into angry black eyes.

"Have you been in *Poble Sec* looking for the *sudacas*?" her captain asked.

Montse shook her head and said, "We think our victim was killed by a group of Englishmen," maintaining an even tone and eye contact.

"I know the English are hooligans." Her captain snickered, as if saying a stereotype was the same thing as telling a joke, and showed her his back. "But what makes you think that?"

"The evidence, sir." Montse told him about Jared's connection to the illegal business called "spanking," the witnesses' confirmation of a group of Englishmen at the beach prior to the incident and their probably location later tonight.

Xavier Fernández frowned at the news as he sat behind his desk and glowered at Montse. "I thought I told you the *sudacas* were our primary suspects."

Pep stepped in. "Believe the correct term is South Americans, isn't it?" No response at his admonishment so he continued, "They still may be responsible. We just need to rule the English angle out first."

The captain's intimidating glare remained fixed on Montse until he grabbed a pen from a Barça cup on his desk. "You can use two officers off the clock," he informed her, as he started to fill out a report.

The sides of Montse's mouth quivered from trying not to grin. "Thank you, sir."

"But, Sergeant..." her captain wagged his plastic pen at her as he spoke, "if I catch you going behind my back and disobeying orders again, I will have your ass. Do we understand each other?"

"Yes, sir."

Xavier Fernández turned his attention to Caldet. "As for you, Grissom. You need to stop watching so much *CSI*. You're place is in Sabadell with other scientists, not on Barcelona's streets with *Los Mossos*."

The burly Spanish owner was leaning on a brass tap, chatting to a patron, when Montse, Caldet and two other plain-clothes officers entered. She wore contacts instead of glasses, jeans and a t-shirt, which swallowed a figure starved from having any resemblance to the female form.

"You're back?" The bar owner did little to hide his disappointment at their arrival.

"Yes. But stay calm," Montse commanded, as she sat at the top of the bar, on the same stool as that afternoon.

Caldet tugged on his beige cardigan and looked around before he sat down next to her. An hour before kickoff saw the front area empty and only a few couples near the big screen in the main room at the end of the narrow bar.

"Are you here to arrest those English boys?" a nervous looking bar owner asked.

"We want to talk to them at the station." Montse squinted to see, not an ex-boxer, but a coward. "What's the matter?"

"It's just... I don't want any trouble, you know?"

"Relax." Montse's lips spread into a forced smile that was the opposite of reassuring. "That's why we're here early — we'll grab them and leave."

All of the bar owner's bulk did little to hide the worry in his heavy eyes as he looked at the female sergeant, no doubt wishing she would change her mind.

"Now, go act normal," Montse ordered, shushing the hovering man away. She waited for the bar owner to leave before turning to a pale skinned officer, with a hyper-alert stare and cropped black hair. "Thanks for coming, Pau," she whispered Catalan in his ear. "Owe you one."

His brow softened. "How about that dinner I've been after?"

"How about a coffee to start?" Montse patted his bicep pumping underneath a tight polo-shirt. "Been working out I see."

The muscular police office blushed.

A wiry officer, in a red track suit, spoke to them in Spanish. "We should order something while we wait."

"Good idea, Alfonso," Caldet seconded in the same language. "I'm having a Guinness."

Montse cut him a judgmental look.

"What?" the veteran forensic scientist protested. "You're worse than my daughters. Fifteen years ago, we would have been drinking a bottle of wine while we waited. Besides, I doubt these men are armed."

"Assume the worse." Montse spoke in *Castellano* as well so that everyone understood. "Also, I think *we* would've been you three, with me at home cooking and cleaning."

"But we are undercover, Montse." Pau joined the conversation and put a hand on her spiny back.

The female sergeant flinched. "Suppose one won't hurt," she conceded, with a shiver, as Caldet called over the skinny Neanderthal looking bartender to order a round of Guinness.

"Man, the English can drink," Alfonso declared, nodding his smooth chin at an tiny man with a square head at the far end of the bar. "That guy's on his third bottle in five minutes."

The front door creaked open, interrupting their conversation. The chatter of English shook the mist of cooking oil as a group of boys and girls entered, wearing the navy-blue and burgundy scarves of Barcelona Football Club.

"Here you go." The bar owner handed the officers four pints of Guinness. "On the house."

Montse took a sip. Her mouth curled, her ivory skin wrinkling in disgust. "This is horrible! It's so bitter."

"It's an acquired taste." Caldet spoke in English and noticed the bar had reached full capacity. He tried to tune into the enthusiastic television commentators who hyped the match to a crowd that was 90 per cent Barça supporters. Replica jerseys, hats and scarves colored the scene. None of the small contingent of Chelsea fans, in electric blue and white, matched the suspects from the picture back on the wall.

After a few minutes, the door flung open again. "Blue is the color; football is the game," boomed through the bar. The owner's skin lost its brown Spanish tint, telling the police officers all they needed to know.

Caldet turned to see what confronted them. One of the suspects wore a Chelsea jersey stretched over a flabby upper body and skin-tight jeans. His red-headed partner had the build of an awkward adolescent and dressed in an extra large pink polo-shirt and baggy shorts around his hips.

The three police officers pushed away from the bar. The muscular Sergeant Pau Llorent put a hand on the bigger suspect's back. "Excuse me," he said in confident English. "We are *Los Mossos d'Esquadra* and would like you to come with us."

"Fuck off, cunt," the spanker cursed, nodding at the bar owner. "I'm here to watch..."

Pau grabbed the man's wrist, twisting his flaccid arm up and behind his back. The younger suspect turned to run. Montse followed Pau's lead. She grabbed a bony wrist. She spun the boy around, shoving him into a cigarette vending machine that rattled. His droopy shorts slid off his hips, down to his ankles. A torrent of verbal abuse spewed from his mouth. Montse boxed his ear to bring silence before applying the handcuffs she carried in the front pocket of ill-fitting jeans.

Caldet tuned into the ticking of the clock mounted on a pale-blue wall as he sat at a desk, doodling on a notepad he had found. He had been at the police station near the Glòries Roundabout for over two hours. A person's mumbled cursing drowned out the sound of a second hand. Caldet looked over his shoulder to see Montse, rubbing the bridge of her Toucan nose.

"Doctor," she huffed, pausing to redo her tight ponytail, which accentuated a face in need of a good meal and sleep. "Pau is in with the fat one. Do you mind talking to the skinny one? He doesn't speak *Castellano*. Alfonso and I don't understand him."

"Sure. I'd be happy to." Caldet dropped his pen and followed Montse into an interrogation room where the handcuffed suspect sat at a table under a light so bright that Caldet's head began to pound.

He squinted and pulled out a chair to sit down. His eyes darted to the manila folder on the table. He picked it up to skim the notes on loose sheets of paper before beginning the interrogation, "You are Andy Johnson, correct?"

Silence. Caldet gave his name and rank, as he tossed the folder back on the table.

The suspect laughed. "Getting interviewed by the Spanish Grissom, am I?"

He let the mock slide. "Do you know why you are here, Andy?"

The boy's thin lips spread into a taunting smirk. "Because you think all British are hooligans?"

Caldet shook his head and delivered the news, "Because we know you killed Jared Stewart."

"No, we didn't." A nervous laugh punctuated the denial as the spanker glanced over his shoulder at the closed door behind him.

"Show me your hands," Caldet ordered.

"Don't I get a lawyer?" The Englishman no longer smiled as he made eye contact and squirmed in his chair.

"No." Caldet snatched a pair of handcuffed wrists and twisted them in opposite directions. The kid's palms were scraped. The forensic scientist let go and shook his head again. He lied about his legal authority, "Tell me why you did it, Andy. I can get your sentenced reduced."

"We didn't do nuffin." The young suspect pounded the table, jingling his handcuffs.

Caldet leaned back in his chair and studied the freckles on rosy cheeks. "Tell me, Andy." He spoke in a more personable tone as he tried a new track. "How long did you work for Jared?"

The kid's green eyes darkened at the change in interrogation tactics. "Was one of the first people he brought over. Why?"

"You were close then, no?" Caldet wanted to gauge their relationship. Friends usually didn't kill each other except over a woman, maybe money or drugs.

"Guess so." The spanker's tone lightened as he spoke about his deceased colleague. "Jared would always let you know who was the boss, though."

"And who's the boss now?" Caldet felt the pull of a developing theory steer his questions.

"Dunno." The kid shrugged in his sloppy pink polo-shirt. "Imagine the top-earner will take over. That's usually how it works."

"Is that you?" Caldet believed the person before him was too much of a runt to be a leader.

The suspect's guttural laugh was easy, sincere, confirming his suspicion.

Cadlet remembered the conversation with the bar

owner, the constant churn of employees who had worked for Jared. "What happens to the ones who don't earn enough, Andy?"

"They look for new work."

"That means there are always new people looking to take your job, correct?" Caldet's eyes probed the wiseguy grin across the table in search of information during a long pause. He got nothing. Time for some more deceit to jump start the conversation:

"Your friend says it was your idea to kill Jared to avoid getting sacked."

"No, he didn't." The not so cocky suspect chuckled again. "Besides, it was 'im that was about to lose 'is desk. I 'ad *anuvver* mon*ff* to prove meself."

Caldet struggled to understand an English accent that was far different than what he heard on the BBC or at forensic conferences. The only noise in the interrogation room was the electric current feeding the blazing light in the ceiling. The forensic scientist watched as the expression in front of him shifted from one extreme to another. Each movement, whether the deepening of a line or the twitch of a lip, reflected the conflicting thoughts and emotions Caldet imagined swirled in the head of someone, facing a murder charge.

Had my inquisitor spoke the truth? Did my mate really sell me out?

"Is that offer for less jail-time still on the table?" the suspect eventually asked, his harsh English accent bouncing off the stone walls.

Caldet nodded and listened to the spanker explain that when he and his friends first arrived, Jared had given them golden leads, telephone numbers of pensioners which hadn't been picked over and called thousands of times.

"Problem was..." the freckled face kid spoke with the whiny tone of an aggrieved employee, "youse got to stay in the top five on the sales board." He drew a deep breath and screamed, "Do you know how fucking hard that is?" describing other spankers as men who could convince a dread-locked Jamaican to join the right-wing British National Front.

The ginger boy and his friends weren't very adept at *spanking* so they ended up with leads so marked up that it was impossible to make out the telephone digits. "But that's fucking with a geezer's livelihood, innit?" the young suspect finished, with a huff and rattle of his handcuffs, as he tried, unsuccessfully, to fold his arms.

Caldet was still trying to translate what he had heard into Spanish. "More or less," he grumbled, mulling the pieces he did comprehend. "What I don't understand is — why not go to another company?"

"'Cos Jared wudda made sure no *uvver* place'd 'ired us. He was a cunt like that." The kid's soft features hardened into the killer that he was. "He was also kicking us outta one a da flats the company ren'ed and we wudda 'ad to go back to merry ol' fucking England."

"Why not look for another flat and a new type of job?" Caldet suggested, thinking that was a better solution, than committing murder to stay in Barcelona.

"'Cos I don't fucking speak Spanish, mate."

One Step Forward, Three Steps Back

On the top floor of one of the majestic buildings along Passeig de Gràcia, a mousy man in a brown suit enters a prestigious lawyer's office. There is no warm welcome of a possible new client or even an acknowledgment of his arrival. The man raises a fist to his mouth and coughs. The lawyer licks a bejeweled finger and flips the page of a newspaper he reads by the afternoon sunlight, shining though the French doors behind him.

"Excuse me," the man says, brushing the long strands of his comb-over from his squinting eyes.

The lawyer burps and grumbles as he folds the thick daily along its creases before setting it down. "How can I help you?" he addresses the man in Catalan.

The kinship from speaking the same mother tongue lifts his spirits. "I'm your five o'clock appointment," the man announces.

A moon face crinkles in a way that suggests both irritation and confusion at what seems to be an unexpected visit. The lawyer slaps his knees and rises from his wingback chair with the enthusiasm of a husband being summoned by his wife during the middle of a tense football match. The tailored suit on his bubbly figure is a shade darker than his wavy gray hair and he has the lazy waddle of person not accustomed to moving from the table to the sink with his dirty dishes.

The man forces a smile as he speaks to stop a memory from flooding back and the severe indigestion the associated guilt brings. "I'm the one who attacked the state employee."

A gasp, which the distinguished lawyer tries to cover up with a cough. "Yes, um, er, well... I know who you are," he mutters, waving a short arm at a small wooden chair on the other side of his imposing desk. "Been expecting you. Take a seat."

The man says, "Thanks," but wonders if the lawyer is lying or if he treats all potential clients with total indifference, like the employees of *El Corte Inglés*, the department store where the man purchased the faded mud brown blazer, which he hangs on the back of a wooden chair before he sits.

The lawyer wears a bemused smile, slanting up in the direction of mocking. His lips show no sign of moving to speak. The man breaks eye contact and looks at full bookshelves, framed diplomas and pictures of local dignitaries.

The longer the silence the more uncomfortable the man feels and he is the first to speak. "You have to study a lot to be a lawyer, don't you?"

The lawyer nods. "And take many, many exams," opening a desk drawer. "Tell me—what on earth possessed you to attack someone? You don't look the violent type."

"It's a long story."

The lawyer tiffs to show his disappointment at the answer as he sets down a leather folder in front of him. "Well, um," he starts, pausing to stare into the man's languid wood-colored eyes, "if you want me to represent you, you'll have to tell what happened because right now you're facing ten years in prison for attacking a state employee."

"Ten years!" The man's face stretches and he smacks his scalp. "That's half what murders get. I didn't try and kill anybody."

"The sentence is a third of what you'd get if you were a terrorist," the lawyer delivers the statement as if it is good news. "The fact is, according to law X.564.P.907/N, a government employee is, in essence, an extension of the State. And as such, any attack on them is punishable by a minimum sentence of ten years in prison." The lawyer pauses for dramatic effect and adds, "Blame ETA," reminding his potential client of the special status *funcionarios* must have to discourage them from becoming targets of domestic terrorists. "A State Employee is treated no differently than the Prime Minister of Spain or the President of the *Generalitat*." The lawyer ends his lecture with an ironic smile. "Although, politicians can lose their jobs after an election while not going to work for months won't get a *funcionario* fired."

"I know, I know." The man doesn't need to be reminded about the perks of state employment. Like most of his friends, he once wanted to be a *funcionario*. But, like many adults (despite studying the thousands of arcane rules and regulations, written in Spanish and Catalan legalese, hours a day for decades), he never passed the series of exams known as *las oposiciones* to qualify for his dream, even after ten attempts.

"Okay. I hit a state employee," the man concedes. "But don't you think ten years is a little much? For fuck's sake! The Pedophile of L'Eixample got out in six. And that was after his fourth conviction."

"That was due to good behavior." The lawyer defends the judicial decision, "We're not America. We don't send people away for life or execute them."

"But six years for raping a kid?" The man, who has a son and a daughter, closes his eyes and shakes his head to rid himself of the disturbing images that come to mind.

He hears the lawyer open the folder and take a pen from a cup. "We might be able to reduce your sentence," his pitch projects hope as he writes, "but first you must tell me what happened."

The man opens his eyes and asks, "Where should I start?"

"The beginning is always good," says the lawyer, with a thin smile that adds, *I'm glad I'm not you.*

The man charged with attacking a government employee sighs at his predicament. "You know the new law that went into effect this year?"

The lawyer squints as the thinks before he seeks clarification, "Which one?"

"The one that requires all Barcelona residents to get a new identification number and card."

The lawyer nods and writes. "Law 20.210-19X."

"Yes," the man confirms. "I believe that's the number. How did you know it so quickly?"

"I'm a lawyer. I must know the law."

"Yes, of course." The man smiles and shakes his head in admiration. "But it is truly remarkable. You must be very intelligent."

The lawyer replies with a grin that beams false humility. The man breaks the silence and explains how he once wanted to be a lawyer. His scores on his high-school tests, however, determined he was better suited for the maths and sciences, leading him to study economics at university, and now he works as an accountant at a French multinational.

"A respectable job, no?" The lawyer's intonation registers confusion at the relevance of the man's educational and vocational background in relation to the crime with which he has been charged.

"Yes, suppose so," the man grumbles. "But the pay is shit."

"Enough to live on, isn't it?"

"Barely." The man stares at a shiny face that conveys as much sympathy as a Lladró doll. He imagines taking the folder on the desk and smacking the porcelain cheek, hard enough to make it shatter. "But nothing like yours," the man seethes, hearing a clenched jaw pop.

The lawyer senses the change in mood. He chuckles nervously and glances at his notes. "Enough about me," he says. "We were discussing the new law and why you attacked a *funcionario*."

"Yes, of course." The man shuffles his numb tailbone on the hard chair to get some feeling back. He tells of receiving a certified letter at the end of last November, reminding him that he hadn't filed the required paperwork for his new number and card yet.

"Why did you wait so long to do it?" the lawyer inquires.

"Because I don't have time for anything anymore!" The man flails his arms as he sits and rants about hectic days that start at seven and finish at midnight, with the only time to relax being the rare moments he steals his mother's Valium during family gatherings.

The wrinkles on the lawyer's face deepen as he squints again and sets down his pen to re-enforce his seriousness. "This law applies to *all* Barcelona residents. Even I have to follow it so lack of time is no excuse."

"Suppose you're right," the man mutters, unable to think of anything more to say. Sweat trickles from his armpits down his ribs as his body temperature rises. He stands from the hard chair and stretches on his way to the French doors behind the lawyer, in need of a moment to cool down.

Across the Passeig de Gràcia the centurion shaped chimneys of La Casa Milà shimmer in the late afternoon sun, as if they are metal, not stone. The glare stings the man's eyes. "Although," he blinks, long and slow, in concert with a heavy sigh through his nose, "I still don't understand why I need this card. What's wrong with my old one?"

"Aside from the €5,000 fine?" The lawyer doesn't bother to turn around and look at the man.

"Yes," he says, feeling hot again.

"The new number officially classifies you as a *tax-paying* resident of Barcelona." The lawyer explains that the purpose of the law is to entice people from the underground economy to become legal by offering a discounted rate for transportation passes and entrance to most sights, "like La Sagrada Família and Parc Güell."

"Let me guess." The man nods at the view outside the French doors, "Casa Milà, too."

"Of course," the lawyer declares, still facing his desk, not the sarcastic man behind him. "All of Gaudí's masterpieces. Plus Palau de la Música and Grand Theatre de Liceu."

Oh, how the man wishes his glare truly emitted fire. He'd burn the lawyer's swirling silver cowlick down to the scalp.

"I was raised in this city," the man snarls, coming back to reality. "And all my family lives here. We have a car and don't spend our free time sight-seeing or at the opera."

"What!" The lawyer slams his pen on the desk and

swivels around in his chair to confront the man, evil-eying his hirsute scalp. "But Barcelona is the most beautiful city in the world. How could you...?"

"Yes. You're right." The man has heard enough. He brushes the long strands of his comb-over from his wrinkled brow. "Barcelona is the best, like its football club. But I've already told you: *I don't have fucking time.*"

The man stomps to the hard wooden chair and sits in a huff. "May I?" he asks, pulling a cigarette pack out of his shirt pocket.

"Of course." The lawyer nods at a blue crystal ashtray on his desk. "Tell me about this letter."

The man lights a cigarette and takes a long meditative pull. Smoke gushes from his mouth as he speaks, "First I had to visit my local municipal office in L'Eixample. They needed to see official documentation, proving my residency, before giving give me the application."

The man explains once filling out the five page form in blue (not black) ink, he then had to take the application to the Catalan Regional Office, near Drassanes, for someone to stamp and sign the appropriate space. He next had to visit the Spanish Home Office, by *Estació de França,* for another signature and stamp on a different page. After he did all that, he needed to return to his municipal office in L'Eixample to submit the form.

"If approved," the man stubs his cigarette in the ashtray as he finishes reciting the letter, "I could expect the new card in six to eight weeks."

A befuddled lawyer looks up from his notes. "What's the big deal?" he asks, counting his chubby fingers. "One signature for the city, one for the regional autonomy and one for the country." He goes on to empathize with the seemingly infuriating nature of such multiple layers of bureaucracy before shifting to defend the various departments' importance and their vital role within a functioning state.

"Why not just pay someone to do it?" the lawyer suggests, genuinely curious to hear the answer. "It's only €75. That's what I do."

The man says his salary pays the mortgage and utilities; his wife's covers their children's catholic school and other expenses. They don't have any money to spare.

The lawyer closes the folder and leans back in his chair. "If you don't mind me asking..." his hands are behind his head and his tone tries to sound light, but comes across more interrogatory, "how do you expect to pay for *my* services?"

"Don't worry," the man mutters, really wishing he didn't have to be in this situation. "My family and neighbors have loaned me enough to cover your fees."

The man crosses and uncrosses his legs. His tailbone feels tender from sitting on unforgiving wood. He stands and stretches again. A puff of air blows in his ears when he sinks into plush cushions of a couch under a print of Picasso's *Les Demoiselles d'Avignon*.

"Anyway," the man returns to his story with his arms and legs sticking out, feeling comfortable for the first time. "I took the morning off work and went to the L'Eixample Office around ten."

"All state offices close at two," the lawyer's voice rises, "why not go earlier?" He writes in his notebook and screams, "Please, sit in the seat!" waving his free arm at the chair on the other side of his desk. "I can barely hear you."

The man claps to snap out of a daydream, where two bikini-clad females sit on either side of him, but a cold beer on the glass coffee table is the sole focus of his attention. His leather belt pinches his stomach when he reaches for a bowl where the beer should be and grabs a handful of candy wrapped in golden foil.

"Wanted to sleep in a little bit." The man finally answers the question regarding his late arrival. Sucking on a caramel he strolls to the desk. "Also, it makes no sense getting there early," he mumbles, biting down on a hard shell to taste the gooey filling. "You still aren't leaving before noon with everyone and their mother getting there an hour before the doors open."

"Hmm." The lawyer hums for a good five seconds. "You know what? Thinking about it..." he beams a congratulatory smile and waves the pen at the man, "I believe you're right!"

The lawyer's squinting eyes are hidden behind fleshy lids and long lashes, reducing his brown irises to slits. His stare seems to emit psychic waves, however, that put thoughts in the man's racing mind. It's not the lawyer's fault I am where I am, he thinks, before cursing God and Lady Luck for not blessing him with a good enough memory to pass the tests that determine life in Catalunya and Spain.

The man pops a second candy in his mouth, crunches to get the lawyer's voice out of his head and makes a mental note to buy a lottery ticket after the meeting.

"Please, continue." The lawyer reminds him, "You're at the L'Eixample Office."

The man's tongue picks at the crevices of his molars and he smiles. "So far so good. In and out in just 45 minutes. I find a blue pen and fill in the form before taking the metro to the Drassanes Office."

"Why didn't you drive?" the lawyer asks.

The man pauses at the relevance of the question before he speaks. "Decided to leave my car at the office parking lot. It's too expensive to park in the city-center anymore."

The lawyer stops taking notes and looks at the man. "Sounds like you could have used the discounted rate after all."

The clicks of a lighter struggling to catch blocks out the lawyer's snarky remark. The man pulls from a fresh cigarette and explains that he only rode the metro until Plaça Catalunya, electing to walk down Las Ramblas the rest of the way.

"Why do that?" a confused lawyer inquires.

"You really don't ride it much, do you?" The man rants how changing lines makes him feel like, "a rat with hundreds of other rats, in an underground maze of tunnels and steps."

The lawyer roars with laughter. "That's a bit of a poetic exaggeration, don't you think?" He chuckles to catch his breath. "You almost sound *Andaluz*," he teases. "You're not suggesting riding the metro made you attack the *funcionario*, are you?"

The man grits his teeth and his nostrils flare, like an angry donkey. The label *Andaluz* stings for he is a hardworking Catalan from the north, not some lazy southern Spaniard from *Andalucía*, who only sings and dances to flamenco music, when not killing bulls to toasts of sangria, all on Catalunya's dime.

The man takes a deep drag of nicotine and feels the burn as smoke stream through his nose. "What do you now about life?" he questions the lawyer. "You're rich. You can buy anything."

A cough to clear the indignation stuck in his throat at the shift in conversation. "Not anything," the lawyer defends himself against the ad hominem attack. "I'm not Bill Gates."

"No, you're not." The man eyes a sharp letter opener on the desk before focusing on the flabby neck, spilling out over a white collar across from him. "But I bet you have a nice apartment in Barcelona and one in the mountains."

The lawyer gulps and says without irony, "By the sea in Costa Brava, actually. And let me tell you something — it's not easy paying for my two houses, plus my children's private English school and my new Mercedes."

The lawyer takes a deep breath. He stands up from his large chair and declares, "We live in a democracy now," opening the French doors to usher in the strident noises of blasting car horns and revving scooters from five stories below. "If you don't like it," the lawyer's voice soars above the din of traffic, "elect new politicians!"

He directs his booming tone at the man, who sits and wiggles in the hard wooden chair, "Would you rather return to the time of Franco?"

"Of course not!" He shoots to his feet and readies to raise his fists to defend his honor. "No real Catalan would ever dare want such a thing."

"Good," the lawyer snorts, shutting the French doors to reintroduce quiet. "Hurry up. We've been talking for over an hour and I have a tennis match at seven."

The man doesn't know if he wants this lawyer to represent him. But so far he has the most certificates and books. He is also the only non-*xarnego* with an all Catalan surname, meaning no Castilian blood. The man sits back down to ponder his next move. He decides to hold off passing judgment and lights another cigarette before returning to his odyssey through the local bureaucracy.

"Where was I?" the man asks, reminding himself to stay calm. His wife's reaction after his first assault charge is still fresh and he is terrified of a repeat performance.

The perturbed lawyer huffs as he sits in his chair and glances at his notes. "At the Drassanes Office."

"That's right!" The man flashes a smile to say, "Sorry for wigging out and taking us on a detour earlier. No hard feelings, right?"

The lawyer is unmoved by the gesture and exhibits no emotion as the man explains the joy he felt hearing his number called, after a two hour wait. He walked up to the counter and handed the guy working the five page form. Not a word for ten minutes as the functionary's stare lingered over the filled in spaces. Finally, he announced his decision, "I need your income-tax statements, too."

The man taps the cigarette over the ashtray after delivering the line verbatim. "'Where does it say that?' I ask him and the little shit recites some law like it was a pledge."

The lawyers chest almost bursts from laughter. "You hit him for having an attitude?" He wipes the tears from his eyes and continues, "Have you ever met a pleasant *funcionario*? My God, there was an ad campaign about their need for more fiber in their morning cereal to improve their mood."

The man smokes and watches the lawyer's porcelain skin break out into a red rash. "Are you laughing at me?"

"Of course not!" The lawyer shouts to plead his innocence before his tone drops to defensive, "Just saying —it's not easy dealing with the public every day."

"Nor is my job," he man hisses, eying the letter open again. "I actually have to go back to work after lunch and can be fired for not producing."

"Don't you have a full-time work contract?"

The man hears concern in the lawyer's question and watches the spreading redness on a porcelain forehead vanish. "Only been there eighteen months."

"Ah, I see." The lawyer's fleshy eyes display genuine sympathy for the first time at the realization the man is six months shy of his two year anniversary when, by law, the cost of laying off contracted employees almost doubles, from twenty-six to forty days paid for each year worked.

The lawyer's lips curl into a smile of condolences. "What happened after the boy rejected you?"

The man mashes the smoldering butt in the blue crystal ashtray. "I went to work, got yelled at by my boss and returned the next morning to find the ticket machine broken and an even longer line."

"Did you wait?" The lawyer scribbles notes.

"Hell no," the man yells. "Things are iffy at my company and I didn't want to arrive any later than I had to."

The lawyer stops writing mid-sentence and looks up from the folder. "What do you mean *iffy*?"

"These are tough economic times," the man tells him. "Our head office in Madrid is looking to cut costs and rumor has it that Barcelona is first to go under the knife."

"It's always the same," the lawyer bellows, throwing his silver pen that bounces off his desk and hits the floor. "Madrid keeps everything and leaves Catalunya shit. I'm tired of them stealing 10 per cent of our GDP for the rest of Spain."

The man could not have said the common political talking point better. "I know! To hell with the Socialists. They're no better than the PP. I'm voting for the Catalan Nationalist Party next election."

The lawyer nods enthusiastically. "Without Spain holding us back, Catalunya can become the next Holland!"

The man feels similar to the first time his wife giggled at one of his sardonic quips. His smile only hints at the joy he feels at finally finding a lawyer to represent him against charges of attacking the fascist Spanish state.

"We'd have a better football team," the man brags. "Probably, even better than Argentina or Brazil."

The lawyer chuckles to himself and takes a pencil from the cup. "What happened after your visit to the Drassanes Office?"

The man lights yet another cigarette and feels the smoke fill his lungs. He holds it in as he speaks. "Had to wait a week until my boss went on a business trip before going back again."

"And?" the lawyer prods.

The man snarls and exhales out of the corner of his mouth. The smug look on the functionary's face flashes before his eyes. The man snaps the just lit cigarette in half as he stubs it out. "The same little shit from last time said that there was an €8 fee."

"That's not much," the lawyer comments.

"No. You're right." The man pauses and thinks he's figured out the reason for the new ID card—millions of euros in fees for a cash-strapped government. "But I only had a twenty. Asked the guy if he had change. He said 'No, Next,' without stamping the form."

A wide-eyed lawyer leans forward. "So you hit him?"

The man calms down with a shake of the head and a pleasant memory. "Would have, but a nice lady lent me the money. Gave him a piece of my mind, though."

The lawyer laughs at himself for getting excited about nothing and sits back in his chair. "Good for you. What happened next?"

The man readies to light another smoke and stops. He crushes the cigarette in his hand, squeezing it like a stress ball. "When I got to the Spanish Home Office for the second stamp and signature," the man seethes, "the clerk told me that the son-of-a-bitch didn't initial the seal and to go back to Drassanes."

"Easy there, my friend." The lawyer chuckles as he watches the man open his hand over the desk to drop loose tobacco and paper into an overflowing ashtray. "It wasn't their fault."

A rodent face twitches with askance after the statement. Who exactly is this lawyer supposed to represent? Me or the Spanish State? "Yeah," the man sneers, "you're right as usual. Although, I was starting to get a bit paranoid that the guy just didn't like me."

The lawyer holds up a finger and writes a single word in all caps. "Continue, please," he says, looking up to see the man stand and stroll to the French doors.

Outside, the twilight sky is the color of a bruise. The reflection in the glass darkens the man's eye bags and wrinkles while his balding scalp shines from the overhead light the lawyer turns on.

"Anyway," the man sighs and feels his shoulders sag to his ribs. "This is now turning into a five day ordeal if I was lucky."

"What's one more day?" The lawyer returns to his desk and plops down on his comfortable chair.

A tremor shoots from the man's ankles, up his legs, jolting his heart. Warm spits sprays from his mouth as he unleashes a blistering critique of an asshole for a boss who rides him about everything, forcing him to get home at nine or ten, just to keep up with all of his busy work.

The lawyer wipes his lips with the back of his hand and shrugs. "That's only an hour later than me."

The man sees not a human being, but a giant brown pig in a suit. He starts to salivate at the prospect of stabbing the swine and carving him up with the letter opener on the desk, like a leg of *Jamón Ibérico*. His stomach roars with encouragement; he takes a step toward realizing his fantasy. His wife's shrill voice blares in his head. She makes it perfectly clear that she will explode into another foot stomping, plate throwing tantrum, if she gets a second call from the police.

The man gulps spit to commemorate the death of another dream. "Do you have kids? he asks, running his shirt sleeve across his mouth.

"Two sons and a daughter," replies the lawyer.

"Your wife doesn't mind you coming home late?"

"No. She doesn't work and we have a nanny."

How can you not respect a person who has everything you want? Envy twists in the man's chest, cutting off the oxygen supply to the anger he feels at the injustice of it all. "Well, we can't afford that luxury." The man keeps his tone even to mask the bitterness he feels toward life. "When I get home late, my children are asleep and my wife's in a mood that would put the fear of God in a wild game hunter."

"My wife has a temper, too." The lawyer snickers and chalks it up to, "that Latin blood." He stands from his chair and puts an arm around the man, leading him away from the French doors and the five-story drop to Passeig de Gràcia below.

"You sound like you need a drink," the lawyer tells him.

"I need a whiskey," the man jokes.

"Atta boy!" The lawyer pats him on the back and states, "Someone after my own heart," pushing him toward the hard wooden chair. "Now sit down."

"You have whiskey?" The man's voice squeaks with surprise at his sarcasm being taken seriously.

"Do I have whiskey?" The lawyer struts to a standing wooden bar in the corner of his office. "Just one of the finest single-malt Scotches ever made."

The man wanders over to take a look. "Really?"

"Yes." The lawyer shushes him back to the desk before continuing, "My family and I went to Edinburgh last year," pouring two tumblers from a crystal decanter.

"My wife and I went to England once," the man says. "I hated it."

"It isn't Spain or Catalunya. That's for sure." The lawyer hands him a half full tumbler and toasts, "*Salut.*"

"*Salut,*" the man seconds, as they clink glasses and take sips.

The lawyer smacks his lips and lets out a satisfied 'ah' on the way back to his leather chair. "A fine whiskey, isn't it?" He beams with pride as he explains, "It's the Highland water and malting process that makes it so special. The bottle cost me over a €100."

The man sits on hard wood. He doesn't notice the difference between this whiskey and the one he usually buys at the store for a tenth of the price. "Normally take it with cola," he tells the lawyer, who laughs as him again.

"Don't tell a Scot. That's like putting ketchup on *paella.*" The lawyer sips his drink and opens his folder to read his notes out loud, "You were having a bad week at work and a frustrating time with a *funcionario* over a law you didn't agree with." The lawyer pauses and flashes a smile. "I think it's safe to say most people have probably suffered moments like this. What do you expect? The *funcionario's* job is to find problems where there are none."

"I know, I know," the man gestures for patience, "but even you will have to agree what I tell you next is shear provocation."

The lawyer perks up and takes a pencil from the cup on the desk. "All ears," he says.

The man drinks his whiskey like it's a shot of *orujo*

and feels the burn as it travels from his throat to his gut. He shivers and lights yet another smoke before he continues with his story, "Either I got the little shit's signature or started the whole fucking process over."

He explained that the wait at the Drassanes Office was only an hour, but he didn't feel lucky or blessed. He walked to the counter, clutching not just the form, but a folder stuffed with a copy of every piece of documentation, from his birth certificate to his most recent income-tax statement. The person working was not the boy but a woman who looked like a prison librarian. She could have been the other guy's twin, though. She repeated the same steps. She took the five page form, flipped through it front to back, three times, reading the fine print twice. At the end of her little show, she sighed with *faux* disappointment and informed the man, with the relish of a waiter telling an obnoxious customer that their credit card had been declined:

"Sorry, sir. I obviously can't initial something I didn't stamp. You'll have to see my colleague who's working on the second floor."

The lawyer grabs the edge of his desk, bracing himself for the answer to his question, "You didn't hit a woman, did you? It's not like it was a few years ago when there was no punishment. That's a real no-no now. And five years in jail."

"No," the man says evenly. "I waited another forty fucking minutes in a different line." He grinds the burning cigarette against the mountain of butts in the ashtray as he continues in a neutral tone, "As you can imagine, I wasn't in the best of moods when I finally got to the counter and asked the kid to please initial."

"What happened next?" the lawyer asks.

The man's voice quakes as he tries to remain calm, "I

got another long pause before the son-of-a-bitch explained that due to not working in that capacity today, he wasn't authorized to initial the stamp and to come back on Monday." The man pauses and shakes his head. "That's when I lost it."

"What do you mean, *you lost it*?"

The man pulls out another cigarette before deciding he has smoked enough. "To tell you the truth," he says, with a smirk stuck between apologetic and embarrassed, as he slips the cancer stick back in the pack. "Don't remember much. I shrieked: 'I shit on this fucking form', and went for the ticket dispenser."

The man stops and tries to piece together exactly what happened that fateful day. "The guy broke out in a red rash and the next thing I know — I'm getting tackled to the ground by security and the *funcionario* is holding the top of his head, crying that I attacked him."

"And the ticket dispenser?" the lawyer inquires, as if the machine is an innocent bystander.

"Ripped off its stand and by the counter." The man taps his bony chest and it echoes. "Listen. I'm not a hard guy. Have no clue how I did it."

The lawyer stops writing and chews on the end of his pencil. "Well, I must say," he finally announces, "it does seem like you had a bit of really bad luck. Could probably knock the sentence down to a five years." The lawyer glances at his notes to see the word, CRAZY, and adds, "On account of acute mental distress," looking up from his desk. "It's a bit of a reach and you'll have to see a psychiatrist."

"Five years," the man yelps.

"With good behavior, you'll be out in one."

"Can't you get me off completely?" The man clasps his hands in prayer. "What would a normal assault charge get?"

"A first time offense?" The lawyer cocks an eye to the ceiling and does the simple calculation. "Maybe a month or just a fine."

"You can't get me that?"

The lawyer shakes his head. "The law is the law. It must be followed to the strictest letter, otherwise we have anarchy. The fact is—you attacked a state employee."

"Haven't you been listening to a word I said?" The man screams, "He drove me to do it!"

The lawyer smacks the table with the folder and raises his volume to get his point across, "Look. Even if you were innocent, which you aren't, it makes no difference. The law clearly says that a state employee is *always* in the right."

The lawyer offers an anecdote about an old lady to support his point. She is hit by a speeding police car while crossing a street. The light is green and there is no crime that necessitates such haste. Nor are sirens used as a warning to stay clear of the intersection. The police are employees of the state and she is just a citizen. This indisputable fact absolves them of all culpability, without the need for a trial or hearing. The grandmother of four, meanwhile, has to pay for all damages to the squad car that knocks her over and breaks her hip.

The man remembers hearing the story on the nightly news. The blood flows to his numb tailbone as he stands from his chair and shuffles to the French doors one final time.

Casa Milà is awash in the yellow spotlights of night. The man thinks how he has never visited any of Gaudí's monuments as an adult and how pointless it has been to take on a state employee. It doesn't matter that they are petty and incompetent, that they gain sadistic pleasure from denying service and making everyone's lives miserable. The law is the law. There is no question of guilt or innocence. The *funcionario* is always right; you are always wrong. End of story.

I should have been more patient, a defeated man decides, with a heavy sigh. He turns from the view and faces his future legal counsel. "What's the next step?" he asks, worried about staying alive long enough for his court date, once his wife learns of his fate.

The lawyer flashes a smile and picks up his folded newspaper. "See my assistant this week, pay my retainer and she'll give you a form." He explains that the man then needs to go to the judicial office in *El Born* for a signature before taking the form to his municipal office in L'Eixample, at which point they will begin legal proceedings.

The Witch from Bilbao

I remember the first time I saw her. It was early for Barcelona, just past ten at night. Most locals were in the middle of dinner at home or at a restaurant, leaving the hundreds of bars throughout the city open, but empty. The exception was a hole in the wall called Sugar, in the heart of *Barri Gòtic,* not too far from a street made famous by Picasso.

The lighting inside the bar was dim and tinged red while the dense fog of tobacco smoke shook to the thumping disco music. I rubbed my itchy eyes. When I opened them again, the crowd around me had melted into overlapping dots of different colors. Except for her, that is.

She was as lucid as a cut-out of a photograph pasted in the middle of an impressionist painting. She sat at the opposite end of the bar counter, her back against a stone wall. Shadows shrouded her like a cowl as she sipped a blue concoction through a straw, but her face was aglow from the candle, burning in a red glass under her chin.

The girl wasn't statuesque or radiant, more like a raven haired fairy. Her sloe-eyes latched onto mine, causing the 62 per cent of my body weight which was water to slosh and crash, as if her gaze had the power of a full lunar eclipse.

I blinked and readied to flash a disarming smile to acknowledge her from afar. A forearm shoved me from behind, a waft of too much cologne irritated my nose. I cast a quick glance over my left shoulder to find a bronzed man, using my upper back as a prop, as he flagged down a bartender.

A soft elbow to the sternum was my usual remedy for such situations. Nothing vicious. Just hard enough for the person leaning on me to notice the nudge, but not sharp enough to provoke a violent response, unless they were a biker. The twat on top of me spent hours spiking his hair with gel and shaved his sideburns into points. I doubted he liked to get dirty and change a crankshaft. My elbow poked his chest and he mumbled an apology as I stretched to clear some more space before my eyes darted across the bar.

The dark fairy had vanished during the commotion. My bodily fluids were still, but my head was a tempest. My neck snapped as I searched to see where she had gone. She wasn't standing at the counter or sitting on one of the stools along the stone walls. I took a long sip of my sweet minty mojito as my sights set on the bathroom door at the back.

She had gone to powder his nose. I was sure of it. I would've seen her had she left. But by the time I'd finished my drink, there was no sign of the mysterious beauty. Could my mind be playing tricks on me? Was she a figment of my imagination, like the vivacious bat-winged succubus who had appeared in a recurring dream last week?

I slurped the last watery drops of my overpriced cocktail and hailed the bartender, not sure if I was in the mood to get drunk or call it a night.

"Do you have a light?"

A female's accented English strummed my eardrums. I turned to see it belonged to the raven-hair fairy and felt the firing synapses in my brain shoot my tongue full of

Novocaine. "Um, er, sure," I muttered, fumbling in my pocket for a lighter, as I rose from my stool to greet her.

"Has anyone told you—you're the spitting image of Harry Potter?"

I was too focused on the flutter of her succulent lips to catch every word of her question, except for the last two. The answer was yes and my English accent didn't help. My usual reply to anyone, who cited my uncanny resemblance to the boy wizard, was to point out the ugliest celebrity doppelgänger the person speaking looked like. But this Spanish pixie didn't remind me of any actress or model. She barely reached my shoulders, yet her deep-set astral eyes would've unnerved Voldermort, rendering his dark powers useless.

I stood there in a trance, speechless and thus unable to answer her question about my resemblance to JK Rowling's most famous character. I was able to think, though. And I laughed silently, without even a quiver of my lips, as I remembered how proud the Basques were of their *pintxo* sniffer.

It wasn't "spike" shaped, like the English translation of the word implied, more like something found on Pinocchio, after he had told one or two lies, but before the branches and leaves sprouted, à la the Disney version of the story. I explain this because the famous Basque snout was on full display when the girl turned her head and lifted her chin to blow smoke into the ceiling that I could touch without fully extending my arms.

"What's your name?" Her voice broke the spell she had cast over me and her dark stare was once again the sole focus of my attention.

A minty tidal wave crested and crashed inside my belly. I gulped and stuttered, "S... Sa... Sam," nodding at her for a reply.

"Edurne," she said.

I still couldn't form a complete sentence, let alone pronounce her name correctly. Her bucolic perfume sparked images of the dense forests and jagged hills of the Basque Country. Its people were the Scots of the Iberian peninsula, famous for their brute strength and games, which consisted of heaving heavy objects as far as they could, in a clearing of an ancient Oak forest.

My mind unable to function, my mouth took over and I blurted, "Do you lift rocks?"

The Basque girl caught the reference to her homeland and laughed. "Only when I swim," she quoted the punch line to a joke about her people. "Have you been to *Pais Vasco*?"

"I went to Bilbao once." The words now slid off my nimble tongue. "Loved it. Getxo had a great beach."

The girl's stormy eyes flashed. "I come from a small village near Bilbao."

"What brings you to Barcelona?" I followed up with the usual first question when meeting a fellow transplant.

"The same thing that brings you."

"The weather?" I laughed at myself for giving the most common answer and noticed Edurne smirk. "How long have you been here?" I asked.

"A year this Halloween. And yourself?"

"Seven years this Christmas."

"Wow," she said. "That's a long time for a *guiri*. Do you speak perfect Spanish?"

"Not fluently, but I get by." Edurne didn't speak English with the abruptness of most locals, whether they were Basque, Catalan or *Valenciano*. But she did have a trace of a strange accent. "Your English is impeccable by the way."

She repaid my compliment with a smile. "Tanks. I

lived in Ireland for a few years."

That explained the lack of a "th." "Whereabouts? Dublin?" I asked as if I knew, when the Emerald Isle was as remote to me as Transylvania.

"A village near the Wicklow mountains." Edurne ended the sentence with a light sigh before her lips curled at the edges. Her teeth weren't so much crooked as offset, with sharp incisors behind the top row, giving her smile a hint of vampire or maybe even werewolf, the night before a full moon.

"Let's go somewhere quieter," she suggested, her Irish tinged cadence striking a cord in my brain that rendered my prefrontal cortex catatonic. Her back was toward me now, her hair up in a pony tail. Her flowing skirt swished and I zoomed on the lines of a tattoo, peeking above the collar of her red and black corset. What was the picture etched on her milky skin? A vampy Betty Page? A ninja geisha? One foot went before the other without any orders from me as I tried to imagine her marking. The balls of my heels stomped on shoes and my shoulders barged into backs, but I didn't catch people's glares or their warnings to, "Hey! Watch out." Same went for the distant shouts of the bartender, telling me to come back and pay for my drink.

Edurne took me to Pipa Club, which overlooked Plaça Reial. The place was just as packed as Sugar, although the fog of smoke was tinted yellow, not red, and the music wasn't thumping disco, but old school punk rock played at a volume you'd expect to hear in an elevator. Encased ornamental pipes adorned the walls, relics of a past time, when the converted flat had been an exclusive smoking club, not a Sherlock Holmes themed bar, which was open to anyone who could find it.

Off the main corridor was a small wood paneled bar where a couple sat in the corner. They stopped their conversation at our entrance and stared. Not at us, but at Edurne. I couldn't see what type of look she gave them. It must've been some sort of an evil eye that hinted at being part gypsy because the couple pocketed their cigarette packs and left in a hurry. This Basque girl definitely had something about her. I'd never been so lucky getting a seat this close to midnight in Barcelona.

Edurne brushed my arm to get my attention and waited until our stares met. "Sit down," she commanded. "I'll buy the first drink. What would you like?"

"Um, er," I stuttered, incapable of an opinion, too worried it might offend her. "What are you, um, having?"

"Have you ever tried *pacharán*?"

"Yeah." I didn't need to tell a lie, "Love it."

She smiled and said, "Okay. Wait here," holding up her hands to re-enforce the point. "I'll get you a glass. It's not as good here as we make back home. But it's perfect for autumn nights."

I sat on a stool at a table, both seemingly built for toddlers, not adults, but didn't notice my knees constantly knocking into the wooden edge. I watched Edurne's backside move with an almost feline slink under her flowing skirt. I tried not to think about her or what the rest of the night entailed. I didn't want to get my hopes up and curse the possibility of something positive happening.

My attention turned away from my date, vanishing into a black-clad crowd. A small pool-table stood near the open door of the small bar. A lithe girl in baggy jeans stuck coins in a slot and pushed. The clatter of pool balls interrupted the fast-paced song wafting softly from the bar's speakers. The girl had dirty-blond hair and carried herself with a nonchalance typical of the French. My ears strained to pick up on her voice to see if I'd guessed her nationality right when she whispered, what I imagined, were sweet nothings in a scruffy man's ear.

Moments like this usually reminded me how lonely life could be for a single male in a big city.

"Here you go."

Edurne's slight Irish accent reminded me that I wasn't alone so I should stop trying to eavesdrop other women's conversations.

I sniffed to clear my head. A floral, almost perfumy, aroma floated up my nose. I turned toward the scent and saw a rose colored liquor, served over two ice cubes, in a highball glass. I took the drink. My stare lifted from my hands and tethered to Edurne's supple frame as she walked around the table and sat down across from me, with the grace and class of a Parisian.

"Thanks," I whispered, taking a sip of a familiar licorice-and-berry flavor before my cheeks met in the middle of my tongue from an unfamiliar bitter aftertaste.

"What do you think?" she asked.

I gulped the strange tasting *pacharán* and lied, "It's good."

Edurne's cryptic grin made it tough to tell if she believed me. "I didn't think they sold that brand outside of the Basque country," she said. "It's supposed to have hallucinogenic qualities, like *Absenta*."

"Really?" It was getting harder and harder not to get lost in her bewitching gaze and nod in agreement to her delectable intonation. I took a bigger sip of what tasted like a bitter, berry-flavored cough syrup.

"What do you like best about Barcelona?" I mumbled, sucking on an ice cube to rinse my mouth.

Edurne laughed a delightful little chirp of a laugh. "I love its beauty and the people it attracts," ending her sentence with a sip of red wine and an enticing smirk. "And you?"

"The beach being close to the city." I was no longer looking into her enchanting eyes but at silver rings on nimble fingers. "And the chance to meet girls, like you, who are as beautiful as the buildings," my mouth spouted, without any permission from the Broca area of my brain.

Edurne's lips curled and peeled from her teeth to show her offset fanged incisors again. "Ah, that's sweet," she said, the cheesiness of my pick-up line seemingly lost in translation. "Do you believe in witches?"

I tried not to laugh out loud at the randomness of the question. Was it a test, like when a girl asked if I believed in astrology, karma or fate? If I said no, was Edurne going to say: *adios, adéu*? (or whatever good-bye was in Basque.)

Her flickering eyes and silence told me that I had to say something so I asked, "Like the Golden Witch of Sort?" bringing up the famous witch from outer space who was said to bless the Christmas lotto tickets sold in a small town called Sort, or *Luck*, in Catalan.

"That's just a marketing ploy." The sharpness of Edurne's tone hinted at annoyance at my glib treatment of the fairytale subject matter. "Witches are only for children's stories here," she sneered before her voice softened again. "It's a shame because there's such a rich tradition of magic in Catalunya. But Catalans today take themselves, and life, too seriously."

I chuckled at a statement I'd heard all too often from other transplants, both from within Spain and outside alike. "You got that right," I confirmed, with my most charming smile. "What kind of witches are there in the Basque country?"

"Many types." She grinned cryptically again. "Do you know the *Sorgin Dantza*? It's one of our national dances."

"Can't say that I do. Is it like the one they do here where everyone joins hands and moves really slowly in a circle, to the music of flutes and tambourines?"

"The Sardana? You call that a dance?" Edurne leaned forward, looking like she was about to crawl across the table and rip my throat out with her sharp teeth. "The *Sorgin Dantza* is more burlesque." She sat back with an apologetic smirk after a flash of anger. "We've been doing it since Pagan times."

I pictured my date setting down her glass before slowly stripping off her corset to reveal a buxom chest, swaying to a rhythmic bongo beat. "Can you show me?" I blurted, hoping to turn a fantasy into reality, because as my mother always told me, "You never know unless you ask."

A quick chirpy laugh and Edurne bit her bottom lip. Silence. A cold draught blew away the hanging smoke, brightening the deadened yellow-light. Our stares joined like two magnets that charged my puckered mouth and pulled me across the small table for a kiss.

"I see you liked the *pacharán*."

Edurne's comment killed the gravitational spark. I sat back and blinked. A new punk rock tune played before being drowned out by the noise of a cue-ball, slamming into the racked pool balls. At least she hadn't ruled out giving me a private dance, I thought, looking down at my glass, surprised to find it empty. Maybe it was all the talk about witches and burlesque dancing, but the *pacharán's* effects felt more like a potion than a cocktail.

"Are you ready?"

The sound of a stool scuffing the floor lifted the rosy haze that clouded my thoughts. I looked up and felt my jaw relax into a drunken grin. "For another *pacharán*?"

"No." Edurne cut me a smirk calling me cute but slow before looking over her shoulder at the corridor, leading to the front door. "To walk me home. Barcelona's not safe for a single girl this late at night." She faced me again and asked, "You are a gentleman, aren't you?"

My mother had tried to raise me one. She had also attempted to instill the need of a university education in order to find a steady nine-to-five job. I had no degree and worked a few hours a week conducting bicycle tours to supplement my weekend deejaying gigs. Edurne was right, though. As any tourist guide will tell you—Barcelona wasn't the safest city this late at night, especially for a girl carrying a bag big enough to conceal an infant.

We walked down Carrer Ferran to the jangle of closing metal shutters. The street was just wide enough to be classified as one-way and cars lined up to turn right onto Las Ramblas behind us. Along the pavement, kids with fliers targeted groups of inebriated tourists who huddled outside overpriced Irish pubs to discuss which club to visit.

"Psst," a voice called from a pitch-black side-street of *Barri Gòtic*. "Coke, marijuana, hash, charlie."

"*Cerveza*, beer," chimed a man, who weaved through the stalled traffic.

A muscular woman in a pink mini-skirt stepped from the shadows, into the glow of a street lamp. "Hi, *papi*," she said, with a kiss. "*Jou* lookin' for a good time?"

I put my arm around Edurne's shoulder to bring her in close, sandwiching her stuffed bag between us. I felt the thieves hiding in plain sight, watching us, their eyes crawling over our persons, like probing fingers. Edurne cast an appreciative glance at my attempt at chivalry, but her gratitude didn't diminish the tension in my teeth, which lasted until Carrer Ferran opened onto Plaça Sant Jaume.

A blue moon shone down on bumblebee colored taxis parked outside the majestic white buildings of the regional and municipal governments. A group of armed police officers stood in the middle of the square in navy blue uniforms and black jackboots. Statuesque in their appearance, they showed the same effectiveness stopping crime as the stone gargoyles on the outer wall of the Cathedral we passed.

A burst of confidence charged through me. I pulled Edurne in for a kiss. She spun away, twirling with her bag in the air.

"Easy there, tiger," she teased, skipping ahead.

I gave chase down Carrer Ferran. The stone beneath my feet dissipated with each step and the street lights dimmed into the silhouettes of trees. There were no buildings with balconies, wasted tourists or parasitic peddlers of vice. We had gone back in time to before there was the first church, let alone a Cathedral, becoming two love-struck, tunic-wearing inhabitants of a Roman colony before Constantine saw the cross of light, when witches and magic ruled the land.

The roar of traffic brought an end to my antique inspired fantasy. I grabbed my knees and panted to catch my breath as we waited to cross Via Laietana.

"Exercise much?" Edurne's eyes stroked me from my moptop hair to the canvass sneakers on my throbbing feet.

"Ride my bike everywhere," I wheezed. "Don't know

what's wrong with me."

On the other side of Via Laietana was *El Born*. Like *Barri Gòtic* and *El Raval*, the neighborhood was a mess of tiny alleys which viewed from a satellite looked like a Minotaur's lair. Edurne led me past the squat and convex wall of the Santa Maria Del Mar, the star of a historical novel set during medieval times, when Catalunya had been the Crown of Aragón.

A right, a left and then another right before we stopped at what I assumed was her building. The click of Edurne turning a key opened the box in my brain where drunkenness had held my conscience captive. My inner voiced reminded me that first night hook-ups never turned out well. Either I wanted something more or she did. Rarely did we both want a relationship. Even when we thought we had something in common, a pairing born in an alcohol induced stupor usually ended a few weeks later, with a head-splitting hangover and one person wondering — why have I done this again?

I glimpsed Edurne's tattoo, peeking above the collar of her corset as she disappeared into a ticking light. I put my conscience in a choke-hold and stuffed it back in a box that I locked before swallowing the key. There were times in a man's life when future concerns and questions of character became subservient to present desires. These moments caused us to lose touch with our rational and sentimental human side, turning us into animals driven by primordial needs, like lust and hunger.

"Here we are." Edurne's voice snapped me out of another trace-like state. We stood outside her attic flat. Her breathing was effortless. My lungs and hamstrings burned as if I'd just climbed to the top of the Sagrada Família. But unlike the one and only time I'd scaled the

350 steps of Gaudí's masterpiece, Edurne's slaying presence made sure I didn't complain as I followed her though the door.

The walls inside her studio flat were a crimson red, the wood trim and ceiling beams, black. Those seemed to be her favorite colors, judging by the thin fabric covering lampshades and her corset. I sniffed to breath. The pungent potpourri of incense, hashish and tobacco smoke was thick enough to leave me a little lightheaded.

"Have a seat," Edurne suggested, as she sauntered behind a kitchen counter with a vase of dead roses in fresh water.

Maybe the contact buzz I got walking in had sobered me up because I ignored Edurne's order for the first time that night. "Those from last *Sant Jordi*?" I asked, nodding my chin at the macabre floral piece, as I joined her in the kitchen.

No response, not even a "Huh?" or glance over her shoulder as she opened a refrigerator. I cleared my throat to repeat my question in a louder voice, but decided against it, fearing Edurne might've already thought my remark too lame to justify with a reply.

I sighed and slunk away from the kitchen. The futon couch I sat on was too comfortable to be from IKEA, but I didn't relax. I needed to get a better feel for my cryptic host. The crimson walls had no decoration. The titles on the spines of books on shelves were written in a language I had never seen before.

My sights fixed on a side-table where candles and a Celtic Cross flanked a wooden frame, which I picked up for closer inspection. The black and white picture was of Edurne in an overcoat, standing in a field near a flowing stream. Barren mountains jutted into the stormy sky behind her. Her black hair sweeping across her face reminded me of those classic snapshots of European models in the 1960s. The white border was stained an almost mustard yellow, giving the image a vintage feel. Was my host a "nostalgic" who always claimed life had been better in the past and tried to replicate their favorite era by imitating the clothing, art and slang?

A deep caterwaul disturbed my thoughts. I put the picture back where I'd found it. A scrawny ginger cat, with fully dilated eyes and flattened ears, crouched at my feet. I didn't fear the small beast leaping and scratching my cheeks. I was, however, petrified of Edurne asking me to leave because her pet obviously didn't care for me. But she didn't kick me out. She barked at the animal in some harsh language that wasn't Spanish, Catalan or English, flinging open a rickety door near the kitchen.

The cat hissed at me one last time and disappeared into the night.

"Sorry about that." Edurne's lips curled into a coy smile as she shut the door. "Seamus gets jealous sometimes."

I wondered what type of relationship they shared to make her feline possessive of men, but knew better than to touch such a subject on a first date. "No problem," I replied, glad to finally be in complete control of my Broca area again.

Feeling pleased with myself I got off the couch and moseyed over to the kitchen counter where another glass of rose colored *pacharán* perspired near the dead flowers.

"I made this batch myself," Edurne said, full of pride.

"Really?" I took a sip. The bitter aftertaste lingered in my mouth, like a throat lozenge, but I lied again, "It's really refreshing. By the way, what language was that?"

"Basque." She had a modesty to her that made her red aura glow. "I like archaic languages. I speak Gaelic, too."

"Wow." I was genuinely impressed. "I barely speak English and Spanish correctly." I glanced at the closed aluminium door near the kitchen. "Is the terrace yours of communal?"

"Mine. Go take a look if you like."

"Your cat's not waiting outside to attack me, is it?"

"No." Edurne giggled. "Seamus won't be back until the morning, probably with a dead bird or rat as a peace offering."

"That must be a pleasant sight first thing in the morning."

Another chirpy laugh that made me want to perform a standup comedy routine. "Come," Edurne commanded, with a wave of her hand. "People say the best way to see Barcelona is from the roof of a building. Tell me if it's true while I wash my face."

I tried to reply with something witty, but she pushed me onto a concrete roof and slammed the rickety door.

In a bit of a rosy *pacharán* daze, I walked past gnarled potted plants and toward the low wall at the edge of the building. The spindly beige spires of the Sagrada Família skyed above the dense blocks of the city. Surrounded by cranes and stadium lights, the famed church's completion inched closer with each passing week. Optimists predicted that construction would even be finished within my life time, nearly a hundred and twenty years after it had started. I hoped so, because even from this distance, the Sagrada Família was like something from the world of Tolkien.

Beyond the city skyline was the rounded silhouette of Barcelona's foothills. My sights fixed on the flaming beacon of yet another church, this one atop Tibidabo Mountain. I recalled the passage from the bible that gave the place its name, the mountaintop where Satan offered

Jesus the world for his soul. It was a deal I didn't think I would've been able to resist, especially if the devil was a becoming woman who found me funny.

My head didn't feel light anymore. My gaseous brain had condensed into a dense mist, like the one I remembered always blanketed Bilbao in the mornings. I thought about all of the churches in the Barcelona. There were the famous, like the Sagrada Família, Cathedral and Santa Maria del Mar. Lesser known ones, like the other Santa Maria in Plaça del Pi and the church that opened onto a small square in *El Born*. Then there were the ones, often closed and dark, midway down a tiny side-street, monuments to a monastic life which was going the way of the various Pagan religions. The telluric forces in all of the churches' stone and spires walls must have seeped into my foggy consciousness because Edurne's voice rang like bells before a royal baptism.

I turned around to find the door open. I lifted my heavy leg to clear a raised step. My shin smashed into the corner of the futon, now folded out into a bed. It was a hard knock, which would've usually provoked a yelp or curse, but I didn't let out a peep. I sunk my teeth into my bottom lip and rubbed my moist eyes to make sure the sight before me wasn't a *pacharán* and pain induced hallucination.

Edurne lay across her fold-out bed in a racy slip, looking like a raven-haired Tinkerbell who moonlighted as a madam in Neverland's bordello. The fragrance of burning incense scented the air. Flickering candles cast dancing shadows on the walls and Edurne's milky skin. The hanging smoke from the flames was joined by the thin wisp, billowing off the rolled-up cigarette, she held between ringed fingers.

Swarms of buzzing dopamine neurotransmitters

rushed through my synapses toward the oily, perfumy odor. My head the weight of helium again, my vision clouded. I felt high from the aroma, Edurne's red aura, the steamy situation. She cut a smile that sliced through the smoky haze and matched the naughty glint in her eye. My body no longer moved on my command, but on her psychic orders, and I climbed onto the soft mattress, which seemed stuffed with the same air used to form the atmosphere.

"That's a good boy," Edurne said, handing me the spliff.

I took a deep drag and coughed. The queasy feeling was a reminder why smoking hashish after drinking liquor was a big mistake. The closest sensation I could equate to it was being locked in a spin ride that pushed the centrifugal force to the point an astronaut threw up.

I grabbed my mouth to stop from upchucking the calamaris I'd eaten for dinner marinated in *pacharán*. A blasé Edurne began to remove her silver jewelery. My eyes trailed her doll-like hand as she placed each piece on the side-table. The wave of nausea passed with a gulp. One ring had a small compartment where the villain would store the poison to kill the victim in a mystery film.

I choked on the possibility Edurne might have drugged me. My conscience broke out of its locked box and I jerked away, ready to leave.

"What's wrong?" she asked, her tone genuinely concerned, a well-manicured hand on my shoulder.

I faced Edurne one last time or so I thought. Her entrancing stare and erotic allure overpowered my drunk and stoned conscience without much of a fight. All decision making authority now rested with the growing power between my thighs and *that* head shot a faint electric charge up my spine, ordering my mouth to pucker up and lean in for a kiss.

My mother always told me a gentleman never engaged in pillow talk because sex was the one experience that lost its power the more people with which it was shared. I had proven to be a disappointment when it came to making her proud. "Part-time bike-tour operator in Barcelona," wasn't something a parent wanted to say when people asked about his or her son's current job status at age thirty-three. So to honor my dear old mum, there will be no words such as vulva, tantric or cunnilingus to describe that night. But I will say Edurne's tattoo was of a black cat climbing an Oak tree and it was one of those rare moments in life that wiped away the sempiternal memories of staggering home alone, cursing tourists and friends alike who had been struck by Cupid's arrow.

***

The morning sunlight cut through the hanging cloud of hashish, incense and candle smoke. My closed eyelids warmed and turned pink and I rolled over to toss an arm around Edurne for a little spooning action. No one was beside me but a damp pillow. A steady purr stroked my ears and I peeled apart my crusty eyelashes to see a silver ball of fur curled up, level with my nose.

The cat lifted its pointed face to reveal the mask of a Siamese, but with black and gray markings, rather than the traditional brown and tan. It yawned and showed its pointed teeth before staring at me and making love-eyes, the way felines did when they were satisfied.

What the...? I sprang up from the bed and grabbed my clothes from the floor. The scratches, running from my neck down to my thighs, stung while my rectum felt like those mornings when a bowel-movement brought tears to my eyes.

I rubbed my hands down my face and blinked. My bleary sights fixed on the side-table. The framed photograph was in color, not black and white. The image was of the same barren mountains, running stream and stormy sky. But instead of a raven haired fairy, there was a silver haired witch who was old enough to be Edurne's grandmother.

Mónica & Juan

Mónica had never been a morning person, believing early-risers sanctimonious and uncivilized, but she no longer groaned at the sound of an alarm clock. Her eyes popped open of their own freewill to see darkness before the first ring chimed. She then sighed through the nose for her first breath of the day and rolled onto her side, doing her best to stop the mattress from squeaking, as she crawled out of bed, mindful not to disturb a snoring husband.

Juan wasn't prone to angry outbursts if woken up early, but Mónica saw no point in rousing him to join her out of a misplaced sense of solidarity. She respected sleep more than any other human activity and worshiped it more than God. She didn't know if there was a scientific study to back her theory, but she was convinced that ten hours with the Sandman worked better in the fight against Father Time, than the best cosmetic cream, maybe even plastic surgery and certainly praying to look young again.

Mónica did feel a tinge of envy at her husband's blissful position, though. She did what she always did in such situations—she sighed a heavy sigh, as she slipped on her bathrobe before sneaking out the dark bedroom.

In a perfect world, she would still be under the duvet, with a silk blindfold, but such a pampered start was reserved for the privileged few in Spain. The inherent unfairness of it all had been one of Mónica's common complaints until she had learned not to like, but appreciate, the atmosphere of dawn over dusk.

Sunset and night signified the end and brought a day's worth of memories, stress and regrets. Morning arrived with a calmness in the air that foreshadowed the start of a new cycle, which offered the chance of something different happening, even if the probability was that it would be the same old routine.

Mónica wanted to think about how much life had changed since her revelation, but she needed coffee to jump start her still sleepy brain. The days of a relaxing cup before work, however, were now distant memories, like sleeping past 6:15am and late nights out at discotheques, with girlfriends. She cracked open doors along the corridor to peek in on the reasons she never went out on the town or got enough rest anymore. Both small bedrooms were awash in the soft glow of nightlights. Her son's a blue hue, her daughter's a shade of pink. Their mother made sure they, like her husband, did not stir at her ghostly presence when she closed their doors and left.

The shuffle of slippers was the only noise Mónica made as she continued down the corridor, but her head was far from quiet. It wasn't just time that was tighter now, but money. The world seemed to be getting more expensive, stretching the financial limits of her and her Juan's salaries. She had cut out all vices by the time of her second child in an attempt to improve their economic situation, only to discover her good deeds were merely symbolic gestures that did little to dampen the sound of pressure, which had started playing in her head after the first baby.

Mónica heard the familiar ticking of a clock, even when she wore no watch, sometimes even in her sleep.

She stepped into a beige bathroom and flipped the switch. Tick. Tick. Tick. Her long eyelashes fluttered from the sudden introduction of a harsh artificial light. Showers long enough to wash her hair were reserved for Sundays, with the price of water rising faster than the cost of cooking oil. Now, her internal timekeeper said when three minutes were up, at which point Mónica turned off the taps with a sigh and shudder from the brisk air on her wet skin.

"Juan, honey," she said, clutching her robe to ward off the early morning chill, as she entered the bedroom. "Time to get up."

Mónica turned on the overhead light and her eyes didn't flinch. Tick. Tick. Tick. She rushed to pick out that day's outfit.

Well-worn clothes, grouped by article, crammed her small closet. The plastic hangers she slid along the rails, clattering into each other. She struggled to find a skirt, a shirt, jeans, a sweater, something, anything, which she hadn't already worn twice in the last month. God, how she couldn't wait for the Christmas season to be over and post-holiday sales to begin. It was the only time Mónica allowed herself to relapse into one of her bad habits.

A sigh of frustration vibrated her lips. There was still close to a month left before the start of sales season. First Christmas, then Kings Day, on January 5th, had to pass.

Juan's snoring continued to sputter. Mónica stormed to the bed and rocked his limp body back and forth. "Come on, Juan," she said. "Have to get the kids up now."

He snorted, rolled onto his side and wrapped himself up tighter in the blanket.

Mónica stamped her foot. "Juan," her volume rose to the level of an alarm clock, "I'm starting to get angry."

"Okay, okay," he grumbled. "Just five more minutes."

Mónica hated how it was the same struggle every morning. Did other women have to put up with lazy husbands like this? She knew the answer was yes, and sometimes worse, based on conversations with colleagues and reports on the nightly news.

The sound of running water five minutes later meant that Juan was in the shower. He did listen to me, Mónica thought, feeling her long face lift with a thin smile. The sense of elation was fleeting. The gray wool dress she wore felt snugger than she remembered. She frowned at the possibility of moving up a size or God forbid, two, and sucked in her stomach while ushering her yawning children into the dining room.

Her six-year-old son, Juanito, sat at the round dinner table under a shining chandelier as Mónica buckled her three year old daughter, Alba, into a high-chair. In front of both were glasses of poured juice, bowls of cereal and plates with fruit that Mónica had cut into the crude shapes, all tenderly prepared between her shower and getting dressed.

"*Mami*," Alba whined, shaking her long brown curls. "I don't like this cereal."

"Sweetie." Mónica tried to sound soothing, like her mother had recommended for such moments. "You have to eat it to be big and strong." She strolled up to the high-chair and lifted a spoon. "Zoom, zoom," she added, pretending the bite was an airplane as Juan did when he got Alba to eat.

The toddler screamed with a set of lungs of a future opera singer, "I don't like it!" swinging her arm into the bowl. It, along with the plate of fruit and full glass of juice, flew through the air and crashed to the ground, spraying Mónica in the process.

"Albaaaa!" she shrieked loud enough to wake the priests in the church on Mount Tibidabo. After a deep breath to simmer down, Mónica was still fuming. "Eat. Your. Food."

The little girl had her mother's big brown eyes, which narrowed into a familiar scowl of defiance. She pointed a chubby finger at the box of Sugar Puffs on the dining room table, where her brother sat, and screamed again, "I want that one," her voice reaching an octave, not even Mónica could achieve.

She tried, though, "You can't eat those! You'll get fat."

The puzzled look on Alba's face meant that she didn't understand the comment. Mónica breathed a sigh of relief. She didn't want to give her baby a complex about her body, not now or ever. She remembered what her mother had said the other week, about trying to have more patience, which like time, money and moments of absolute silence, seemed to be in shorter supply nowadays.

"Do you want me to make you a fruit smoothie?" Mónica suggested an alternative to cereal as a website on stubborn babies she had read recommended.

"No!" Alba folded her arms across her chest and stuck out her bottom lip.

"Sweetie," Mónica begged, "pleeease."

"Nooo!"

Mónica readied to scream her daughter's name again when Juan stepped into the kitchen. "Hey, honey," he said, straightening his tie. "Mind taking the kids to school today? Meeting some guys from work for breakfast so need to take off a little early."

Mónica hated how he had almost an almost superhuman ability to tune out the chaos and stress. Her long black hair whipped through the air as her eyes slit and latched on to her husband's stupid smirk.

"You're taking them to school," she snapped, ordering Juan to finish getting the kids dressed, with her next breath. He had to make sure Alba wore a skirt, not pants, like she always wanted to do lately. "Need to put on my makeup and find a new outfit," Mónica added, gesturing at the stains on her gray dress so that her dimwitted partner got the complete picture of her morning so far.

"But honey..."

"No buts, Juan." She stopped him before the excuses started. "I do everything around here. Can't you just do this *one* thing?"

Mónica took his silence and guilty expression as a yes and went to the bathroom. Her husband's towel and pajamas lay on the wet floor. She bit her lip to stop from slamming the door. A haggard reflection in the mirror told her what she already knew—the ten days off between Christmas and King's Day needed to arrive now. Although, she realized, the reprieve would be from work, not home, which meant no time with the Sandman to reverse the aging effects from a lack of sleep and too much stress.

Mónica wanted to cry from the sense of hopelessness, the feeling that time, money and patience were fast approaching zero before her body reached its expiration date. She sniffed. The ticking between her ears stopped her from acting on her bubbling emotions. She had to get ready for work and didn't want to show up late or looking like a mess, becoming a topic of office gossip.

Even though Mónica had already turned the dreaded forty, she still tried to keep up with the latest trends and starved herself most of the year so that she could fit into the same size she wore when she was twenty-five. She stepped from the elevator into her building's lobby, strutting in a knee-length pencil skirt, pointed-toe boots and a tight-fitting sweater. The ensemble was all the rage that winter, as it had been ten years prior, when Mónica purchased her well-worn outfit.

"Good morning, beautiful," a blue-haired woman seated behind a desk said. "Just saw your husband and kids."

"Hello, Carmen." Mónica gave the *portera* a polite smile. "You're here early today. How's everything?"

"Good. There's a new couple in the building."

"Really?" Mónica always enjoyed a bit of gossip, as long as she wasn't the subject.

"Yes, *guiris*."

"Where from?"

"*Nórdicos*." The elderly lady shrugged her shoulders to admit her confusion. "Maybe Swedish. Maybe Norwegian or Danish—I can't tell the difference between them. Everyone is tall with blond hair and blue eyes up there."

"I went to Norway once." Pre-baby memories flooded Mónica's head. "It's sooo beautiful."

The *portera* shuddered. "It's too cold for me."

"Not in summer."

"I suppose so." The grandmother of three's warm face darkened behind her round glasses after Mónica's defense of another country. "Why ever leave Spain? It's the best. We have everything. Good food. Good weather. Good people."

"I didn't mean to live," Mónica reassured the offended patriot.

"Yes. I know." The *portera's* expression warmed again. "Off to work?" she asked, taking off her glasses and wiping the thick lenses on her wool cardigan.

"Unfortunately," Mónica sighed at the thought of twenty-five more years of waking up at dawn to pay the bills and glanced at the slim watch on her wrist. The second hand ticked as the minute and hour hands read: 7:45. "Alright, listen..." the exasperation she felt was at herself, not the meandering nature of the conversation, "as always, running late so must go."

"Okay." The blue-haired lady put back on her glasses and saw Mónica off with a smile and a wave. "Have a good day and kiss that adorable daughter of yours for me. She looked soooo cute in that skirt!"

No rain or drizzle fell from the black clouds, but Mónica opened the umbrella she had brought from home, just in case the weather changed. The street lamps were off, amplifying the glow of the local bakery's window. The nidor of fresh pastries scented the heavy air and an empty stomach growled, demanding a hot ham and cheese croissant.

Tick. Tick. Tick. Mónica didn't need to look at her watch to know she had no time to stop and get breakfast to go. She closed her umbrella and hurried down the stairs of Putxet Train Station. It was the second stop of the Tibidabo Line, direction city-center. Cushioned seats were always available and for eight minutes, there was not silence, but peace, when Mónica closed her eyes and listened to the rollicking rhythm of the underground train.

At Plaça Catalunya, the ticking in her head started again. Mónica rushed out the sliding doors, down the crammed platform, up escalators, through a turnstile and down stairs.

The beeps from the closing metro doors pierced her ears. She pushed her way into a standing room only carriage. A young girl, with a backpack on her lap, readied to give up a seat against the wall. Out of the corner of her eye, Mónica spied a woman with a double chin who had also spotted the chance to escape the claustrophobic confines of a metro carriage at rush hour.

Tick. Tick. Tick. The female student stood and eased her way through the forest of commuters as wheels ground to a stop. Mónica used her svelte figure to slip through the cracks between passengers, beating the heavily jowled woman to the seat.

The businessman next to her was immersed in one of the free dailies. Mónica peered over his pinstriped shoulder to read the bold headline: *La Crisis Económica Afecta a España más que al Resto de Europa.* Below the depressing economic news was the mugshot of *El Vigilante del Raval* from last summer's brazen attack on the pickpockets who had become as synonymous with Barcelona as Gaudí.

Mónica felt a blend of anger and sadness manifest behind her narrowing eyes as she read what was happening to her city and country. It wasn't supposed to be like this. Local and national politicians had pledged Barcelona would be the jewel of the Mediterranean after the Olympic Games in 1992. They promised a standard of living equal to the Nordic countries once Spain joined the euro. Ten years later, the only people who had benefited from the single currency were politicians of all political persuasions and their cronies in construction, the media and finance.

The businessman rose from his seat, leaving the thin daily behind. Mónica needed to take her mind off the state of the world and snatched the wrinkled paper from a teenage boy's hand to read some fluff pieces.

The lead story inside was about the Santa Lucia Christmas market in front of the Cathedral and which personalities were to receive *El Caganer* treatment this holiday season. The Pope, the Presidents of the US and France, the Coach of Barcelona Football Club, were just a few of the famous faces who were set to become anatomically correct figurines that squatted and crapped on a ceramic patch of ground.

Mónica's family, like millions of others, had left their home in Southern Spain, coming to Barcelona in search of food and work. She and her parents loved Catalunya for the opportunity the region had given them. Catalan toilet humor, however, was something that they would never get used to.

Her children, on the other hand, adored the traditional *El Caganer* and his partner, *El Cagatió* – a small log, propped up on two arms, with a red stocking hat, googly eyes and single-tooth smile. Her children, like millions of others, fed the goofy face on Christmas Eve and tapped the bark with a stick, singing a song to help the digestive process. The next morning, a small pile of trinkets magically appeared from "The Shitting Uncle's" rear-end.

Mónica finished skimming the Christmas in Catalunya article and read the latest Hollywood gossip. A special insert, dedicated to the luxury apartments for sale near Diagonal Mar Beach, was next. The homes were so modern compared to her flat. Mónica couldn't wait to win the Christmas Lottery and buy a place with a sea view and central heating. She smiled, despite accepting the remoteness of the possibility, and turned to another section, with color photos of packaged vacations.

She and Juan had visited all the major cities in Europe and a few in the US before their kids were born. But not the Caribbean or Far East. Scenes of tropical beaches and the Great Wall of China formed before Mónica's eyes, blotting out the commuters in the carriage. At first she envisioned going on vacation alone. Then she thought, how boring, and pictured a chiseled blue eyed Swede for a little fun before her husband and kids arrived as her final, definitive choice.

Most of Mónica's colleagues arrived between nine and ten. She liked getting to work at 8:30am. The atmosphere still felt like dawn, not the start of the morning, and she could drink her first cup of coffee without interruptions, either in the whitewashed breakroom or on the adjacent 11th floor patio, with easterly views.

Before the economic crisis hit last year, her company had splurged on an espresso machine for the employees. The strong aroma of an Italian blend stimulated Mónica's groggy imagination, transporting her to the location of a gourmet coffee commercial, starring a silver-haired fox for an actor.

A sip from a plastic cup returned her to reality. Her lazy stare looked past the overhead lights reflecting in the window. Dark clouds threatened to storm above a choppy Mediterranean Sea, but no drizzle sprinkled the glass. Can't wait for summer, Mónica thought, as she finished her coffee. She saw the Human Resources Director outside, lost in thought, as she smoked near the low patio wall. Her good looks and young age made Elena a frequent target of office gossip, but Mónica had always gotten along with the raven-haired Ice Queen.

"Good morning, Elena," she said, grabbing the collar of a fleece cardigan she kept at the office to protect her from the arctic air-conditioning. "Why are you out here without a coat? It's freezing."

"Oh. Good morning, Mónica." Elena's tone chirped with surprise at the unexpected company. "How are things?"

"Really, really tired."

Elena grinned and took a deep drag of her cigarette. "Me, too," she said. "I didn't get home until almost ten last night. My husband wasn't too pleased."

She rolled her eyes as she blew smoke toward the ominous sky and rocky sea. Mónica laughed. "He sounds like me when it comes to Juan."

"Does he come home late a lot?"

"Sometimes. Usually when the kids have been acting up."

Elena beamed at the subject of children. "And how are your little angels?"

Mónica described her morning, from waking up at 6.15am, without the need of an alarm clock, to Alba's tantrum at breakfast, to her clueless husband who asked to leave early, when his wife was covered with food, milk and juice.

Elena's face slackened at the intimate details and her agape mouth said, "Oh."

"Do you have kids?" Mónica asked, knowing little about her superior's personal life.

"Two teenage step-sons." Elena grinned to show she had regained her composure. "They just think about girls and football."

Mónica shuddered. "I am not looking forward to my kids becoming teenagers. They are a handful as it is, especially my youngest—she's a monster."

"Being the step-mom..." Elena took a final drag of her cigarette. She exhaled and continued, "I let their father do most of the discipline and stay out of complicated issues," stomping the burning butt on the ground. "Alright, Mónica." Elena flashed a polite smile and tapped her watch. "Time to work. Have a good day."

The caffeine sped up the rate of the ticking in Mónica's head as she sat at her desk and focused on a computer screen. Her inbox was full of unread emails. The ones from the German multinational's Munich headquarters were in the official company language, English. The rest were in Spanish. Her boss, the Finance Director, hadn't arrived yet, but his presence was felt. There was a stack of new papers on what had been an organized desk when Mónica left work yesterday.

She dug through the mess to find a hand-written note. She had to prepare a two hour PowerPoint presentation for tomorrow's Steering Committee meeting. It was the same one she had scheduled on her boss's agenda three weeks ago. Why not give me the task then, not the day before? she wondered. Everything was always last minute and urgent with him, as it was with every head honcho in the office.

Mónica huffed and picked up the pile of papers, messing up her normally organized desk. Her boss had been with the company since its Spanish branch opened twenty years ago and still liked to work as if word processing and personal computers didn't exist on a mass scale. Scribbled drawings on torn out notebook pages diagrammed the slides he wanted her to create, along with chicken-scratch notes, with additional instructions.

Mónica set down her work and opened up PowerPoint to start on the presentation. The patter of her fingers hitting the keyboard drowned out the ticking in her head as she zoned out on work.

"Do you want to grab breakfast?"

The question broke Mónica's concentration. She looked up from her computer screen to see the Sales Director's Assistant, Mar, with the big fake smile she always wore.

The time was 9:20am. Mónica had finished the layout for about half the slides, but she had yet to receive any of the requested figures. "Sure." Her mouth curled into a thin grin as she readied to ask for a favor, "But do you think you could email last quarter's sales and costs before we go?"

Silence and a blank look. Her colleague had obviously yet to check her email. "Um, can I do it when we come back?" Mar clasped her hands to beg for forgiveness, beaming her big fake smile again. "Swear. It'll be the first thing I do. Just starving right now."

"Fine." Mónica frowned and wagged her finger in fake anger. "But first thing. It's for the big bosses in Germany."

A chastised Mar grew tight-lipped and nodded.

The bar everyone in the office went to was just around the corner from their building, but the walk was long enough for the Spanish women to open and close their umbrellas, both worried about being caught in a rain, which had yet to fall.

"Did you hear the rumors?" Mar asked, as they sat at a small round table in the far corner of the bar and waited to be served.

Mónica shook her head and tuned into her colleague's squeaky voice through the racket of people talking and banging plates:

"Germany's ordered staff reductions."

Mónica was curious to discover how Mar had unearthed such classified information. "How do you know?"

"Overheard Elena and the General Manager talking on the patio. How long have you been with the company again?"

"Fifteen years." Mónica tried not to sound irritated, having told Mar this many times before. "Started as the receptionist."

"That's right! You'll get a nice severance package then."

"Suppose so." Mónica sighed at the thought of losing her job. "We couldn't afford to live without my income, though."

Her cellphone on the table flashed. The ring tone for the song, *Mr Sandman,* played through tinny speakers. Most of her friends and colleagues had never heard of the tune dedicated to her one true love. Mónica first discovered it while watching the original *Halloween* movies in high-school. She and Juan had just started dating. He was a big fan of horror, she a love struck teenager. Now, she refused to watch slasher flicks and made him sit through romantic comedies.

The opening bars of *Mr Sandman* played for a second time as her boss's name, Manel, flashed on the cellphone display.

Mónica cringed and answered, "Yes," feeling her shoulder muscles tense.

"Where are you?" a sharp voice demanded to know.

"Having breakfast."

"Did you see my note?"

"Yes. Making progress. Just waiting for people to get back to me with the numbers."

"Very good." Manel paused and she heard him chewing on the other end of the line. He sipped and gulped before he continued, "You also need to translate it into English and send it to Germany by five today."

Again, could he not have told me that earlier? Mónica wondered. She could have had the English teacher do it during yesterday's class. "I'll try," she said.

A disappointed sigh blew in her ear. There was a rumbling on the other end of the line as her boss's voice rose to place blame on anyone but himself, "They were supposed to have gotten it three days ago!"

Whose fault was that? Mónica held the phone from her ear to stop from asking that question. Mar offered a sympathetic smile. Her boss was flighty and spent most of the work day entertaining. Manel might have been a monster at times, but at least he came into the office and did something.

"Can you call the other departments and tell them to send me the info?" Mónica thought people might be less apt to blow off a member of the board.

"No. Have a conference call with Germany."

"I'll see what I can do." Mónica hung up as a waiter arrived to take her order of a ham and cheese croissant, with a freshly squeezed orange juice. She took her time eating, gossiping and complaining to Mar about colleagues, lack of sleep, celebrities and family. When they finished breakfast, Mónica enjoyed a second cup of coffee in a proper ceramic, not plastic, cup, which reignited what had been a dormant ticking in her head.

Mónica had completed all of the layout and the design of the presentation in Spanish and translated most of it into rough English by the time lunch arrived. Of the required information, Mar had sent the figures for the Sales Department and the Logistics Assistant, theirs. The usual suspects: Marketing, HR, and IT had failed to reply.

Mónica picked up the phone to see what the holdup was before she went to eat with Mar and a couple of other assistants. The tinny melody for *Mr Sandman* rang. She set down the receiver to see the flashing number for the catholic school where her son attended first grade and her daughter daycare.

"Yes?" Mónica answered, wondering what Alba had done this time.

"This is the school nurse. Your son, Juanito, has been throwing up and started running a fever." An image of her precious boy, alone and shivering, flashed in Mónica's mind during a brief pause. "He should probably go home. When can you pick him up?"

"At work now." Mónica thought of her usual solution to such family emergencies. "Let me call my mother."

She hung up and pressed one on her cellphone, speed-dialing her parent's home. "*Mamá.*"

"Yes."

"Juanito's ill and I'm up to my ears in work. Can you pick him up from school and watch him? I'll try to leave the office a little early if I can."

"I'm so sorry," her mother said. "Don't you remember? Your father's scheduled for cataract surgery this afternoon. We're just on our way out the door."

Mónica had forgotten about her father's trip to the hospital, but dared not admit it, "That's right! Give him a big kiss for me."

"What are you going to do?" The worry in her mother's tone was evident. "Can Maria watch him? She is his other grandmother after all."

"No." Mónica shook her head, as if the conversation took place in person, not over a cellphone. "She and Juan Senior are at their home on Menorca. They won't be back until next week."

"And Juan?" her mother suggested.

"Going to call him right now and see."

"Okay. If not, I could do it while your father's in surgery. Juanito would have to come to the hospital, though."

"Don't worry about it," Mónica told her mother. "Take care of *Papá*. I'll call you tonight."

She hung up and pushed two to speed-dial Juan. His voice-mail kicked in after two rings. Mónica hung up, without leaving a message, and drew a deep breath to quell the rising anger she felt toward her unreliable husband. The ticking was just a whisper but a constant reminder. She had to talk to Manel; she needed to stay unemotional. She listened to the whoosh of a long exhale and rose to her feet. The glass wall behind her was close enough for her back to sense. She turned around to see the blinds up and her boss sitting behind a disaster of a desk, with his feet up, talking on the phone.

Mónica knocked on the door. Manel straightened in his large chair, hung up and waved her in.

"Yes," he said.

She explained the situation.

"Are you kidding me?" her boss erupted. "We still have a lot of work to do. You can leave a little early. But not before lunch!"

"Please, Manel." Mónica's voice rose as she again tried to explain the gravity of her problem, "No one else can watch my son and he is really, really sick." She tried to overcome any future objections by adding that the only work left was inputting the numbers, which Mar could do.

"Mar," her boss spat. "All she does is smile. She doesn't know her head from her ass. Everything is impossible and a struggle with her." Manel motioned for Mónica to sit and continued in a more even tone, "If I still wanted Mar as an assistant, she would be, but she isn't. Do you know why?"

Mónica sat down and shook her head.

"Because Elena told me you were the most competent and professional assistant here."

"Really?" Manel had never complimented her before.

"Yes," he said. "And it seemed she was right. Now, I'm not so sure."

"I know it's not a good day," Mónica agreed. "But it's an emergency."

The hard look in Manel's blue eyes conveyed little sympathy. "Have you finished translating it?"

"Almost. Thought Johnny might be able to do it. It would sound much better written by a native English speaker."

"Who?"

"Your English teacher," Mónica said. "Remember?"

Manel stroked his weak chin as he studied her. "You saw in the presentation that the Germans are ordering staff-reductions, correct?"

Mónica debated how to respond to such a blanket threat. She could remind Manel that it would cost the company more to fire her than any other assistant because of her tenure. She could also bring up the fact that she was the only one who hadn't complained to Elena about his temper.

Tick. Tick. Tick. thundered between Mónica's ears as images of her sickly son flashed in her mind. She didn't have the time, nor the energy, to get into an argument with her boss. "Listen, Manel," she said. "Got to go. I'll tell Mar to input the figures and call Johnny to do the translation," adding for a peace offering, "I'll also try to come in a bit early tomorrow," as she walked out of the glass door.

Mónica began to second-guess her decision to up and leave as she rode on an empty metro carriage. Another of the free dailies lay on the seat next to her. *La Crisis* was written in big bold letters. A flashy graph underneath the headline projected unemployment rising above 25 per cent, with a list of companies and factories whose layoffs had contributed to the jobless numbers.

Mónica looked at the phone in her hand, expecting a call from Human Resources, saying that she was fired for insubordination. The ring-tone stayed silent the whole journey underground and above ground, too, where large rain drops began to pelt the pavement beneath her feet.

Mónica opened the umbrella and lifted it above her head. She started down a steep incline. The smooth sole of her pointed-toe boot slipped on a slick spot. She felt the grooves of the umbrella's plastic handle fly out of her hand and the purse she carried on her shoulder weigh her down as she fell back in slow motion, arms out, circling in the air.

"I shit on God and his whore of a mother," Mónica shrieked the common expression Spaniards belted in anger, after she sat in a puddle that did little to cushion the blow, when her tailbone hit the pavement.

A group of construction workers in blue overalls rushed out of a bar. "You okay, beautiful?" they asked in Spanish, helping a shaken Mónica to her feet.

She wiped the back of her soaked skirt and tender derrière. "Just a little embarrassed," she said, squeezing her teeth as she grinned, to dull the pain shooting up her spine.

The youngest of the group put his arm around her. "You single, beautiful?" he inquired, bringing her in tight.

Mónica pulled away and cut him a flirtatious look. "You picking me up?"

The guy was cute in that bad boy kind of way, with piercings and tattoos, but she preferred more professional and clean-cut men.

"It's not every day I get to help out a beautiful woman!"

Mónica laughed. She waved and winced from the stabbing sensation running down her legs. She never got one, let alone two, compliments in one day. The unexpected surprise put a pep in her step as she strutted down the street toward her children's school, with her broken umbrella above her head.

The ticking boomed between Mónica's ears again to the same images of Juanito, ill and alone, flashing before her eyes, killing her light mood. A shot of adrenaline numbed the flaming sensation below her waist and she sprinted across an enclosed courtyard, up a set of steps, through a large wooden door.

The clicks of heeled, pointed-toe boots rose from the tiled floor to the overhead florescent lights. Mónica raced down a long corridor, bursting into the nurse's office, to find no one behind the counter. Her eyes darted in search of a person to ask about her son. The door behind her slammed shut. Mónica wanted to sob at the sight of her ghostly-looking boy, slumped in a chair, in the corner of the waiting area, all alone.

"My poor thing," she cried, holding her little Juanito tight, running fingers through his matted hair.

"Are you taking me home, *Mami?*" he murmured.

"Of course, I am." Mónica touched a burning forehead as the nurse appeared behind the counter. She nodded for Mónica to take the boy that she lifted in her arms until his head rested on her shoulder.

Halfway down to the corridor, her back burned and her legs shook from carrying the dead weight. She set Juanito down and stretched. A familiar voice pricked her ears and she turned to see an ajar door. Through the crack, a defiant Alba stood before a crying boy, with a toy in her hand. Mónica led Juanito to a chair next to a water fountain and looked into his listless eyes. "Wait for me here, okay?" she told him. "Be right back."

He blinked and nodded in confirmation.

Mónica limped to the classroom where the teacher scolded her daughter in Catalan, the sole language of instruction and parental communication. The exceptions were private English, French and German institutions, which were out of most people's budgets, but popular with local politicians.

Mónica knocked on the door to push it open. The young girl stopped her lecture and turned around. "Yes," she said, glowering to show her disapproval at the interruption.

Like the majority of Barcelona's residents, Mónica spoke Spanish, not Catalan, although she read and understood it.

"I'm Alba's mother," she said. "Is she doing anything important today?"

The teacher's probing eyes moved from Mónica's water stained boots and skirt to the makeup smudging her face and the damp hair, dripping on her tight-fitting sweater.

"No." The scowling girl spoke to Mónica in Catalan. "Why?"

"Can I take her from class?"

The teacher's sour face glowed, as if she had discovered she was getting off early from work. "By all means," she yelped, switching to Spanish.

She turned to a room of screaming toddlers and belted, "Alba," through cupped hands.

The little girl spun around. Her big brown eyes widened and her mouth dropped. "*¡Mami!*" she cried, throwing down the toy by the still sobbing boy, as she started a long sprint into Mónica's outstretched arms.

"Hello, sweetie," she said, kissing her daughter's soft cheek, lifting her in the air. "Have you missed me?"

Alba pushed off her mother's shoulder and her face contorted into an exaggerated expression of suspicion. "Why are you here? Am I in trouble again?"

Mónica shook her head and smiled to calm her daughter's fears. "We're going to spend the afternoon together."

"At home?" Alba asked. "Can I watch *Pocoyó*?"

"Of course."

"Yeeeaaaah!"

The few rain drops had turned into a steady downpour by the time Mónica and her two children left the school's front door. She gathered them in close, opening the broken umbrella, in a vain attempt to shield them from the rain.

"What's wrong *Mami*?" Alba pointed to her mother's limp as they came down steps and crossed an enclosed courtyard.

"Had a little accident," Mónica said, trying not to grimace from the burning pain that flared from her toes to her waist, with each step.

"Are you hurt?" her son asked, as they pulled open the door and stepped onto the pavement of a busy avenue.

"No. I'm okay." Mónica lied and gave them a reassuring smile. "Come on. Let's get a taxi."

"*Papi* said no more taxis," Alba reminded her.

"*Papi's* not here, is he?"

Mónica stood at the curb and hailed a cab, spraying water from its sides, as it raced down the rain drenched street. The taxi slid to a stop before an outstretched hand, sparing Mónica from a drenching. She ushered her children into the backseat and climbed in with a slam of the door. After giving the driver the address, she sat back and did what she always did when she could, she sighed a heavy sigh, in the nose, out the mouth.

Her son's head laid on her lap while her daughter kept busy drawing smiley faces in the condensation on the taxi's window. Mónica hadn't felt this relaxed since the train ride from Putxet to Plaça Catalunya. She closed her eyes. First, there was the rollicking rhythm of a train in her head, then silence.

The opening bars of *Mr Sandman* chimed. Mónica cursed seeing the world again. She dug her phone from a purse, which was still damp after her fall. Juan's name flashed on her cellphone screen. He was the master of bad timing.

"Hey, honey." His tone was contrite. "Sorry about missing your call. I was stuck in a three-hour meeting. You know how it is. What's going on?"

"Juanito is sick." Mónica kept her answers curt, hoping her husband realized how angry she was at his unreliability.

"Is he with your mother?" he asked, slightly concerned.

"No."

"Is he with you?"

Stupid questions did not help Mónica's mood. "Yes."

"Manel didn't mind?" Juan seemed worried now.

"Not sure," she told him. "We'll see if I have a job tomorrow."

"Oh." A two second pause. "By the way, got some good news."

Only winning the lottery would cheer Mónica up and there were no numbers drawn today. "What?"

"Mom and Dad said we can use their house on

Menorca for the Easter holidays."

"The water's too cold to go swimming then."

"I know." Juan's voice cracked from the disappointment of her rejection. "Just thought it'd be nice to get out of Barcelona."

"We'll see."

"Um, okay," he muttered. "Let me know. You okay?"

"No. I fell and I'm in pain." Mónica gritted her teeth to keep from crying. "Look, Juan. I'll see you tonight, okay?"

"I'll try and leave work early," he said it as if he meant it. "A big client's just cut the budget so every one's running around and..."

Mónica hung up the phone before she called her husband a liar. The only times Juan had followed through on his word and left work early were: the week after she had an emergency appendectomy, when she almost miscarried with Alba, twice, and the two weeks following the birth of each child. Five times out of at least a fifty. That was it. Then again, Mar's husband missed the birth of their only daughter while at a Barça football match and was incapable of putting a dish in the dishwasher. Like everything in life, husbands were relative, Mónica decided.

After getting home and tucking her children into bed, Mónica headed to the kitchen to pop two Ibuprofens for her stiffening back and legs. The tinny melody for *Mr Sandman* scratched her eardrums. Her eyes darted to the spotless counter top to see a blocked number flashing on her cellphone.

"Yes," Mónica answered, knowing it was either a salesmen or her office.

"Hello. It's Elena. How are you?"

She would have preferred a hopped up voice, pitching

a service she didn't need, to the concerned tone of the Human Resources Director, asking about her well-being. "I'm fine, thanks," Mónica lied before telling the truth, "Juanito's sick, though."

"Yes, I heard. Is it serious?"

"Think it's just the flu. If he's not better tomorrow, I'll take him to the doctor."

"Are you coming to work after?"

Mónica's father had outpatient surgery, which meant that she could leave Juanito with her parents, like she always did in these situations. She had also told Manel she would come in early and he needed her. Germany had promoted a young regional head. Mónica had been around long enough to know when there was a new chief, somebody had to be sacrificed, and a Financial Director who didn't know SAP, let alone Excel, made the most logical target, despite the high cost of his severance package.

Mónica readied to tell Elena: *Yes* out of loyalty to the only company she had ever worked for. A photo of Juanito and her on the refrigerator gave her pause. The image captured the moment after a his first violin recital. Juan thought their son's instrument of choice was a bit on the sensitive side and always found a reason to get out of attending concerts. Mónica had never missed a show and sobbed from joy at her little boy's improvement during this year's Christmas pageant.

"I don't think so, Elena." Mónica explained the situation with her parents and the need to take care of a sick son.

Silence after the answer. "Um, er, okay," her superior eventually muttered, then sighed, "I understand."

"Will I still have a job?" Mónica asked.

Elena laughed as if the question were a well-timed·

joke. "Of course you will. Manel will be upset, but I know how to handle him. Mar will help out, along with Ana at reception."

"Thanks, Elena."

"Don't worry. Just make sure to bring a copy of the doctor's note and dock today and tomorrow from your vacation time."

"Will do." Mónica hung up and saw an icon for a text message on her screen.

How about Paris for Easter? Claudia can watch the kids and we'll spend a weekend in the City of Lights? Juan.

Mónica was touched by her husband's clichéd attempt at being romantic. It wasn't his fault all Spanish men were the same. It didn't matter if they were Catalan, *Extremeño*, or *Asturiano*, their mothers had babied them until they married and left the nest, creating the proverbial boy trapped in a man's body, for wives and daughters to then raise.

The idea of her two babies, alone with her twenty-five year old sister-in-law, made Juan's offer a nonstarter for Mónica, despite the obvious appeal. She texted back her preference for a quiet night at home, maybe a dinner and a movie out. Juan confirmed their date in under a minute and promised to watch the kids on Saturday so she could lie in bed.

His heart was in the right place, but their children demanded to have their mother in the mornings. There was no arguing with irrational beings. Nor would Mónica want their preference to be any other way, even if the wrinkles in her face deepened and multiplied from a lack of time with the Sandman.

As she walked down the hall and listened to the sound of falling rain, Mónica tired to remember the last time it had felt like dawn at two in the afternoon. Inside her bedroom, Juanito was curled up under a blanket on her side of the bed. Alba was propped on pillows where Juan usually slept. Her eyes drooped shut and didn't open again as she watched her favorite cartoon on the flat-screen on the wall. Mónica smiled and turned off the TV. It was a question of seconds, not minutes, before all three of them were sound asleep.

Running the Gauntlet

Four men, sickened by the plague that terrorized their beloved Barcelona, marched down dusty Carrer Ample to the clatter of cans sliding in an almost empty duffel bag. Meaning "Wide Street" in Catalan, the road was narrower than the Las Ramblas promenade and dated back to the Middle Ages when a towering wall protected, not always successfully, the old city from sieges, infestations and attacks. Nowadays, busy avenues carried two-way traffic around Barcelona's historic heart. This openness left Carrer Ample, and other ancient streets, vulnerable to the sinister forces which the four men had come to battle that summer night, maybe even to the death.

They entered a bar called Hook, not because they were fans of JM Barrie, but because it was the first place someone had suggested. As the two wooden statues of Indians in full headdress implied, and the name on the sign above the front door confirmed, Peter Pan's arch-nemesis, the pirate with one hand whom Long John Silver feared and a saltwater crocodile desired, Captain Hook, served as the locale's inspiration.

Inside, dimmed yellow lights dotted peg legs hanging from the rafters. Eye-patches and nautical steering-wheels decorated dark wood paneled walls. Bartenders clad in puffy white shirts served cocktails and beers to tanned patrons in t-shirts and shorts. No one paid attention to the four men as they gathered at a round table near an old sea chest, with an incendiary plan to save their cherished city.

"Right, chaps." The leader of the group, George, spoke with the regal intonation of an English gentleman. "Glad to see everyone is *he'ah*."

"*Sss...* what about Johnny, Frans and Alex?"

George stared at the bruises on the bronzed face of his right-hand man, Tommy, who whistled through a missing tooth.

"They are obviously cowards." George glowered through bottle-cap glasses at his friend's greasy blond afro. "Would you please use shampoo next time you shower? You might be from Africa, but you don't have to look like Tarzan."

Tommy was the third generation of his family to have been born and raised in Nigeria, but the first to have received his education at a posh boarding school in rural Massachusetts. This gave him a New England accent that, like the English, often dropped *r's* in the middle and end of words, although with a distinctly nasal American sound when he spoke.

"They say *hai'ah* washes itself *aftah* six months." Tommy paused and stuck a rolled cigarette in his mouth. "But you don't have to *woa'wey* about that, do you?"

George inhaled a cloud of rich tobacco smoke as he rubbed his freshly shaved head. The bristly patches of gray hair pricked his fingers, but he felt mostly smooth scalp. "Baldness is hereditary," he explained. "I have no control over it. You choose to look uncivilized. Do you think women like men who look like they were raised by wolves and a lazy bear?"

"Is *Estham* coming?"

George heard a familiar lisp interrupt his and Tommy's conversation. "I've already told you, Paco, " he snapped at a dark-complexioned Spaniard, with a potato-shaped head and bulbous eyes. "Sam's phone is off and I haven't seen him since his date with a Basque girl."

"When did you tell me that?"

Was the little turd taking the piss? George had told Paco at least five times that the part time tour-bike operator had dropped out of sight since their decision to implement the final solution to rid Barcelona of the evil forces which terrorized the city's innocent citizens.

George turned from the Spanish humpty-dumpty and faced the final member of the group—a pock-marked man, with a new Louis Vuitton baseball cap cocked to the side, a shiny puffy jacket popular with hippity-hoppers on his slender shoulders.

"Have you spoken to Jared and his crew?" George asked Morgan from France, aka the French Slim Shady.

"'ave you not 'eard? Jaraad iz dead."

"What?" George gasped. "How?"

"They killed 'im at *Po-art Olímpic* last week."

"Then it'll just be the fou' of us?" Tommy's voice cracked, as if the answer made a difference to tonight's plan.

"That seems to be the case." George shook his head to rid himself of the chill that stroked his ribs whenever the conversation turned to death. He had only met Jared at their meetings. His agreeing to join their operation had felt like a Faustian bargain. George perked up from an inappropriate sense of relief at the tragic news until he realized Jared might have been a spanker and a thug, but he didn't deserve to die so young. Who knows? He might have found Jesus.

George tried to focus on the task at hand, not a dead hoodlum, as he stood to address his troops. He was a rail-thin man with a pronounced Adam's apple who ironed his clothes and liked to wear button-down shirts tucked into hiked trousers. On his upper lip was a trimmed silver mustache, which had been in vogue in Britain before the facial hair became associated with Adolf Hitler, although it remained popular with World War Two veterans, like George's recently deceased father.

"Four men committed to a cause is better than an army of a hundred mercenaries," the proud son of a soldier declared, clapping and rubbing his hands together. "Right, chaps. Who wants a drink? My shout."

The three men raised their hands and George picked Paco to help with the order. They came back ten minutes later with four small cola bottles and highball glasses, three-quarters full of Cuban rum.

George poured some of the cola into his glass. The two ice cubes bounced around as he stirred the cocktail with his finger which he then sucked before he spoke. "Guess they attacked someone again. One of my teachers near Bar Marsella."

"They're such *fuckahs*," Tommy cursed, his tongue touching the stitches on his bottom lip.

They were the dark forces that seemed to run Barcelona. They attacked tourists, pimped streetwalkers and sold bad quality drugs. Their most famous source of income, however, came from thieving and pickpocketing. Anyone on the metro, at the main city sights, looking for a good time at the hundreds of bars and clubs, were their prey. They had become such a part of Barcelona life that they even inspired a website, RobbedinBarcelona.com, with its own popular Facebook page.

"Did you read the article in *La Vanguardia* last week?" Paco asked.

"Don't read the Spanish press," George snorted, finishing his drink. "It's just propaganda for the different nationalist factions."

"The mayor said that the rise in crime and violence was the tourists' fault for getting so drunk."

"Is that so?" George crunched on a melted ice cube and chewed. "Look. I'm not proud of my British brethren's behavior when they come here. But that's a bit rich to put it all on us."

George gave the common conspiracy theory, involving a deal between the city police and the local mafias, as the most likely reason for the rise in crime. "As long as the criminals don't target locals and pay a kick-back," the middle-class Englishman ended with some cockney slang, "the Old Bill looks the other way."

"But I'm from here." Paco eyed George with a mix of suspicion and disbelief. "And they robbed me, twice."

"Are you calling me a liar?"

"He'ssss right, Paco." Tommy's whistle broke the tension. "*Aftah* they got me, I went to a *bah* and the *ownah* said that's why they *nevah* report anything to the police. It'd make no difference and piss off the mafias."

Paco looked into his drink and slurped. "Dunno. Sounds paranoid."

George felt the 50 per cent of his DNA that came from his father manifest in his eyes. They squinted into the same scolding stare his old man had given him as young boy as the forty-five year-old George focused on the troglodyte Spaniard for insinuating he had a mental illness.

"What?" a confused Paco asked.

Like his father, George believed silence was more powerful than berating. It eliminated the chance of a prolonged argument, forcing his opponent to squirm and look away, as Paco did, signaling defeat.

George wanted to grin after his victory but expressed

no emotion. He reached under his seat and raised a deflated duffel bag into the air. "Right, chaps," he said, the contents inside clanging together when he set the bag on the table. "I've made us all shirts."

He pulled a zipper and produced a black t-shirt, with *Taking Our Streets Back,* printed on the front in big white letters.

Morgan took the clothing and held it up to his XXL paisley polo. "Why do we need these, George?"

"So when the police ask who did it, this sentence will be what they report."

"What *happenz* if they do not speak English?"

George's expression stiffened to hide the fact that he hadn't thought of the possibility. "Sure one of them will," he muttered, snatching back the shirt before he zipped up the duffel bag and slung it over his shoulder. "Right..." he had the tone of an authoritative leader again, "time to get a move on. We'll put the shirts on right before we run the gauntlet. Don't want to attract too much attention along the way."

Carrer Ample was bedlam. Revelers staggered in and out of the kitsch bars popular with locals, transplants and tourists alike. At the bright light of a late night convenience store, a group of Americans stumbled out, shouting, "This place fuckin' rocks, man," with tall beer cans in hand. They were so enthused at being, "totally *muthafuckin'* wasted in Barcelona," they staggered blindly past a blond girl with her head buried in her knees, sitting on the stoop of a closed Spanish shoemaker.

The click of a camera joined the background noise and George looked down to see Paco, with his cellphone aimed at the girl. "What on bloody earth are you doing?" the Englishman screamed.

The crustacean-eyed, lispy Spaniard stepped back and snapped, "*Whaths* wrong with taking pictures of beautiful women?"

"She's fucking smashed, mate."

"*Shee'ths ethstill* pretty."

The French Slim Shady laughed at the Spanish *Mr Potato Head* dressed in skin tight jeans on sausage legs. "Aren't you gay?"

"No," Paco protested. "I loooove women. Look at all my pictures."

He showed Morgan his phone and flipped through photo after photo of different unsuspecting females that ranged from jail-bait to geriatric, plump to anorexic, comely to homely.

"Who *iz* that?" the Frenchman inquired.

"*Whooths diths*?" Paco stopped at an image of a girl with long strawberry hair. "My new flatmate."

George had heard enough and pushed the perverted Spaniard away. "Get away from this woman, you sick bastard."

"What?" Paco whined. "I don't understand. *Whaths* wrong with...?"

George tuned him out. He bent down to help the distressed platinum blonde with dark roots who sat on the shoemaker's stoop. "Miss, are you alright?" he asked, tapping her shoulder. "This isn't a good place to be in this state."

The girl lifted her head from her knees. The stench of vomit, vodka and diet cola blew from her mouth when she groaned, "Huh?" as her blood-shot eyes opened and rolled back into their sockets.

George began to shake the girl to coax some more information. She slurred a popular hostel's name. He stood. A floating green light creeping down a congested

Carrer Ample meant that the approaching taxi was free. George hailed the cab. He put the drunk girl in the backseat and told the driver in Spanish, "Nothing better happen to her," giving him a €20 note, which was five times the fare. "I've got your taxi number memorized."

It was a lie, but George wanted to plant the seed of the possibility in the driver's mind. He banged the roof of the cab and waited for it to leave. "Where's Tommy?" he asked, turning around to see Paco and Morgan.

"He had to go to the *bathrooom*," the French Slim Shady said, flicking the cigarette he had been smoking into the street.

"For fuck's sake," George shrieked. "Hold this," handing Morgan the clanging duffel bag.

Back at Hook, a beanpole took advantage of his height to peer over the heads of the puffy-shirted workers and tanned customers. Tommy's greasy blond afro poked up at the far back, near the toilets. George put on imaginary blinders and marched through the crowd.

"What on earth are you doing?" he barked, finding his right-hand man with three tall blondes.

Tommy had a fresh rum and cola in hand and beamed a gap toothed smile. "May I introduce you to Ingrid, Olga and Kirstin? They're from Sweden."

"Allo!" the three girls said cheerily.

George had eyes only for his wife. He yanked Tommy's arm, pulling him to the side. "What are you doing?" he repeated. "I said we had to get a bloody move on."

Tommy kicked the ground and muttered, "Yeah, I know. It's just..."

"Just what?"

"There's only fou' of us and I..." Tommy lifted his

doe-eyes from the grimy floor and offered George a weak smile for an apology, "I just don't think tonight is a good idea *anymoah*."

"Is that so?"

Tommy nodded.

"How many times have you been robbed?" George's voice boomed as he brought up the four muggings his right-hand man had suffered during his year in Barcelona, two of which had sent him to the hospital. The Englishman also reminded his young friend how he had sworn on his beloved grandmother's grave that he would seek revenge after the last attack.

"Now, Tommy," George continued to lecture. "I know you're only twenty-one, but there comes a time in every man's life, when he must either stand up and fight or shut up and stop complaining. What are you gonna do?"

Tommy set his drink on a cigarette vending machine and pulled out a pouch of tobacco from his back pocket. "I'm only in *Bahcelona* a few *moah* weeks," he paused mid-sentence to pinch some stringy brown tobacco and roll his smoke, "before I go back to Africa and work at my parents' hotel. Just wanna have fun, you know?"

Tommy lit his cigarette and exhaled into the ceiling.

"I see." George did little to hide his disappointment in his tone. The blond Tarzan had been the first person to answer his ad in the Barcelona Connect, looking for "noble men who were sick of being victims to scum." Tommy was also the only member of the group, other than Jared, who had attended all five meetings where they discussed how to rid Barcelona of the evil-doers who beat tourists and robbed old ladies, like George's favorite auntie.

"Alright, then." He sniffed to dry his moist eyes and turned on his heel to leave. "I'm not going to beg. Good luck to you, son."

"Listen, George..."

He didn't bother to turn around. He bit his hairy lip and plowed through the packed bar toward the front door that he shoved open hard enough for it to bang into one of the Indian statues.

"Where's Tommy?" the French Slim Shady asked, handing George the duffel bag, as he stormed toward the corner of one of the many alleys, branching off the festive Carrer Ample.

The Englishman threw the strap over his shoulder and tucked the canvass sack under his arm. "He ate some bad seafood," he always spoke quickly when he lied, "and isn't feeling well."

"He looked okay to me," Paco said.

George scolded him with the famous Hastings' glare that had intimidated each generation of Hastings men and women, dating back to before the Normans crossed the English Channel in 1066.

His icy expression warmed as George turned to Morgan and said, "Right, Frenchie. Let's get a move on."

"I *'ave* to meet some people at Bar Tequila."

"For fuck's sake! We all agreed to treat tonight seriously." George paused and glanced at Hook's wooden Indian statues with their arms crossed in defiance. "Now Tommy's dropped out and you've gone and made plans."

"Relax man." Morgan reached out to put a reassuring hand on George's shoulder. "It'll be quick and it's on the way."

"That's not the point!" He shrugged off the Frenchman's gesture. He ranted about planning this moment for two months. After each meeting, George had asked if anyone wanted to back out. No one did. In fact, everyone claimed that they were as committed to the cause as him. "I need to know I can count on you," George cried, the frosty Hastings' glare directed at Morgan for the first time that night, "because if not—fuck off! I'll do it myself."

"You don't 'ave to worry about me, man." The French Slim Shady's thin lips stretched into a tough-guy grin as he took a cigarette from its pack. "They got my little *sistur*." He paused and struck a lighter before continuing, "And the last *motherfuckur* to hurt my *sistur*, I put in the *'ospital*," blowing out a cloud of smoke

"You know what, Frenchie?" George threw an arm around Morgan's shoulder. "I take back everything bad I ever said about you frogs."

"I won't leave you either," Paco chimed in, looking up at George with moist eyes, the same shape, color and size as his wife's Pug.

The rarest of sights from an English gentleman—a smile which showed his small, slightly crooked, tea stained teeth. "The Three Musketeers it is then," George declared, full of righteous and noble pride. "Follow me, men."

They marched from Carrer Ample, down the first of many dark alleys that had cut through *Barri Gòtic* since its time as a walled city. The dull bangs of cans, sliding with the shirts in the duffel bag, joined the rhythmic stomps of footsteps until they arrived at Plaça de George Orwell.

George scanned the scene. A modern sculpture of an orange globe on top of a twisting metal pole rose from the middle of a raised concrete platform. Men and women chatted, drank and smoked at the metal tables, belonging to the bars along the square's perimeter. Junkies with their mangy dogs, meanwhile, begged for money under the watchful eye of the cameras on the walls.

George's stomach turned as if he had drunk sour milk. "Where is this bar, Morgan?" he asked, wondering what the square's namesake would think of such a vile place.

"You've *nevur* been to Bar Tequila?" A French accent registered surprise. "It's an institution."

"Try and avoid the city-center."

"I know where it is," Paco interrupted, strutting to the front, leading them to a bright red door with the word, *Tequila,* written in slanted black letters.

They entered a dark front room with glistening bar counters on either side and an arched door near an empty DJ booth at the back. The only lighting came from the red neon tubes, shining on framed heavy-metal posters. The music of Metallica played over speakers, at a volume one notch louder than you would hear in a waiting room, as a scantily clad female bartender stopped washing glasses and approached the three men.

"What would you two like to drink?" George asked, trying not to stare at the girl's dress, consisting of strategically placed latex straps.

Morgan took a pair of headphones that hung from the glass rack above the bar counter. "Tired of rum. Too sweet. How about a whiskey and cola?"

George was about to agree but felt Paco pulling on his shirt sleeve. "I want an apple martini."

"Are you sure you're not gay?" George snapped at another interruption from the roly-poly man in a skin-tight tank-top and jeans before his mood warmed. "It's no big deal if you are. A relative of mine recently came out."

"I swear," Paco protested. "I love women," reaching for the cellphone bulging in his front pocket.

"You know what, mate?" George shook his head before wagging his finger. "You need to stop doing that. It's creepy."

He turned to the bartender and ordered their drinks in Spanish, with a thick English accent, "*Dos whiskeys cola, y un apple mahtini, poh favoh.*"

The young female bartender strained to understand the pronunciation, revealing the first signs of crow's feet around heavily mascaraed eyes. "Um, *Vale*," she eventually muttered.

She had enough piercings to qualify as a pin cushion. George tapped Morgan on the shoulder. "What?" the Frenchman asked, removing his padded earphones.

George nodded at their bartender who made their cocktails. "I don't understand why pretty girls feel the need to ruin their looks with piercings and tattoos."

Morgan laughed as the subject of their conversation returned with their order. He waited for her to leave and asked, "You don't like them?"

George shook his head.

"You've come to the wrong city then."

"I know." George paused and noticed Paco on a stool, banging his shiny potato-shaped head to the music of Iron Maiden, which now blasted through the headphones covering his ears. George's voice was louder than the music from the overhead speakers when he spoke again. "He's a strange one, isn't he?"

Morgan poured the cola into his glass. "Very," he admitted, as he sipped his drink through a straw. "How do you know him?"

"He's my wife's younger brother."

The French Slim Shady almost fell off his stool. "*You're* married?"

George nodded and retorted, "Why?" feeling offended

at the incredulous reaction. "Do I not seem the marrying type?"

The bar's front door opened to a blast of people shouting and glasses breaking. A group of three men in hooded sweatshirts and camouflage pants entered. The door closed and the only sound was their footsteps until a song by Rage Against The Machine faded in.

"*Bonsoir*," the men said in unison.

As George sipped on his drink, he watched Morgan and the three men chat. He didn't understand their conversation, having not studied French for almost twenty years. A minute later, the men set down their half-drunk beers and slipped Morgan some money under the counter. In return, he gave them a small plastic bag of white powder when he shook their hands.

"*Merci*," the men belted, leaving the bar to another blast of street noise before the front door closed.

"You're a drug dealer?" George blurted, wondering why he hadn't screened the people who answered his classified in the Barcelona Connect. "Thought you were a French rapper."

"Shhh." Morgan put his finger to his lips. "Is there a problem?"

George stared at a hard, pock-marked face and lied, "Suppose not."

"You don't do drugs?"

"Tried E once in the nineties." George shuddered from the memory of having the chills, wanting to throw up, but not being able to purge the toxins in him. "Drugs aren't really my thing," he added, downing his strong *Cubata*, as if it were just cola, not 90 per cent whiskey. "Think I'm the only one in Barcelona who doesn't take something, though."

Morgan confirmed the statement with a knowing grin

and pointed his chin at the female bartender, who took the orders of a group of South Americans, with a couple of *guiris* thrown in. "Another drink?"

"Alright, but this is the last one." George turned his attention to the arched door by an elevated deejay booth. "We should probably sit down somewhere more private," he suggested to his new right hand man who nodded in agreement.

Rock You Like a Hurricane by the Scorpions provided the soft background music as the three men moved to Tequila's empty backroom, near the toilets and their bright florescent lights.

"This is the plan," George announced, as they sat at a small rectangular table. He spread out a city map, which he had pulled from his back pocket, and pointed to a street at the bottom of Las Ramblas. "We're going to attack them here."

"Why there?" Morgan asked, staring at George's stoic face, as he continued to lean over the table, with his finger on the location.

"There's been a reported surge of muggings on this street at the same time every weekend. Not sure why." George folded up the map and returned it to his back pocket. "Guess we're about to find out. Any questions?"

"Yes." Paco sipped his second apple martini. "What exactly are we going to do? I have never been in a fight in my life."

George unzipped the duffel bag and produced a jumbo-sized can of hairspray that he had converted into a flamethrower. "We'll use these," he stated, trying not to smile, as he handed the contraption to Morgan who studied the homemade weapon, with a look of shock and awe.

"As you hold down the nozzle," George pointed at the front of the hairspray can where electrical tape secured a blue flamed lighter, "strike the lighter and that will ignite the flammable spray."

Morgan smiled in appreciation at the lethal device in his scarred hands. "You're like Q from James Bond, George."

"Thank you." The Englishman beamed with patriotic pride. "British ingenuity was what drove the greatest empire the world has ever seen."

Morgan smirked and gave the weaponized hairspray back to George who put it back in the duffel bag, with the four others he had made, along with the black t-shirts with *Taking Our Streets Back,* printed on the front.

Paco hadn't blinked the whole time George discussed the plan. "But won't we burn them?"

"That's the idea," he quipped, finishing his third and final drink of the night. "Hopefully, they'll be smart enough to run once they smell singed hair."

"I don't know." Paco closed his golf ball sized eyes and shook his spud-shaped head. "It seems a little crazy to me."

George took a deep breath. "I know it's a bit extreme," he admitted, "but they have the numbers on their side." He contemplated what to say next, breathed again and continued with a cliché, "Look. I abhor violence as much as the next man, but desperate times call for desperate measures."

"But this is really, *really* crazy."

George took off his bottle-cap glasses and rubbed the bridge of a broad nose. "Paco," he said, putting back on the specs so that he could see clearly. "If we don't stand up to these men and put the fear of God into them, no one will."

"He's right," Morgan seconded. "They only understand violence."

"But we could go to jail!" Paco's moist eyes latched onto George's stiff mustachioed upper lip that finally moved when he spoke.

"How did you feel when these men held a knife to your throat and took all your money?"

The Spaniard murmured, "Violated and afraid."

"And what did you tell me the day after it happened?"

"That I was tired of always being the victim."

George prodded, "Do you still feel that way?"

Paco nodded.

"Well then..." The righteous Englishman waited until he had his brother-in-law's full attention. He then banged the table and waved a long arm to re-enforce his point, "here's your chance to stop being the victim and show these subhumans that their days of preying on the innocent are over!"

"What about the police?"

George scoffed at Paco's question, "Where were they when Tommy was beaten, Morgan's little sister was mugged and my auntie was robbed?"

The dumpy Spaniard shrugged and George told him, "In a restaurant having a coffee."

"You don't know that for sure."

"Maybe not." George slung the duffel bag over his shoulder, causing the hairspray cans with lighters inside to collide. "But I do know the police don't care about what's going on because if they did, we wouldn't be here tonight."

The lights of the bar flashed on and off, indicating 2:30am, closing time. "Right, chaps." George felt his heart drum against his chest. "The time is upon us. Let's roll as the Yanks say."

He led his men out of Bar Tequila, onto Carrer Escudellers. During time of the walled-city, the street had been where potters spun clay into plates, cups and statues. The closed ceramic knick-knack stores were a testament to this time in history. The hoards of inebriated tourists, spilling out of the bars that closed their metal shutters, were a more modern addition to the city landscape.

"We should probably wait until the crowd thins," George whispered. He felt tense as he tried to avoid making eye contact with two nearby police officers. Their stares were currently focused on the perky bums of the young girls who staggered around, searching for their missing friends, not him and his duffel bag of dirty ticks, which was how he wanted the situation to remain.

"George," Morgan said, as he spied three men pick the pocket of a kid in a baseball cap, within spitting distance of those in charge of protecting the city and its people. "Can I ask you a question?"

The disgusted Englishman shook his head at the police incompetence and said, "Sure."

"I know your favorite auntie was robbed. But why are you really doing this?"

"Well, Frenchie," George opened, with the intonation of a loquacious man, "because when I first arrived, they got me."

He had just moved to Barcelona to live with his Catalan bride, whom he had met in England the year before. They were strolling hand-in-hand as they passed Palau de la Música, on their way to a place that served trendy tapas in *El Born*. His eyes were fixed on the white statues with gold trim carved in the red-brick façade of the music hall when a young boy zoomed past on a wobbly bicycle, skidded and crashed to the ground.

George dashed to help because, "There's nothing like the feeling you get from being a good Samaritan." He told Morgan his mood then soured at the discovery he felt lighter without his wallet in his back pocket. This epiphany came just as he caught sight of a second man, hopping on the back of the bicycle before it disappeared down an alley.

George carried most of his cash and credit cards in a hidden money belt so the thieves didn't get much. "But they prey on the decency of men," he said. "And then when they robbed my auntie and I saw Tommy's split lip and missing tooth, I just couldn't let it go anymore."

A grinning Morgan pointed at the duffel bag. "Are we going to put on the shirts now?"

George smiled a warm smile before his face snapped and he cast a furtive glance to assess the situation.

Only a few drunken stragglers populated the trash littered Carrer Escudellers and no more police were present. The men donned their black shirts with white letters, under which they hid their homemade flamethrowers, before setting off toward their confrontation with Barcelona's dark forces.

"Coke, marijuana, hashish, charlie," the famous chant heard throughout the old city came from the huddled groups of Moroccans and Nigerians in the shadows of crisscrossing alleys.

"*Cerveza*, beer," sang one of the many Pakistanis, who patrolled the beach during the day, *Barri Gòtic* and *El Raval* at night, with a six-pack in one hand, a plastic bag full of more cans in the other.

George turned to Morgan. "You seem like a bright young chap. Have you ever thought about doing something else? You know—not drug dealing?"

Morgan grinned, as if he had heard that question

before. He compared himself to a *"bartendur"* and pharmaceutical sales-rep. "My clients are adults," he continued, with quintessential French indifference at the morality of his actions, "who can spend their money as they wish."

"Yes," George conceded the existentialist argument. "But booze is legal and drugs aren't."

Morgan laughed. "And what we are about to do is?"

George could only say, *"Touché, "* as Barcelona's Three Musketeers reached the end of Carrer Escudellers.

On the Las Ramblas promenade, cross the one-way street carrying traffic in the direction of Plaça Catalunya, city workers in green uniforms wielded high-powered hoses. Between them were slow moving trucks, with spinning brooms under their chassis. The blasting water acted like the Catalan sheep dog. Revelers tried to stay one step ahead of the nipping spray as they were herded away from the seedy old city toward the bright lights of L'Eixample.

The minute the three men started to cross the slippery pavement of Las Ramblas, prostitutes manifested out of nothingness. They whistled. "Hey, Papi," they shouted. "I suck dick." Their toned muscles and prison hardened expressions in the glare of ornate street lamps, provoking more dread and loathing in the testicles, than sexual desire.

On the *El Raval* side of the historic promenade, muscular transvestites emerged from the shadows to offer their services in deep baritones.

"Remember when they were old fat Spanish and Catalan women?" George hugged his bag as they stood at the edge of the wet pavement. "Now, look at them."

"I think they're quite pretty."

Paco spoke his first words since Bar Tequila, but

George ignored the asinine comment, for they had reached the end of their quest.

On the other side of a one-way street, tucked between two buildings, was Carrer de l'Arc del Teatre. A blend of nationalities, complexions and sexes stumbled beneath the white stone arch that spanned the entrance to the alley. The wall mounted lanterns guided the way for those who wanted to keep on partying as they staggered down cobblestones toward one of the knock-knock bars and after-hour clubs, hidden deep in *El Raval*.

Then the bulbs in the lanterns cut. The white arch and alley vanished, leaving a black gap between the twinkling buildings. High-pitched shrieks and cries pierced George's eardrums. He shook; vengeance was at hand. Not for him—but for his favorite auntie, for Tommy, for Barcelona. "Ready to run the gauntlet," he wheezed, feeling short of breath.

"*Oui,*" Morgan said.

"Ready, Paco."

The dong of a can bouncing off the pavement answered George's question. He turned and caught sight of the third Musketeer, shoving a manly girl of the night, into the backseat of a taxi, direction the beach.

Morgan chuckled. "And then, there were two."

"He was useless anyway." George paused and listened to the rising volume of the shrieks and cries join the city's dissonant wall of noise. "Remember, wait for my order."

Morgan nodded and they sprinted across the street, into pitch-blackness, where feral barks and whoops bombarded the ears in surround sound. Women's bloodcurdling squeals, men's aggressive growls, added to the House of Horrors atmosphere. Flicks of lighters. Flashes of fire. Demonic grins behind the flames.

George's neck snapped. He searched the bursts of light that dotted the blackness. Where was Morgan? A hand reached deep in the Englishman's trouser pocket, filled with thumb-tacks, in anticipation of such a moment.

A yelp and the pricked fingers stopped stroking his thighs.

"Now!" George ordered, pressing the nozzle of his flamethrower. Gas hissed; the lighter clicked. The would-be pickpocket yowled and clutched his face. The alley was aglow from the fiery spray. Muggers and victims ducked for cover. They later reported that the stiff man showed no emotion during his brief rampage, not even the second before the metal can exploded in his hands.

***

George awoke to steady beeps and a dark world. The warmth of the dressings acting as a blindfold told him it was day. The skin beneath the bandages, wrapped loosely around his fingers, wrists and face, bubbled and tingled, especially his seared upper-lip and his right palm.

But much to George's surprise, he wasn't crying in agony. Not from the open wounds, nor from the tubes and needles stuck in his veins. He felt strange, nauseous but giddy, like he did when he flew in a hot-air balloon as a young boy. His old man had likened the sensation to being on morphine, a drug which he had first discovered during his six months in a military hospital, recovering from shrapnel wounds.

A familiar fruity perfume tickled George's singed nose. He sneezed. A high-pitched whistling filled his head before the beeps of the monitors returned and the slaps of sandals stopped at the edge of his bed.

"How do you feel?" his wife asked him in Catalan.

He sucked on his tongue to generate spit, which he then swallowed to sooth a charred throat. "Like I've been grilled and put in warm water." George spoke Catalan more fluently than Spanish, but with the same thick English accent. "How long have I been here?"

"Nearly two weeks." His wife inspected the bandages he imagined gave him the appearance of a person who was being mummified and embalmed at the same time. "They induced a coma until the severity of the burns lessened."

George listened to his wife take a deep breath as she stood over him. "My God, George," she said and he detected her rising anger. "What have you done? The police were just here. You're going to jail."

That possibility had never crossed his mind. Nobody served time for their crimes in Barcelona. He was hoping for a few singed thieves at most. A writeup in a free daily about a mysterious band of vigilantes, taking Barcelona's streets back, the best case scenario.

"I'm sorry, honey," a raspy George said, wondering what had caused the hairspray can to heat so fast and detonate. Was it the pressure? Did he shake the gas inside too much, making it combustible? He knew better than to pose such questions to his fuming wife. "Didn't think it'd go this far."

"What were you thinking?" She laid into him about the insanity of his dangerous and illegal actions; the price that she and their teenage daughter had to pay. "For crying out loud, George," his wife roared. "There was a feature on the local news last night, you're in all the papers and our neighbors think you're certifiably insane."

George apologized again and listened to his wife storm away from the bed, taking the fragrance of her perfume with her. "I don't know, George." She sounded distant when she spoke again, as if she had turned her back on him in both a literal and figurative sense. "I can't have a criminal for a husband."

Her words reminded him of the other member of the dynamic duo, his right-hand man, the drug dealing French Slim Shady. "What happened to Morgan?"

"Who?" his wife shrieked, her footsteps thundering in the steamy darkness, as she charged his bed. "The police say it was just you, George. You're the only person in Barcelona crazy enough to try and be a hero."

He didn't go through with it. The realization rendered the pain-killing effects of the morphine impotent. Where there was once skin on his upper lip, palms and arms, George felt the heat of flames, the flavor of smoke and hairspray in his mouth tinged with the salt from tears, welling in his bandaged eyes.

Gaudí's Crypt

1897

Antoni Gaudí felt the irritation at his situation fester in his chest as he sat behind a cluttered desk in the Sagrada Família's recently finished crypt. Sunlight flooded through windows high on white walls covered with sketches of the last great sanctuary of Christendom. Particles of plaster and dust glistened in the air, tickling his throat down to his lungs. He wheezed and coughed into a handkerchief, which he had pulled from the pocket of the green wool coat, he wore to ward off the January chill.

The crypt's completion could not have come at a better time. The lack of donations for the Sagrada Família's continued construction meant that there was no money to spend on lighting, heating or renting a proper workspace. In fact, since Gaudí had taken on the church's commission fourteen years ago, he hadn't earned enough to go to a bar for a coffee, like he once enjoyed doing, not that he had noticed the sacrifice.

He designed the colossal monument not for his usual industrialist benefactor, the Vatican or members of the Spanish Royal Family. But for his most important client—the Lord Almighty, He who had endless patience, He whose reward of eternal salvation was greater than any earthly possession or prize.

Gaudí sighed with frustration as he drummed his long fingers on the wooden desk. His intense blue eyes studied the markings on a thin piece of cardboard that was unlike any on the walls. There were no sharp charcoal lines, sketching one of the eighteen bell towers for the Twelve Apostles, Four Evangelists, Jesus and the Virgin Mary. Nor were there drawings of the façades that were to trace Christ's life from birth to resurrection. Instead, Gaudí's stare lingered over the equations and diagrams he had scribbled while his mind puzzled over the math.

All of his calculations predicted tragedy. The Sagrada Família would sink into the ground and crumble from the amount of stone needed to reach such celestial heights. The traditional method would have been to build a secondary wall and add flying buttresses to support the weight, but God's architect saw such a solution as a waste of space and too conventional for such a glorious edifice and client.

Gaudí stood from his chair in a huff. His fingers stroked the rosary-beads in his trouser pocket to clear his mind of all emotion and thoughts. In the corner of the crypt was a small shrine honoring Luke, the patron saint of a circle of fellow artists who, like him, had refused to paint nudes out of respect of the Catholic Church's pious teachings.

The architect felt his knees creak as they bent and rested on the stone floor. Before him was a wooden stand with a black velvet cloth and a medieval rendition of his favorite saint on top. He closed his eyes. His clasped hands rested on his woolly beard. He spoke words only he and God could hear.

Oh, Heavenly Father, I have failed you. I am incapable of devising a solution equal to your vision. I feel your spirit whether awake or asleep, looking at someone or at a blank piece of cardboard, but do not believe myself worthy of your presence. Please, Dear Lord, show your humble servant the way.

The darkness lifted like a building tarp blown away by a gust of wind. Gaudí saw himself as a young boy, running through a forest on a late summer afternoon. The bat he chased into a cave was the only thing in his sights. Wings fluttered ahead as daylight faded to a memory. The ceiling brushed his bobbing head and racing footsteps pounded the rocky ground that vanished.

Splash. He plunged into a frigid lake. A sickly child, his mother had never taught him how to swim and kept him away from other children who might have shown him how to stay afloat. He sank face first, bubbles streaming from his nose and mouth, past his ears. Subterranean rivers brought a glistening light, illuminating towering stalagmites below. The warm glow enveloped the boy. In the spindly peaks and valleys, tips and dips, he saw the mirror image of what came to him when he dreamed.

A current rippled through the sparkling water, flipping a young Gaudí on his back. Tiny spheres of air carried his fading breaths toward the lake's surface. It grew smaller, brighter. The boy smiled and felt himself floating in tepid water. It was like looking through a microscope. He could see the stalactites on the cave's ceiling with such clarity. They were an exact reflection of...

"*Senyor* Gaudí."

A boy's high-pitched voice popped the vision, bringing back the black canvass of closed eyelids. Many things annoyed the architect: bourgeois opulence, *Castellanos* who refused to acknowledge Catalans as different, men who frequented prostitutes, being just a few of his pet peeves. Nothing, however, irritated Gaudí more than having his concentration broken, for it always happened just when everything was about to come together, resulting in a moment forever lost and impossible to reproduce.

"What?" Gaudí snapped, feeling his lungs rumble. He gripped the sides of the wooden shrine that shook as his shoulders heaved and his head rocked from the violence of a hacking cough.

"*El Senyor* Güell requests your presence," squeaked a boy no older than thirteen in an ill-fitting, black-wool suit.

The mention of Gaudí's benefactor lightened his mood and his coughing fit eased.

"He's sent one of those new horseless carriages from Germany to fetch you." The boy stood and watched as the architect struggled to rise from his worn knees to his cramped feet.

"Is that so?" Gaudí wiped the spit from his mouth with the back of his hand which he ran through flowing blond hair above his ear in one smooth motion. His blue eyes twinkled before they closed and he massaged his neck as he pictured the machine.

"Yes, sir," the boy interrupted. "He's the first person in Barcelona to have one."

Gaudí looked at an eager face. "Good for him," he grumbled, brushing past his young visitor on his way to the crypt's door.

There was not a cloud in the January sky as Gaudí and the boy walked past mounds of uncut rock and stacks of stone slabs, near empty benches and barrels. Cloth tarps flapped and lifted in the blustery wind to reveal the abandoned scaffolding, which traced the perimeter of a barely laid foundation. The boy's mouth opened to comment on the lack of human activity, but he recalled his boss's warning not to mention the halted state of the church's construction.

"What do you think of all the changes happening to Barcelona?" the boy asked instead, too impatient to wait for a reply. "*El Senyor* Güell says, there are now balloons that can take men across oceans!"

"Is that so?" Gaudí muttered his favorite expression when he had nothing else to say.

After they crossed a semi-paved Carrer Mallorca, the architect found his eyes drawn to a new park. Freshly planted saplings with olive trunks had thin branches that looked like skeletal arms capable of holding up the heavens. He had seen such trees, but older, along Avenue des Champs-Elysées, during the Paris World Fair almost twenty years ago, and he thought back to that memorable day.

The Comella Glove shop had hired him to design a case for their most exclusive product. He took oak, iron and glass, forging, carving and blending the materials, into a decorative display that seemed to be an extension of the jeweled glove. Most of the fair's attendees looked at Gaudí's work with the patronizing curiosity of an adult admiring the project of a precocious child at a county fair. The glove failed to sell, but it did attract the attention of one wealthy Catalan industrialist.

"Sir? Sir?" The young boy tugged the architect's frayed coat sleeve, bringing Gaudí back from the fond memory of how he had come to know his main backer. "What do you think? *El Senyor* Güell calls it a *motorwagen*."

Gaudí ignored the boy with the annoying habit of not waiting for answers to his questions. Before him was a topless steel carriage, with four wheels and no animal. Unlike something nature would create, the man-made machine was totally symmetrical. The four bicycle-like wheels were round, held together by perfectly intertwined spokes. The only difference was the size, with the wheels at the back, being larger than the ones at the front.

"Why is there no top?" Gaudí asked.

"*El Senyor* Güell says it would fly off because the machine is so fast."

Gaudí would rather go slow and be comfortable. He ran his fingers along the polished black metal frame that curved and bent on either side. He stopped and looked up to see a two person leather bench mounted on a vibrating wooden and metal trunk. In front was a straight brass pole with a wheel mounted on top. A dark skinned Spaniard, with a thick black mustache, manned the controls behind a windshield that stopped at eyelevel.

"What's your name?" Gaudí asked in Catalan.

"José, sir."

"Where are you from?"

"Sevilla, sir."

Despite being fluent in Castilian, Gaudí would not change from his mother tongue for any man, not even the king. "What brings you to Barcelona?" he continued his small talk in Catalan.

"Work, sir."

"Ah, yes, the pursuit of the all-mighty peseta. How do you find Catalunya?"

Gaudí felt a repetitive tap on his shoulder and spun around to glower at the trembling teenager who carried goggles and a scarf in outstretched arms.

"What's your name?" Gaudí growled.

"Arnau, sir."

"Has your father not taught you to only speak when spoken to?"

"No, sir." The teenage boy's voice hushed as his quivering eyes darted to the floral pattern on the new pavement tiles. "My father died a few years ago."

Gaudí understood what it was like to have lost a parent. His dead mother continued to haunt and inspire him, for he knew if he fulfilled God's plan, a heaven where she awaited was what followed this life.

"Thank you, Arnau," Gaudí said, his face straining to smile, he did it so infrequently lately. He patted the boy's shoulder and took the scarf and goggles. Arnau offered a wary grin as he helped the architect bundle up and climb into topless *motorwagen*.

Most of the roads of L'Eixample remained loose gravel. The *motorwagen*'s thin wheels kicked up dirt to the jangle of small pebbles, ricocheting off the metal frame. Men with caps and pipes, walking along side donkeys or pushing wheel barrows, stopped and gawked at the sight of the horseless carriage, barreling toward them in a cloud of dust. Everyone, man and animal alike, then scattered at the blast of a horn when they realized the shimmering machine wasn't going to stop.

Gaudí felt the skin between the dusty eye-goggles and moist scarf start to burn from the wind. The pounding of hammers and chisels thundered in a sky shaded brown from the smoke of steamrollers. All around him were signs of Barcelona's golden age. Cloth tarps draped scaffolding attached to hidden façades undergoing cosmetic changes while exposed steel frames showed the skeletons for new edifices to be erected.

The architect thought about his beloved Sagrada Família: neglected, forgotten, decades behind schedule. He slumped in his seat, cursing the materialistic leanings of the emerging bourgeoisie, who would rather spend their money turning flats into palaces, instead of donating to the last sanctuary of Christendom. Did they not understand without Christ, Our Lord, none of their wealth would be possible? That all their material possessions meant nothing when they arrived at Saint

Peter's Gate?

Gaudí rued the decline of true men of faith, like him and Eusebi Güell, but didn't get a chance to dwell on his disappointment. His body leaned to one side and slid down the cushioned backseat as the automobile turned off Las Ramblas, onto Carrer Nou de la Rambla.

Prostitutes, their clients and panhandlers clogged the shadowy *El Raval* street. The driver honked; smoke plumed from the exhaust pipe. The steel *motorwagen* plowed through the congestion before stopping midway down at a somber stone wall with the flattened curve of two catenary arches. The wavy bars of wrought-iron doors gave the illusion of being Arabic mosaics. In the middle were the scripted initials "E" and "G," the latter letter disappearing as one of the doors swung in.

The black *motorwagen* drove into a courtyard rife with the stench of hay and horse manure. Gaudí noticed the wooden doors for the stables below ground were open. The odor reminded him of his family's farmhouse outside Reus where he had spent much of his childhood alone, wandering through the forest in search of bats.

The rattling engine cut, ending the lucid memories streaming in Gaudí's mind. He took off his scarf and goggles and watched as Arnau climbed down from the *motorwagen* and extended a helping hand.

"This palace is the first building you designed for *El Senyor* Güell, isn't it?"

Gaudí ignored questions when speakers already knew the answers. He shunned the boy's gesture and got out of the *motorwagen* himself. The wavy wrought-iron door began to swing to a close. Through the shrinking gap, he noticed people stopping and staring at an opulent iron eagle mounted between the two catenary arches. Most onlookers had wide-eyes and slack jaws; others snickered and pointed as they mocked. The architect tried to dismiss the critics as uneducated and ignorant masses, but the sting of seeing his work belittled burned more than the skin of his chapped cheeks.

***

Eusebi Güell sat at his desk in the glow of an electric lamp. The collection of poems and essays he read were written by his friend Joan Maragall. The tales were set in the Catalan countryside during medieval times. The descriptions of local forests, mountains and villages were easy to picture and Güell caught himself laughing at the satirical and scatological humor of the unpolished prose. The influence of Nietzsche in the vitality and symbolism of the words and national themes was a bit too obvious for Güell's liking, the industrialist being a devout Catholic. The German philosopher, the Antichrist.

From one of Barcelona's wealthiest families, Güell took tremendous pride in the book's publication and the role he had played in his hometown's recent metamorphosis, from Spain's forgotten second city into a modern European metropolis. Only a few years earlier, speaking or writing in Catalan, displaying national symbols, like the dragon or bat, meant imprisonment in the castle on Montjuïc Mountain. Now, thanks to the greater freedom he and his fellow industrialists had negotiated with the King of Spain, those repressive days were over! A great renaissance had begun with the Güell name to go down as the Catalan Medici.

He thought about his friends who doubted and ridiculed such grandiose statements. They cited his irrational affinity for the crazed architect Antoni Gaudí, the fantastical nature of his work and prickly country temperament. Their pretentious derision only cemented Güell's faith in his friend. He might not have understood the art or the man from Reus, but as a student of history, he knew that it was the original and the creative, like Gaudí and Mozart, who withstood the test of time. Not men, like Lluís Domènech and Antonio Salieri, who only reproduced the fashion of the moment, even if beautifully.

A knock on the door and Güell set down the book of poems. "Come in," he said, watching his young personal assistant, Arnau, enter his office.

"*Senyor* Güell," the boy announced. "*El Senyor* Gaudí is here as requested."

"Fantastic." Güell pushed the arms of his leather chair to lift himself from the seat. He straightened the snug vest he wore, which like his shirt, tie and suit, had been handmade by an English tailor during his last trip to Manchester. "Send him in."

Gaudí walked with a slight hunch and wore a rare warm smile. "Hello, Eusebi," he said, as the two men embraced and pecked the skin above the long beards on each other's cheeks. "It's been a long time."

"You're frozen," Güell blurted, grabbing his dear friend's arms. "Are you alright? You look knackered. Let Arnau get you something warm to drink."

"I'm fine for now." The architect peered over his benefactor's shoulder to see their reflection in a window. "As you've probably heard, donations for the Sagrada Família have dried up for the time being."

"Yes. I'm sorry to hear that." Güell nodded at Arnau to leave and waited for the boy to close the door before he spoke again. "You know, Antoni," his tone was sterner now, "when people pay for buildings, they don't expect sketches."

The architect stopped warming his hands near a fire under a marble mantle. His eyes narrowed and darkened as they focused on his patron. "Is it my fault Bocabella's original plan was flawed?" Gaudí sneered, feeling his inflamed chest heave before he hacked into a clenched fist.

"No, of course not." Güell patted his friend's back with an bejeweled hand as a benevolent master did when his favorite servant choked on their own spit. "Let me call my accountant and see if we might be able to offer a donation to get things started again."

"You are too kind, Eusebi." Gaudí's burning glare cooled as he dabbed his lips with the stained handkerchief he always carried with him. "I don't know what I'd do without you," he sighed, dropping the balled-up rag back into his jacket pocket. "You seem to be the only person who likes my work."

"I don't like it; I respect it," Güell cracked as he sat down behind an engraved desk and opened a box by an inkwell. "But enough woe-is-me talk. How about one of Spain's finest cigars from Cuba?"

Gaudí felt his joints grind as he crossed the room. He not only designed buildings and glove cases, but furniture, too, including the chair on which he sat. "You're supporting Madrid's colonialism buying those," he quipped, feeling the contours of the wooden back and seat support his body like well-made shoes did the feet.

Güell had a smug smirk common with men of power. He pulled a silver lighter from his vest pocket, puffing the cigar until the tip glowed. "You've been reading too much Marx." A cloud of tobacco smoke blew from the industrialist's mouth as he spoke. "One can be for the people and still enjoy the finer things in life. You once indulged."

Gaudí refused the offer with a dismissive wave of his hand. "A sign of an impetuous youth."

The industrialist looked at his friend who had aged faster than a king during a time of war since taking on the Sagrada Família's construction. "We've missed you at Mass lately."

"*You* have," Gaudí corrected, feeling an irritating tickle in his lungs, but not enough to trigger another coughing fit.

Güell looked away from his friend's accusatory glare. His mouth puckered as he blew a succession of smoke rings toward the fire under the marble mantle. "Don't you like what they've done to the Cathedral?" he inquired, eluding to the recent renovations the city's main church had undergone, as the possible reason for the architect's absence.

"It looks like a poor replica of something built in Gothic France." Gaudí told himself to stay calm and not excite his temperamental lungs. He looked at the window behind his benefactor. Beyond the maze-shaped iron bars was a view of the courtyard, the front wall and the street where people gathered to laugh at his iron eagle perched between Arabic-inspired gates.

"But that's not the reason I don't attend service there." Gaudí's attention returned to his one and only fan. "I've been going to Santa Maria del Mar to hear Bishop Josep Torras i Bages' sermons."

The industrialist chuckled as he stubbed his half-smoked cigar in a crystal ashtray. "You like your proverbs mystical and about donkeys, eh?"

"What animal better represents us?" Gaudí snorted, wondering if his benefactor's tone had been glib or sarcastic. "A bull? That's the epitome of blind recklessness and *la rauxa.*"

Güell stretched his arms and named the lean rat as his preferred animal symbol for the defining Catalan personality trait, *seny*. "Level-headed and alert," he explained, "able to stay alive surrounded by predators, just like us."

Gaudí shook his head and tiffed. "Too small. The donkey can carry more weight and what a kick! Even wolves are wary of him."

Güell's chuckled again. That was all the time it took for his favorite architect's eyes to cloud, his usually alert stare, withdrawing into another world. The industrialist had seen the distant look come over his friend before. The Holy Spirit had visited the man from Reus, singing him a song that spurred his genius to transmit God's designs, first onto paper, then into stone.

Gaudí grabbed a fountain pen from the inkwell and pulled a folded piece of cardboard from his breast pocket. Güell felt a blend of admiration and envy as he watched the architect sketch. The industrialist had tried painting, music and writing. None of his endeavors provoked more than sighs and groans of frustration at his lack of artistic talent.

"What's that?" Güell asked, when the fountain pen's metal tip snapped from its wooden stem and the architect coughed to signal that he had finished.

Gaudí showed him a piece of cardboard with sharp lines.

"Looks like something found in a cave." Güell cocked his head to get a different perspective. "Or maybe it's a forest?"

Gaudí gave a cryptic smile but no answer.

"By the way." Güell broke the prolonged silence and nodded at the window with a view of the courtyard. "What do you think of my new toy? A fine piece of German engineering, isn't it?"

"It's a cold ride but better than being behind a shitting

horse." Gaudí set the broken-tipped fountain pen on the desk and folded the cardboard before slipping it back into his breast pocket. "You also have a new employee, I see."

"Who, Arnau?" Güell's voice trailed off as he leaned to the side and reached into a drawer. "His father was one of my better managers until he had an unfortunate accident at a factory." The industrialist set a leather folder on his desk and opened a small brass clasp. He sighed and shook his head, as if he were about to discuss his own son, "As you've probably noticed, the boy's not blessed with too much common sense so I took him in."

"The world needs more men with your generosity, Eusebi."

"Thank you." Güell smiled and offered Gaudí favorite Catalan proverb, "The tight-fisted man is like a pig, only good after his death."

The architect grinned in agreement. "What do you have in there?" pointing his woolly beard at the folder on the desk. "A big check for me?"

Güell laughed at the suggestion. "No, but I do want to talk to you about a new church."

Gaudí sat up in surprise. "Another church? Doesn't Barcelona have enough? There's one on every block."

Güell laughed his hearty laugh again and explained that the location was at the worker colony Gaudí had helped design near Sant Boi. The school and the hospital were up and running. "But, as I'm sure you'd agree," the industrialist continued, "what the people need most now is a place to worship."

He produced a photograph from the folder and handed it to the architect. "I was thinking here."

Gaudí studied the grainy image in his hand. It was of a sloped wooded hill. An picture of stone columns and arches, rising out of the ground, began to form in his mind. "I'm flattered, Eusebi," Gaudí said, rubbing his closed eyelids to clear his head. "but the Sagrada Família consumes all my time."

"You can do both! " Güell pitched the architect on the fact that the new church was to be his creation from the beginning, unlike his other commissions. "Unfortunately, there won't be the same type of budget as my palace." Güell watched an excited man sink into his chair. "In fact, I'd like you to use the leftover materials from the worker colony whenever possible."

Gaudí's bushy eyebrow arched at his benefactor's austerity. "May I ask why?" he asked, tossing the black and white photograph on the desk.

"We're entering a new world," the industrialist told him, "with more and more competition. Really must watch my expenses now." Güell reached below his desk. "Do have a present for you, though," lifting up a wooden box.

Gaudí blushed with a joy that made a sick man look healthy. It was no ordinary box, but one crafted from polished mahogany, with lacquered brass clasps. One side opened to reveal a glass camera lens embedded in the middle of a wooden board. "Thank you, Eusebi," Gaudí murmured, his patron's benevolence lubricating his lungs.

"It's a J. Lancaster Instantograph. I bought it the last time I was in Manchester." Güell relighted his half-smoked cigar and added, "A bonus for helping me with the church," as he puckered his lips to blow smoke rings.

1908

Gaudí stood on a stool in the main room of his new workspace. An array of strings and chains dangled from the flat ceiling, with the intricacy of the finest hand-crafted chandelier. His creation only needed one more piece to be finished. The thought made an aging architect feel nimble and young again as he tied the knot to hold the final pellet-filled sack in place.

The sensation was fleeting. Gaudí placed a hand on a wood wall to keep his balance as he climbed down from a three-legged stool. Another rush of euphoria. The Holy Spirit had paid him a visit again. He hurried toward his camera before the sense of weightlessness and clarity left.

A black-bellow separated the glistening lens in a wooden board from a box mounted on a stand Gaudí had fashioned out of wood scraps. The sense of rapture warmed him as he stood behind a tinted-glass plate. He ducked his head. He closed an eye to line up the perfect shot, one which would finally make him worthy to be called, "A servant of the Lord."

The whine of hinges brought a breeze. The weighted strings and chains rustled, then rattled, when the door behind Gaudí closed. His bottom eyelids rose with the steam bubbling from his lungs. He turned from the camera to find Arnau, who was a young man now in a better fitting wool suit.

Gaudí wheezed and coughed into a handkerchief he had recently bought. "Haven't you heard of knocking?" he sneered, wiping his mouth with the back of his hand, as he ducked under the string model above his bald head.

"I thought you didn't want me to do that anymore." Arnau grabbed a cane near a wooden board, with an etching of the overhead web of weighted sacks, threads and chains, propped against the wall. He handed the walking stick to the architect. "I did my best to stay quiet when I came in as you instructed."

At least the lad tried. Gaudí had come to the conclusion recently that Arnau's perpetual bad timing and lack of *seny* was the Holy Spirit testing a Catalan man's ability to produce one of the nine attributes of a true Christian: patience. The architect grinned to show forgiveness at the interruption and tapped the young man's arm to follow him out the house.

The hazy April sky stung their eyes, causing their pupils to oscillate, as they tried to decide if it was gloomy or bright. Gaudí squinted. Across the street from his modest house, sand-colored walls stood tall enough to have carved holes for future stained-glass windows. The Sagrada Família's nave was almost complete, but the architect didn't rejoice. He had hoped for the first façade to have been finished by now, the figurines and forest imagery chiseled in stone already painted, bringing the Nativity Scene to life.

"*Senyor.*" Arnau tugged his sleeve before waving at the black *motorwagen*, speckled brown with rust spots.

"Where's José?" Gaudí asked, pointing his cane at the front bench.

"*El Senyor* Güell had to reduce staff." Arnau spoke with the cold efficiency of a manager who liked making tough decisions. He pushed the architect up the ladder, onto the front bench, the cushioned backseat just holes in the floorboard after it had been stolen one night. "I handle all day-to-day operations now." A hardened Arnau settled behind the wheel and pointed. "The scarf and goggles are in the glove box."

As the topless *motorwagen* spluttered to a start, a bundled up Gaudí thought about how much Barcelona had changed in the last eleven years. Motorized carriages, streetcars and bicycles clogged the paved streets and bevelled intersections of L'Eixample. Every building sought to replicate the scenes of nature and medieval Catalunya depicted in the poems and essays of Maragall and others. What were once meant to be powerful symbols of a national renaissance had been repeated and diluted, becoming nothing more than a decorative motif for the nouveau riche.

Irritation clawed at Gaudí's lungs. He pressed his fist against the scarf covering his mouth as his chest pulsed from a hacking cough. He turned around, ready to rip off his wool muffler and spit, but decided against it. On the other side of his dirty goggles were the eighteen spindly spires of the last great sanctuary of Christendom, rising above the squat skyline, into the white winter sun. The architect had given up all hope of actually witnessing his magnum opus completed before he joined his mother in heaven, but just envisioning the Sagrada Família complete, warmed his cheeks during the two hour journey.

The first house inside the worker colony of Sant Boi was built of same simple red brick used in the village's outer wall and the cylinder chimneys of the adjacent textile factory. The home's Arabic motif, however, made the layout fit for a sultan and Güell's tubby son sat on the patio that extended from the second floor. A glass of wine in hand, he toasted Gaudí as the rust spotted *motorwagen* puttered down the main street.

Next was a stretch of shops and a bar-restaurant. Then came windows and doors carved into a single stone slab, looking like holes in the face of a mountain. Detached houses separated management's living quarters from the workers' and at the top of a hill, armed soldiers stood guard, near shiny black automobiles, with even sized wheels, metal roofs and windows on all sides.

Arnau parked the topless *motorwagen* and helped Gaudí out before handing him a wooden cane. The architect's arrival went unnoticed until he took off his scarf and goggles.

"Look, look. Gaudí, Gaudí," a male voice shouted, then it became a chorus. A group of photographers hugged their bulky cameras. They turned from their current positions and scrambled for a shot of Barcelona's most famous and polarizing architect. He wished he'd kept his face hidden behind wool stitching and glass lenses. He hated the newfound attention. It wasn't as if there was a tremendous increase in donations to the Sagrada Família as a result.

Gaudí took Arnau's arm. The young man smiled and assumed his latest, and favorite, role. He had transformed into a human shield who protected his high-profile client from the glare of flashing bulbs as they hurried past pine trees that blurred the exterior of the completed crypt, to a still unfinished church.

The entrance sloped with the sylvan hillside, like the protruding mouth of a cave. As Gaudí passed under the overhang, he didn't stop and look up at the black crosses amid the colorful mosaics on the ceiling. He kept his eyes down and shuffled through the forest of slanting columns, stepping over a wooden floor beam, through an open door.

The architect had designed the sensation of entering the crypt to feel like the transition from dawn to morning. Smooth granite pillars, chiseled and sanded into the shape of bones, sprouted from the ground. His favorite shape, the catenary arch, supported the tall vaulted ceilings awash in amber from the candles and the hazy sunlight, shining through butterfly shaped stained-glass windows.

Gaudí's mood lifted, as if he had been possessed by the Holy Spirit, from experiencing his idea erected in stone form. He pictured the lines and shapes around him on a gigantic scale once the Sagrada Família was finally completed. The strings, chains and sacks, hanging from his new workplace's ceiling, had allowed him to map out the stress points and calculate the tension of the arches and pillars. Clay models confirmed the feasibility of his divine inspired plans. Now, it was just a question of money, the devil that ran the world and tested one's faith in a just Lord.

Gaudí leaned on the polished knob of his cane to catch his breath. His lively blue eyes scanned a sparse crowd representing the elite of Catalunya and Spain. He spotted his benefactor, standing by the holy water in a massive oyster shell. Near him stood a short man whose elegance made the industrialist look like a pauper.

"Antoni," Güell beckoned, waving for him to join their conversation. "May I present you to King Alfonso XII?"

"I am a big fan of yours." He wore a sculpted black mustache, twisted into points at the ends, and spoke in the official language of the Spanish nation, Castilian.

A bearded Gaudí bowed and knelt with respect. "How do you do your majesty?" he replied in Catalan.

The King's countenance hardened. "Did you not just hear who I am?"

"Yes, your honor," Gaudí kept his tone even, "and I speak to you as a Catalan loyal to the Count of Barcelona and House of Bourbon."

A wide-eyed Güell gasped and smacked his cheeks. The

King might have tolerated linguistic freedom, but basic diplomacy made not addressing him in the royal language another matter entirely.

"Sorry, your honor." The industrialist spoke in Castilian, to avoid any further embarrassment and shoved the cause of his rising body temperature to the side. "*El Senyor* Gaudí has been under a lot of stress lately."

Güell pushed his snickering friend out the front door. Guards, carrying rifles, loitered under the mosaic overhang and near the stairs leading to the crypt. The enraged industrialist grabbed the ragged collar of a green jacket and dragged the bony architect away from prying eyes to the back of a building, which stood without the support of secondary wall and flying buttresses.

"What's wrong with you, Antoni?" Güell seethed, his chest expanding from his first breath since the incident.

"What?" Gaudí's mouth slanted under his feathery beard as he straightened his jacket. "Is King Alfonso so thin skinned that I must speak in Castilian even when he visits Catalunya?"

The industrialist's visage sharpened. "Are you crazy or just reckless? This isn't the time, nor the place, to make political statements. People have been executed for less!"

"The King won't execute me." Gaudí stretched his arms and felt his hunched back crack. "I'm too famous. They're thinking of commissioning me to design a building in New York."

"You just don't get it." Güell couldn't believe his friend's bullheadedness. "Now is not a good time to be stirring the pot."

"What is it, Eusebi?" Gaudí noticed the raven-black bags under his patron's moist blue eyes.

Güell's sniffled and gazed at the tower rising from the back wall. "I'm afraid we have to halt construction on this church."

"For how long?"

"Until I can sort things out." The industrialist explained how he was trying to gain access to the Morocco territories for a cheaper source of labor. He wagged his ringed finger and added, "I was also going to ask King Alfonso to speak with the Vatican to see if they couldn't help with the Sagrada Família."

"Forgive me, Eusebi." Gaudí looked down at his hands crossed on the knob of his wooden cane. He had put his nationalistic pride above the needs of his precious sanctuary. He wheezed to catch his breath and confessed, "I wasn't aware."

"How could you be?" Güell snapped, tapping his liver spotted skull. "You don't live in reality. You're an artist. You live in the fantasies in your head."

Gaudí's fiery eyes lifted from his cane and burned a hole through the elegantly dressed industrialist. He might have claimed to be the proverbial lean rat who always escaped a trap, but in reality he had grown too fat to flee his Spanish cage. Eusebi Güell i Bacigalupi, you have put the need of money and wealth above your country and worse, your relationship with God.

"You're going to burn in hell," Gaudí told him.

"What!" the industrialist yelped as the architect coughed. "Why would you say such a thing?" Güell shouted, still feeling wounded from the harsh attack. "Because I understand that history cannot be changed? Look at *Perpinyà* and North Catalunya to see how life has worked out under French rule during the last hundred and fifty years. Did you know everyone there speaks French and only French? One language, one nation."

After a deep breath, Güell smiled as he exhaled to help himself calm down. "Honestly Antoni. I wish it were different, just like I'm sure you wish you didn't need capitalists like me to finance your ideas."

Gaudí continued to fume. He closed his burning eyes and the sonorous voice of the Holy Spirit boomed between his ears.

Who are you to judge a man's fidelity to God? A man who has been the only person to have ever believed in you?

"I'm truly sorry, Eusebi," Gaudí whispered, seeing a forgiving smile.

"It's alright." Güell threw an arm around his shoulder and brought him in close. "What's done is done. Go home and I'll see if I can't smooth some easily ruffled Spanish feathers."

Gaudí wriggled away from the tight embrace and cut a man, whom some said had grown to look like his older brother, a leery glance. There was a question the architect had wanted to ask since that day after the World Fair in Paris, over thirty years ago.

"Eusebi, I know we are both Catholic and Catalans, but why me above all others?"

Güell chuckled at the seriousness of the moment and kept his tone light to mask the sting of the truth, "You and your buildings are the reason people will still know my name long after my son and Arnau have run my companies into anonymity."

"Do you really think so?" Gaudí's voice cracked with hope.

"Trust me." The industrialist laughed again as they walked down crypt's stairs. "In a hundred years from now, nobody will remember what I made, just that I was the erstwhile benefactor of not just Catalunya's, but Spain's, greatest architect."

A Brown Christmas

Bernat Fort sat at the bar counter, tucking into a dinner of thick blood sausage and white haricot beans. He loved his wife and children, but there were times, like tonight, when he wanted to start a new life as a solitary troubadour who traveled the land and sang poems that made people laugh and cry. He went to the village bar during such moments, rather than realize these bohemian desires. Being surrounded by fellow married farmers and tradesmen comforted Bernat because their stories and gripes served as constant reminders, that no man's home was always jolly and life could be a whole lot worse.

An icy draught disturbed the torches on the walls and touched the hairy back of his neck. Bernat gulped a second cup of hot red wine to ward off the chill and looked over his shoulder to see what other husband and father had needed a break from his family.

A couple shivered as they huddled by the closed wooden door. The young man was tall with a straggly beard and wore a frayed outer tunic, which looked more like a sack than a piece of clothing, for a coat. There was something familiar about his angular, handsome features, although Bernat couldn't remember a name or how he might have known the guy. Maybe they had met one night at the village bar when he was really hammered, complaining about a nagging wife.

The woman was a complete stranger, but she was as

captivating as a bonfire in a dark field to a sometimes happily married man. Bernat pictured himself a sculptor, carving her long neck and soft features out of a wooden block. The statue would be so magnificent that the entire country would come on pilgrimage to pay homage.

He noticed the round belly under her ragged wool cloak. It was one thing to fantasize about a woman, but not when she was about to have another man's child. Any future involving her now had to include the grating wails of newborn babies and images of them shitting on the floor until they were old enough to go outside.

Bernat had enough mouths to feed and no interest in adding another. He hailed the bartender for a refill on his drink to wash away the ashy taste of guilt in his mouth. He knew it was wrong for a married man to stare at a pregnant woman, but he couldn't let this fetching stranger out of his sight. He sipped his fresh mulled wine and observed the couple as they squeezed between the backs of chairs toward where he sat at the bar counter, out of the corner of his eye.

"My name is Pep and this is Mari." The young man's light voice and expression projected hope as he spoke to a pear-shaped man, in a leather apron, "We've come from Barcelona Ciutat..."

"Yes. And?" The bar owner snorted, folding his short arms across a hefty bosom.

His aggressive tone and posture seemed to unnerve Pep. He hemmed and hawed through the story of the one hundred and fifty kilometer journey he and Mari had made, on foot, to the village so that their son could be born in the same place as his father, grandfather and great-grandfather.

"Do you have any room for us?" Pep's pitch rose with the pride he took from their arduous trek. "We don't have much money, but I'll do whatever you need to earn our keep."

The owner nodded politely and smiled, as if he were about to say, yes. "I'm sorry," he replied instead, "but all of our rooms upstairs are taken, with everyone returning to be registered for the census and all."

"We could sleep on the ground." Pep's eyes darted to the grime and ash covered stone floor beneath the muddy boots of the husbands and fathers who sat at the tables and leaned on the bar. He looked up and clasped his hands. "Please, all we need is a roof over our heads to escape this bitterly cold wind."

"Impossible." The owner's arms remained across his chest and he shook his head. "I cannot allow people to stay at the bar when we are closed. What do you think we are — gypsies?"

Mari shrieked, "Can't you see I'm pregnant?" opening her cloak to show a round belly, which was set to go flat any moment, with the arrival of a newborn baby. "Do you have no pity?"

"Look. I'm truly sorry." The owner continued to stand with his arms folded, although his intonation no longer registered glee at delivering bad news. "If I had room upstairs you could stay, but I don't. You simply cannot sleep in the bar. What would happen if you or the child died? People would blame the food and I'd lose business."

"I can't believe what you're saying." A single tear trickled down Mari's smooth cheek as she turned to her partner for strength and guidance.

Pep's patchwork tunic hung, as if he'd shrunk to the size of a young boy, which contrasted with the glazed eyes of a beaten man who had run out of answers, a man who had failed his wife despite his best efforts. Mari responded, not with curses and waterworks, blaming him for not planning ahead, as Bernat's wife would've done, but with a comforting smile, light brush of the arm and soft kiss on the cheek.

Pep's eyes sparkled, giving his weary expression hope again. He grew back into his clothes and stood taller than before. The way he chewed his lower lip brought back a flood of memories that felt more like an epiphany.

Bernat had known a boy with the same name who had the same habit when stumped for answers. He set down his empty wine cup. He stroked the beard on his pointy chin as he studied the young man who stood next to him.

This Pep had the same bump in the bridge of his nose and soulful brown eyes, with specks of gold. "Josep Jacobo?" Bernat asked, giving his name before adding, "Do you remember me? We used to play in the woods near my father's farm before your family moved to Barcelona."

Pep squinted. He nibbled on his lip, sucking the wiry black hairs of his patchy beard. "Bernat Fort," he eventually confirmed. "Of course I remember you," his mouth breaking into a familiar smile, "we built a tree house together."

"So it is you!" Bernat jumped up from the bar. His head banged a wooden ceiling beam, but he felt no painful vibrations. For two glorious summers, he and this man had spent their days fishing, hunting rabbits and pretending a donkey was a war-stallion who drew their makeshift chariot.

Bernat hugged his old friend and planted a kiss on each of Mari's cheeks. Her pastoral fragrance evoked memories of morning sunlight, catching the dew on green leaves. Bernat rubbed the growing knot on his head, buzzing from the chance encounter. He marvelled how life had brought childhood friends together again after all these years. There had to be a reason beyond luck and circumstance.

"You two are staying with me," Bernat declared, in case their reunion had been instigated by one of the thirty-five gods' divine intervention.

The joyous looks on Pep and Mari's faces warmed his body, like a fresh glass of spiced wine. Not even stepping outside the smoky bar into a wintry December night dampened the enthusiasm Bernat felt at the turn of events, which saw him heading home to his family earlier and less tipsy than usual.

He put on a floppy crimson cap to keep the northern *Tramuntana* wind off his head and lit a pipe to calm down. The embers crackled and burned as he led his guests out of the village's walls, up a steep path. The light from millions of stars dusted the surrounding trees and fields like fresh snow. Bernat looked up to see the pan-shaped constellation his father had once shown him as a young boy. A bright star with a fiery tail streaked across the heavens, as if it were an arrow launched by Sagittarius.

"Did you just see that?" a wide-eyed Bernat shouted, turning to Pep.

He and Mari had fallen a few legs behind. "What's that horrible smell?" she cried, wrapping her arms around her waist before doubling over.

Bernat rushed down the path to help. "We're fertilizing the ground for spring," he explained, as he took their heavy sack and slung it over his shoulder.

"Thanks, but..." Pep sniffed as he focused on his wife who had buried her nose in swollen cleavage, "it doesn't smell like any animal dung I know."

"Animal dung! Who can afford that luxury with all of

the taxes we're paying Rome?"

Bernat had Pep's full attention now. "What is it then?"

"Let's just say we kill two birds with one stone here, so don't go looking for any toilets."

"That's disgusting," Mari squealed, rising from her crouch, with her hand pinching her nose and mouth.

She looked like she was about to deliver the contents of her stomach, not a baby. "What's the matter?" Bernat asked, surprised the strong woman from earlier now acted like a city dwelling princess whose carriage had broken down. "Haven't you ever lived in the country?"

"I'm in pain you idiot!" Mari tightened the hold she had around her bulging waist. "I think the baby's coming."

Bernat felt his body fill with enough strength to carry five plump sheep across his shoulders. He grabbed Mari's arm, putting it around his neck. He and Pep lifted her so that her toes dragged against the ground as they carried her up a narrow path, under the cover of overhanging branches.

They emerged from the dense woodland to a depression in the mountain sprayed white by starlight. On the other side of the shallow valley, perched on a ridge, smoke billowed from a chimney and orange lights flickered in the thin windows of Bernat's stone farmhouse.

He shared it with his three brothers, their wives and children, which meant that even his beloved dog had to sleep outside. "You'll have to stay in the stable," Bernat delivered the news to his guests as he led them off the main path and down a gradual incline.

"No problem," Pep said. "As long as there's a roof and walls to shield us from this wind."

"Yep. You got that," Bernat told him. "Plus the hay

dulls the smell of the fertilizer. I'd originally built it for my two donkeys, but they make a bull seem flexible and prefer to sleep outside even in winter." He ended his pitch with a wave of his hand, "so no need to worry about unwanted intruders," as he showed Pep and Mari to their accommodation.

The stable had three log walls and a thatched roof. Bernat set down their heavy sack by the open entrance and puffed to catch his breath. No one said anything so he decided to continue talking up the benefits, "That makes a perfect place for a bed." He pointed his bearded chin at the stack of hay near a feeding trough in the corner across from the donkeys' stalls. "Had to do it when I get in trouble with my wife, if you know what I mean."

"Thanks." Pep clasped his hands and bowed his head. "We'll take your advice."

Bernat's eyes moved from his old friend to Mari. Her sombre expression made it seem as if her beauty came with a horrible curse. "Are you alright?" Bernat asked, feeling his stuffed belly stir from the burning desire to be her protector.

"Just tired." Mari gave him a faint smile that warmed his heart. "This place is more than perfect. Thank you so much for your kindness. May the Lord bless you."

Bernat grinned to hide his surprise at the revelation his guests belonged to the strange Jewish sect who preached about the imminent arrival of the one and only saviour. He didn't know how many gods there were or if the son of one was about to be born as some said. He was usually too tired and drunk by the end of most days to ponder such profound questions.

"Don't mention it," Bernat mumbled. "You're in good hands. My wife's delivered plenty of babies."

He watched Pep leave Mari's side and begin to lay hay in the trough. The need to prove that he, too, was capable of selfless good deeds jolted Bernat's large frame into action.

"Be right back," he blurted, returning with a tray and blanket over his arms.

Pep rushed to catch an unsteady candle before it toppled onto a plate of bread. "Thanks," he said, walking over to a patch of dirt away from the flammable hay.

Bernat set down the tray before covering Mari with a wool blanket. As he looked at her peaceful face, he thought how she was the incarnation of a delicate strength, like a spider web in the late afternoon sun after a storm.

"Let's pray there are no complications."

Pep's voice reminded Bernat that Mari was not his to admire. He grinned to slow the blood rushing to his cheeks as he turned to find his friend casting a tender glance at his beloved bundled in a blanket.

Pep looked up at a still blushing Bernat. "Well, thanks again for everything. We should get some sleep now."

"Nonsense, my friend." Bernat thumbed toward the open entrance and the woods they had crossed. He didn't want the night to end on him getting caught making love-eyes at another man's pregnant wife. "Did you hear that scream earlier? This will be your last moment of peace ever!"

Pep's eyes flared with surprise at the bad news and stayed wide as Bernat complained about the constant demands on his time, patience and sanity, from both his wife and five children. "Their sole purpose on this earth, it seems, is to drive me to want to become a troubadour. I don't know why. I can't sing or play an instrument, but no ties or bonds seems like an easier life than this."

Bernat paused to give Pep a chance to say something and saw a man shocked into silence by the personal nature of his confession.

"Although, I gotta tell you..." Bernat decided maybe he had painted too negative a picture of married and family life. He told Pep there were moments of joy, too, like the smile on his son's face when he caught his first fish and the way his wife's quirks lifted his spirits whenever in a bad mood. "There are lots of times," Bernat continued, a tear of happiness in his eye, "when I'm reminded why troubadours always sing the blues about never finding a home to call their own."

Pep smiled and Bernat concluded his lyrical monologue with a sniff and a dramatic jerk of his arm. "So you see. It's the beginning of a new life. Now is the moment to celebrate this passage of time with a drink!"

"I can't be drunk for my son's birth." Pep gasped his first words and took a step back.

"I didn't say an entire bottle." Bernat remembered his friend had never been the manliest or quickest person. "One drink to calm your nerves. Trust me, you'll need it."

"I don't know." Pep glanced at his pregnant wife under the blanket. "Should probably stay with Mari."

"Go have a drink," her muffled voice ordered from under the cover. "I need silence to rest."

"Best do as the wife says." Bernat chuckled as he dragged Pep by the arm, out of the thatched stable and up a path to the ridge that overlooked the shallow valley.

"Only pragmatic and hard working people like us could create a prosperous life here," Bernat boasted, waving at the dip in the rugged terrain, as a gusting wind brought the faint jingle of cow bells. "As I told you earlier—we can make plants grow from shit."

Pep laughed as he sat down on stairs which led to the stone farmhouse. "Do you pee to water the flowers, too?" he asked, clutching a tattered tunic to keep the crisp air off his throat.

"Now that would be uncivilized and dangerous on windy days." Bernat's words faded as he jogged toward bushes before coming back with a ceramic jug. "Made this hooch myself," he announced before biting down on the cork stopper and ripping it out. "Drink some so you won't need to sit there hugging yourself."

"Thanks." Pep took a tentative sip from the frosty lip of the jug and shuddered. "Wow. Tha... tha... that's strong."

Bernat snatched it back and took a hearty swig to show his friend how real men drank. "City life's made you weak, Pepito," he ribbed, using his friend's childhood nickname. He pulled a pipe from his trouser pocket and sat down on the steps before asking, "How the heck did a wimp, like you, manage to pull a stunner like Mari?"

Pep responded to the comment by taking a second, bigger sip from the jug. "She found me at my carpentry shop," he explained, with a shiver and heave of his shoulders.

Bernat watched his old friend clutch his mouth. His color waned with the first beads of sweat on a white forehead. "No more hooch for you," Bernat declared, with a strike of a match, puffing to ignite the weed in his pipe. "Promised not to get you drunk and I'm a man of my word."

Pep gagged from the pungent, sickly sweet odor of the smoke.

"Sorry." Bernat turned his head to exhale in the other direction. "My stomach's been a bit clogged lately.

Smoking helps loosen the blockage, if you know what I mean."

"That's okay." Pep forced a smile, but still looked worse than his wife when she had discovered the feculent nature of the local fertilizer. "Feeling better now, but can we talk about something else?"

"Sure." Bernat felt relieved to see the first signs of color returning to his friend's hairy cheeks and asked, "How long have you two love birds been married?"

"We're not married yet," Pep delivered the news as if it were normal, not reserved for harlots and members of the royal court. "We might do it after the baby is born, but I doubt it. Mari says we're married in the eyes of God and that's all that matters."

"What!" Smoke stuck in Bernat's throat and he coughed to exhale before continuing his questioning, "You're letting your son be born a bastard?"

"Well, he's not really mine, you see." Pep's chipper intonation suggested that he was happy with the arrangement. "Mari received a visit from an angel who said her son will be the one who leads us to the promised land."

"She's not the only claiming that," Bernat scoffed. "There are three Joseps, one Adrià, and two Cescs in the village whose wives say the same thing." Bernat explained that these men where happy at first, always bragging about the specialness of their future progeny. "Now, they spend all their time at the village bar, complaining about the noisy pilgrims outside their windows."

"Don't you believe the Messiah's coming?"

Bernat detected the tinge of hope in his friend's tone. "Holding off judgement until spring," he said, with a thin smile, to show that he hadn't ruled anything out.

"Why then?"

"Let's see if the arrival of the so-called Messiah brings the right amount of rain." Bernat looked at the stable below. "If it's dry again next April, I'm blaming people believing in some baby for pissing off the almighty Jupiter."

Pep smiled politely at the reasoning. "Well, I prayed to my Lord for your family's health and protection. May your generosity be celebrated for eternity."

"Thanks." Bernat tapped his ashed pipe against the step. He took another swig from the ceramic jug and added, "Next time pray for golden eggs," wiping his sloppy mouth with the back of his hand.

Pep grinned as Bernat drew a deep breath of the icy air to put out the flaming sensation in his belly. "Can I ask you something?" he asked, feeling his lips warm as he exhaled.

"Yes," a still smiling Pep said, "of course."

"Forget the possibility Mari's baby ends up being a girl. Imagine the father is an albino angel and the boy looks like him. Would you still love him like a son?"

"Why wouldn't I?" Pep seemed more surprised by the randomness of the question, than offended. "He'd still have the face of an angel."

Bernat felt the irritation in his inflamed sinuses as his nostrils flared. His childhood friend was a man without a room in which to sleep and doted over a woman who didn't want to be known publicly as his wife. The child he was to raise wasn't his own but supposedly some "angel's." Yet Josep Jacobo was completely serene with his situation, oblivious to the fact that most people would call him a sap.

Bernat loaded his pipe with dried weeds and muttered, "Guess if my wife looked like Mari, I wouldn't care who the father was either, as long as I got to hit that ass every morning."

Pep replied to the crude comment by maintaining his thin grin. The unruffled response reminded Bernat of another person who had long ago learned that the best reply to an inappropriate remark of his was to say nothing.

"Sorry about the dig at Mari," Bernat said, putting the pipe back into his pocket. "Bit drunk and my wife says I can get surly sometimes."

"No need to apologize." Pep continued to smile in a calm, almost smug, way that made Bernat reconsider the sincerity of his apology. "You've been more than a gracious host. Besides, I've noticed Mari can bring out the best and worst in men."

"Beautiful women will do that." Bernat chuckled as he thought about the baby. "Tell me, Pep—have you decided on a name for this miracle son yet?"

"Jesús."

"Jesús?" Bernat repeated, loud enough to register his displeasure. "Why are you giving him such a strange name? Do you want him to get beat up?"

"There's nothing unusual about it." Pep's tone rose a notch, but remained upbeat, as he explained to his host that Jesús was just a variation of Josuè, which meant, "The Salvation."

"Who on earth told you that?" Bernat studied Pep's placid expression to see if this was just one big wind-up.

"An angel in a dream."

Not even a twitch of an eyelid. The sap actually believed what he was saying. "You're kidding, right?" Bernat blurted. "He wasn't the same angel who knocked up Mari, was he?"

"No." Pep's expression sharpened, hinting at

irritation.

Bernat cleared his throat to stop from giggling. Finally, a little emotion from Mr Serenity. "Here's to Jesús, son of Josep!" Bernat raised the ceramic jug in the blustery air and toasted, "May he live a long life and die of old age," ending his quick speech with a chug of hooch.

A thunderous shriek erupted from the shallow valley, bringing the *Tramuntana* wind to a stand still. Bernat's body tensed. He felt his eyes roll in the direction of Pep who leapt to his feet and yelled, "Mari, I'm coming, honey!" as he sprinted from the ridge to the stable below.

Bernat smacked his knees to stir into action. The booze and wine rushed to his head. Each star had a blurry double and he swayed to find his balance on a ground that moved, as if stone had transformed into a cloth, covering water.

Heavy vibrations stopped on the step behind him, putting Bernat back on solid footing. "You'd better stay here," his wife said, her tone a familiar blend of disappointment and resignation. "I can smell you inside the house and you'll faint like the last time."

Bernat blinked and watched his better half's bleary backside jiggle as she shuffled down the gradual incline, carrying a tray with a steaming bowl and a stack of cloths. "As you wish my dear," Bernat shouted, stopping himself before he added, "Attending childbirth ranks just below working in sleeting rain on the list of things I like to do."

The murmur of a strange language rippled through the still air. Bernat swung his eyes from his wife's backside to the black gap in the trees and the start of the path to his farmhouse. A blazing orange ball atop a golden pole appeared, then a second and a third. Three men in sparkling ornamental robes and hats carried the fiery staffs as they led a procession of strange hump-backed beasts of burden.

Bernat sniffed unfamiliar spices mixed with the scent of the animals' sandy fur. His neck turned with the slowness of an owl in a tree. His eyes widened in amazement as herds of noisy cows, sheep, pigs and goats seeped from the woods, into the clearing, as if it had become the region's sole watering hole.

Bernat recognized some of the livestock's markings, the particular ring of their bells. He grabbed the crimson wool cap on his head to stop it from blowing off from the power of his exploding thoughts. What were the animals' owners going to think? Without any plausible explanation for the miraculous feat, they'll label me a practitioner of black magic and burn me at the stake.

Another shrieked shook the air and ground. Bernat swore he heard the stars crackle before they fell dark and the world silent. If his stomach didn't feel like there was a pile of uncut rocks inside, he would've even thought this was it and he was dead. He bent over and squeezed his eyes, but that did little to stem the tears streaming down his cheeks. Men's faces flashed in his mind, their expressions flipping from joy to sorrow, when the baby they held no longer breathed. Not even Pep "The Serene" could withstand such a loss.

Bernat prayed but not for relief. He offered to suffer the agony in his belly for the rest of his life. He would even stop drinking alcohol and daydreaming of becoming a troubadour to prove his fidelity to the one and only Lord. The only thing he asked in return was that the baby Jesús lived.

The plaintive wail of a newborn cracked the silence; the stars flickered to once again shine. The animals brayed and bellowed while the three men cheered. A gust of wind swooped from the north, carrying the sounds of celebration and the infant's cries over the rounded mountaintops and across the land for all to hear. The weight in Bernat's stomach crumbled from the beautiful noise. He rose up to join the festivities, as anxious to see Jesús as his fourth son. But first, he had to fertilize a patch of ground near the stable.

Barcelona Gothic

ello," Alejandro said, excited at the possibility of escaping his current nightmare of a living situation. "You sent me an email about a room for rent."

"Yes. I saw your ad on *Loquo*." A deep monotone voice delivered the instructions from the other end of the line, "You must come today if interested. It's number four Urquinaona, second floor, first flat. Do you know where that is?"

"Think so," Alejandro muttered, scribbling the address on a piece of paper, as he held a cellphone between his shoulder and ear.

"Good. Come in an hour." Click.

Alejandro Villa was born and raised in Asturias, in Northwest Spain, where the locals spoke *Bable* in addition to *Castellano*. Plaça Urquinaona had always been the metro stop to change from the red to the yellow line on the way to the beach, nothing more. As an escalator carried him above ground, an ashen face beamed, like the overhead sun, from the unexpected surprise.

The location was one of the few shaded squares in the city, a stone's throw from Plaça Catalunya and the nightlife of *Barri Gòtic* and *El Born*. On the other side of a one-way street, sandwiched between a bank and an Irish Bar, a large wooden door announced the address on the crumbled piece of paper in Alejandro's pocket.

He pulled it out to make sure he was at the right place. The gray building was constructed at the end of the 19th century, but hearkened back to the Middle Ages. The ground floor was shaded by the overhang of the two outside windows, which curved out like glass and steel turrets, with balconies for parapets in between. The iron crenellations on top of the convex roofs served as the railings for the third floor's patios while a row of arched windows, with a shared balcony, marked the attic.

Alejandro hadn't had the best of luck when it came to meeting women in Barcelona. Maybe an impressive residence in a prime location would change that? He hoped so. Just like he hoped—he was the first and last person to visit the flat as he pressed the button, 2-1, on the plastic intercom.

A crackle and a muffled, "*Sí?*" blew dust off the speaker's vents .

"It's Alex," he said, preferring the shortened, Anglicized version of his name to the Spanish, "Ale" [Áleh], which was what girls named Alejandra also went by.

Another crackle and long buzz summoned Alex inside. He pushed the brass handle shaped like a limp hand with an apple in its finger tips to open the heavy door. Carved ivory colored frescoes ran down the middle of gray walls and his eyes did the splits, causing him to trip over the floor beam of a polished wood and stained-glass divider.

Alex stumbled into a lobby adorned in more dark wood, although brightened by the light from a hanging chandelier. A stone staircase to his right curled behind a woven-metal elevator shaft, which served as the building's spine. He looked through the window of a booth made from the same wood as found in the lobby. No doorman waited with a visitor's list, just dust and shadows.

Alex pulled the metal exterior elevator door and kept it open with his shoulder as he pushed through two red wooden doors that swung into a space not much bigger than a coffin. The sturdy exterior door sprung shut of its own accord, but the flimsy interior ones remained open until Alex pulled them past his hips, bringing the doors to a close in front of his nose.

He pressed a protruding round button for the second floor. Tight spaces always started ten-times smaller than they really were while shrinking by the nanosecond. He closed his eyes and held his breath to the sound of the rickety wooden box being lifted by a struggling chain. The rolling green countryside of his homeland formed in his mind with enough lucidity that Alex tasted the fur of the famed Asturian mountain cattle with the drizzle.

The trip back home ended when the elevator jerked to an abrupt stop, shaking the floor, ceiling and walls. After a long exhale, Alex saw the red wooden doors again. He pulled them past his waist before twisting his body to push the springy exterior door open with his hip.

"Make sure all the doors are *closed.*"

It was the same deep monotone from earlier until the last word, which boomed louder than the metal door closing. Alex turned from the elevator to face a hunched man, with an island of black hair on the top of a barren crown.

"Hey, I'm Alex. This is a fantastic building."

"Maybe not fantastic," his potential flatmate deadpanned, "more unusual."

Alex thought he could count the number of straggly

hairs on the twitching lip before him. "Don't think I got your name."

"Sergi," he said, unlocking a red leather door.

Inside the entryway, a stained-glass rendition of the patron saint of Catalunya dominated the wall that separated two flats. Alex was about to ask Sergi what books he had gotten for *Sant Jordi* last month, when the profession on a bronze plaque caught his eye.

"That's handy having a doctor across from you in case you get sick," said the self-confessed hypochondriac.

"He died a few years ago and his son is trying to sell the office with our flat."

"Really?" Alex didn't like the idea of looking for another place anytime soon. He had done it twice since his move to Barcelona. His first dwelling, a studio in *El Raval,* had cockroaches in the kitchen and got about an hour of sunlight in summer. The second location, where he lived now, was a few blocks below the mansions in Barcelona's foothills. He shared the airy two bedroom flat with a girl from Zaragoza. Her ex-boyfriend had started coming around last week, resulting in non-stop makeup sex a few days later. Alex thought it was bad enough to be single and lonely, without being reminded what he was missing, every morning.

"Don't worry." Sergi had the smile of someone who had suffered a stroke, leaving one side of his face paralyzed. "No one wants to buy the flat with the economic crisis and the housing market the way it is."

His ugly mug made Alex feel better. He doubted he had to worry about hearing the joyous shouts of passionate lovemaking on a daily basis. The temporary nature of the arrangement was something he'd deal with if/when the moment arrived.

Sergi opened the door on his right and led Alex into a small foyer encased in a thin pane of smoky glass. Beyond it was a dark corridor that stretched like a deep shaft until ending at strips of light, outlining drawn curtains.

"My last flatmate liked to go onto the balcony and throw firecrackers at people so now no one can go outside." Sergi's droll intonation made it tough to tell if he was happy or angry about the situation.

"Um, okay," Alex muttered, wondering what details his potential flatmate had left out.

"This is the kitchen." Sergi opened the first door on the left and flipped a switch to reveal a space bigger than many flats Alex had seen. The tan and brown cabinets reminded him of something from his childhood. The grease splattered walls and appliances showed that it hadn't been cleaned since the late 1970s, either. Still, there was a stove, a refrigerator, a microwave and an electric oven, with a greasy stove top, all in the same location.

"This is great," Alex said. "Do you like to cook?

"I don't eat much. Follow me." Sergi moved the tour down the hall to an old storage closet with a washer, dryer and opened boxes of detergent. Next was a freshly cleaned electric-blue tiled bathroom, big enough to fit a deep tub with a shower, two sinks, a toilet and a bidet. Finally, at the end of the long corridor, on either side of the thick purple curtains that blocked access to the forbidden balcony, were two doors.

"This is my office," Sergi said, waving at a closed smoky glass door across from a plain white one. "And, this is your room."

Alex turned the brass doorknob and squinted as he

left the dark corridor and stepped into a box shaped space, brimming in sunlight. A large desk rested against the shortest wall within arm's reach of the string, tying back the black curtain to the entrance of the steel and glass turret, a beige recliner the only furnishing inside. Wooden closets, more common in an office than bedroom, spanned two walls while a queen-size bed jutted into the middle of a black speckled white floor.

Alex tried picturing the layout another way to avoid tripping over the bed at night. Maybe move the desk to the wall by the door and the bed to the short wall, feet facing the curtain for the sun parlor?

"It's perfect," he said, liking that idea.

"You want it?" Sergi seemed indifferent about his decision.

"At the price in the email?"

"Yes. Plus free Internet and no deposit." Sergi's lazy left eye fluttered. "But you must stay one month. You cannot leave before. Is that clear? It's not always easy to find quiet people."

Alex was curious. "How do you know I'm quiet?"

"You don't smell of marijuana or alcohol." The limp side of Sergi's face jerked to life. His lips spread into a taut grin as he looked at a man without tattoos and piercings, *The Greatest American Hero* symbol on his t-shirt. "You don't look or dress like a playboy or hipster either."

Alex wasn't offended by the comments; he didn't realize he was so easy to read. "Okay. I promise to stay a month. How many people live in the building?"

"We are the only ones." Sergi dropped a set of three large keys into Alex's open hand. "The rest are offices or vacant."

He smiled at the news. "Should be able to get a good night's sleep then. How long have you lived here?"

"Before the euro. The doctor asked me to move in with him after his wife died. That's why the rent is so cheap."

Alex remembered their earlier conversation and the possible sale of the flat. "His son doesn't mind you staying?"

The right of Sergi's mouth curled into a smile as the left stayed lifeless. "Prefers me to a squatter."

"I'm sure he does." Alex chuckled. He was starting to warm up to his new flatmate's sense of humor. "What do you do? If you don't mind me asking."

"I'm a programmer."

"Oh, me too!" That explained Sergi's bad posture and freaky personality. When you spent hours staring at a glowing screen, trying to tap into the matrix, you lost certain people skills and evolved differently, physically.

"Yes, I know." Sergi's tone was as lifeless as his glazed black eyes. "You mentioned that in your ad. Maybe one day I'll show you what I am working on. Right now I must leave town for awhile. You can move in whenever you want."

"Okay." Alex looked forward to spending tonight alone. He could listen to his favorite music and cook whatever he wanted, without offending anyone. "Thanks," he said, smiling at the idea.

"No problem." Sergi exhibited the emotion of a post-stroke mortician. "Just remember, it's an old flat so it sometimes does strange things."

Things. Alex hated that word. What types of things? Blocked pipes and seepage? Intermittent electricity and hot water?

Before snapping out of his thoughts to get specifics, Alex found himself standing by the brass hands pinching apples mounted on the front door. A trace of sulfur lingered in the air. He felt strange, queasy even, as if an unseen force had opened a sliver in space-time and teleported him away from the flat to stop him from getting the answers he wanted.

An ex-boyfriend in boxers and nothing else, sitting on the couch of his current place, gave Alex the strength to overcome his unease at the strange exit. He returned to Plaça Urquinaona with all his belongings as daylight disappeared behind the foothills to the west.

The square glowed from the shining bulbs in the windows of closed shops and in the street lamps along the sidewalk. People lined up at the ATM of the closed bank or straggled in and out of the Irish Bar, opening the orange door to bursts of conversation and music.

Number four Urquinaona, meanwhile, sat silent, almost invisible, amid the bustle and glare of the square. The building's gray masonry had darkened to raven black and none of its many windows (from the glass and steel turrets, to the rectangular patio doors, to the arched windows of the attic) had any lights on.

Not for long, Alex thought, releasing the tight grip he had on two bulging suitcases. He slipped the heavy duffel bags off his numb shoulders, which he then shrugged and rolled, to get back some feeling. He was curious to see if the strange force from earlier would teleport him and his stuff to the flat. He waited for five seconds. Nothing. He chalked up the incident before to getting so lost in his thoughts that time seemed to skip ahead.

Alex sighed and pulled a set of keys from his pocket,

inserting the biggest one into the lock near the brass hands. Click. He pushed open the front door and moved all of his luggage from the sidewalk to the entrance. The volume of his heavy pants drowned out the loud bang, but the wood and stained-glass divider shook from the vibrations, when the door slammed behind him. The bulbs in the crystal chandelier were dark, leaving only the dim light from the elevator shaft at the far back to show the way.

Alex huffed and started rolling his suitcases past the frescoes, without giving the carvings a second glance. The wood and glass booth stood dark and silent. He didn't trust the claustrophobic red elevator to handle the excess weight so he lugged his bags up the slippery stone staircase.

In total, it took three trips. At the end of the first, Alex realized he needed to get outside more and exercise muscles other than his brain. Breathing was like choking. His entire body burned and pulsed. He closed his bedroom door and deposited the last suitcase, wanting to collapse face first on the bed that jutted into the middle of the floor.

A hushed voice said, "Look over there, Alex," drawing his attention to the beige recliner inside the steel and glass turret. "Why don't you sit and relax on your new throne? The world outside this castle is your kingdom."

Alex listened to his inner voice, despite the parlance and accent being different than he usually heard. He plopped down on a dusty seat cushion. His rubbery arms shook as he struggled to push the stiff chair arms and lift up his sore feet.

The recliner jerked into an almost horizontal position. The sky outside was a deep purple, with the end of dusk and beginning of night. The street lamps in the square below had all faded on, shading the black trees and benches in a soft white glow. The bright and bustling Via Laietana streamed with the yellow and red lights of fast moving traffic while the stone-spires of the Cathedral stood, illuminated, above the surrounding rooftops. What a vista, Alex thought, feeling himself sink into the beige fabric beneath him as blackness and silence descended, with the arrival of a sleep.

The dream began with a murmur before the image of Alex as a doctor, in the stereotypical white smock, faded in. His room was the location. The bed was no longer there, but the desk against the short wall remained. There was also a chair in the glass and steel turret, although the type you'd find at a dentist office who moonlighted as an OBGYN, rather than a recliner for a sun parlor.

Alex stood over his friend, Dorothy, a Texan whom he had met through a language exchange his first month in Barcelona. She was the typical American beauty, with wavy blond hair and high cheek-bones. She sat in the contoured leather chair, her ankles in stirrups, eyes closed, breathing light, rhythmic.

The urge to check every centimeter of her body with a stethoscope pulsed through Alex. A sinister smile brightened his face at the idea. The background murmur rose to a steady drone when he reached out to stroke her cheek.

Her skin was so soft, he could just bite it.

The ferocious sound of gnashing teeth and sharp claws scratching tiles rose behind him. Alex spun around to silence and the shadows of the square's trees, swaying on the black speckled white floor.

His attention returned to a still unconscious blonde. A low-frequency buzzing filled the air. Alex felt his body charge as if his insides were swarms of frenzied wasps. He bent down to kiss fluttering lips.

Dorothy's eyes popped open and she barked, "Woof, woof."

Alex jolted awake, out of the recliner, onto the hard floor.

"*¡Coño!*" he cursed, jumping to his feet, then screaming, "Sergi, did you forget to tell me about having a pet?"

No reply.

"Serrrrgggiiiii!"

Alex listened to his voice echo and the patter of claws on tiles fade to silence. He counted to ten. The walls creaked and pipes moaned, but there was no other noise, outside his closed bedroom door. He took a deep breath and grabbed the heavy Spanish-English dictionary on his desk, just in case the feral beast lurked in the corridor, ready to launch a surprise attack.

Door hinges whined as Alex stepped from his bedroom to find the flat mostly dark, except for the glowing glass door to Sergi's office. He knocked to see if his flatmate had come back early from his trip. Maybe it had been a lie to get out of helping with the move.

"Sergi, are you here?"

Again, no reply, so Alex reached for the handle, only to grope air. He crouched and peered through the hole where a doorknob should have been. A ceiling projector beamed as computer fans spun to keep the processors cool. "Must be running some programs of his," Alex muttered, loud enough to hear his voice, not thoughts, to make sure he wasn't still dreaming about his comely friend barking at him, like a chained-up dog.

Back in his room, Alex set the dictionary on the desk and checked the time on his cellphone (11:30pm). There was a new message from Dorothy. His palms began to clam at the coincidence. Had she sensed something?

He breathed to calm down and pressed a button to read the text.

At the Irish Bar by your new flat. Come down and tell me all about it. Besos.

Alex could never refuse her. He was smitten by her Barbie doll looks, the American ideal of beauty that even geeky kids in Asturias grew up salivating over.

The Irish Bar next door didn't seem that big from the pavement, but once inside Alex got a sense of its grandeur. A bright light shined on organ pipes and stained-glass windows on brick walls as tall as those found a former adult movie theater.

He looked away from the church inspired decoration and spotted Dorothy at the front bar. The image of her at his mercy snapped before his eyes.

"You okay, Alex?" She spoke to him in English, already fluent in Spanish. "You look a little paler than usual."

"Yes, sorry." His cheeks warmed as he picked up a coaster and looked at the beer it advertised. "Fell asleep and had a strange dream." He told Dorothy about the dog, but left out him being a doctor, she the unconscious patient.

"There's always something with you, Alex." She chuckled, nodding at the bartender with a pierced bottom lip. "What you wanna drink?"

"A beer and a *chupito*."

Dorothy's perky face wrinkled with askance.

"Thought you weren't a big boozer."

Alex needed something to kill the edge that attacked his nervous system like a new virus strain and he barked, "Just order me the drinks, okay?"

Dorothy's blue eyes caught the overhead lights as did her perfect American smile. "Like this new no-nonsense attitude you've got, Alex."

"Sorry," he muttered, thinking he detected a hint of irony in her tone. "Didn't mean to snap. Just feeling a little unsettled after the move."

"No, honestly," Dorothy brushed his shoulder before continuing, "I like men with attitude." Turning to order their drinks, she added, "And guys who can hold their liquor."

A few tequila shots and multiple beers later, Alex no longer felt the cushioned stool on which he sat. "Wha' time is it, Dorothy?" he slurred, her image dividing into ever blurrier replicas of a smiling American girl, as if she were self-replicating cell.

"Still early." Her nasal accent as enthusiastic as ever. "It's not even two yet. Why?"

"Gonna go home and sleep."

"What about the dog?" Her volume rose, but her sleepy-eyes staying half shut.

"Fuck the dog!" Alex mimed his actions. "I'll kick it out the window onto the square."

Dorothy shouted his name and scolded him with a burning glare. He had forgotten the Texan's favorite saying was: "You can't trust people who don't drink or like dogs."

"I'm too wasted to care," Alex mumbled, gripping the bar counter's brass railing to keep himself upright as he slipped off the stool. "We see each other soon?"

"Sure." Dorothy gave him a quick peck on each cheek. "But call me if anything strange happens and don't go hurting any animals, okay?"

Her powdery fragrance mixed with the smell of booze and tobacco on her breath. Alex was worried if he spoke, he'd vomit. He nodded and staggered out the bar. It was one of those moments he wished he understood space-time enough to teleport to his room. The stairs were ice slick, but his stomach was way too unsettled to handle the jerky elevator ride.

Over the next few days, Alex and Dorothy met every night at the Irish Bar. He had begun to build up a tolerance to alcohol and even taken up smoking. The old flat's creaks and moans served as his lullaby while the room spun him to sleep. But there were no growls or scratches, nor any other unusual noises, until a loud, BANG, one Saturday morning.

Alex peeled open his eyes to a splitting headache and the thumps of stomping footsteps, followed by angry grunts and the violent opening and closing of kitchen drawers. He groaned and rolled out of bed, inhaling a cologne of tobacco smoke, tequila and beer.

He opened his bedroom to find Sergi, squatting outside his office, dripping wet, with a towel wrapped around waist. He hammered a screwdriver, as if trying to jimmy open a lock.

Alex coughed to get his flatmate's attention.

"Sorry," he said, holding a towel with one hand and a hammer with the other. "I can't find my doorknob."

Alex rubbed his eyes, but the world was still a blur. He was too tired and hungover to comment further on such a bizarre situation first thing in the morning, but not to ask the question which had been on his mind since his first night:

"Sergi. Are there animals in this building?"

"Animals? Not mice, I hope."

Alex shook his head. "Heard a dog."

"No animals in this building, just us." Sergi's left eye seemed to develop a tic as he thumbed over his bare shoulder. "Maybe it belonged to someone staying at the hostel above the Irish Bar?"

"Didn't think they would allow pets."

"Maybe someone snuck it in." Sergi gestured at a half-naked body. "Look, Alex. I must get dressed. Is everything okay?"

"Yeah," he muttered, unsure if he believed the answer, but positive hammering was a better noise to wake up to than a girl he coveted, having sex with another man. "Things are fine." Alex tried his best to sound normal, not hungover and irritated at the situation. "Just getting settled in."

"Good. Have to go away for a few days again." Sergi seemed happy to be done with the conversation and scurried into a small interior room with a view of the elevator shaft.

Alex returned to his bedroom and drew the thick black curtain to block out the sun. Another beautiful day wasted, he thought, as he climbed under the covers to sleep off the effects of an evening with Dorothy. The possibility that living in this flat might end up killing him surfaced in his mind for the first time and he squeezed his eyes to fight off the stabbing sensation in his head.

A rumbling in the stomach roused Alex from a deep sleep. He reached for his cellphone on the floor to check the time and found the battery dead. He grumbled. No sunlight leaked under the curtain, meaning that another day had come and gone. Why not lie in bed and sulk to mourn the loss? He liked that idea. The noises deep in his bowels stirred, ordering his lazy ass to get up and put something in his body other than cigarettes, tequila and beer.

Alex went to the kitchen and grabbed an apple from the fruit bowl on the greasy counter. Crunch. The sour taste brought saliva to a dry mouth. After opening a tin can, he put some lentil soup on the stove to cook. The overhead light seemed to deaden everything — the colors, the smells, his mood. He sat on a chair and leaned back, feeling the hair on the back of his head stick to the wall behind him.

He noticed amid the grime were bursts of color. Floral tiles, consisting of five mustard petals around a brown center, were sometimes clustered in a rectangle, circle or diagonal line. Sometimes, a single florid tile stood alone, surrounded by a grease splattered white wall. Alex saw no logical pattern to the flowers' positioning. Nor did he sense his legs move as he strolled to the stove and returned to eat his soup.

The only sensation he experienced was a thick liquid solidifying into a crust beneath his eyelids. Why do I still feel so tired? Alex wondered. I haven't done anything all day but sleep. Yet I can't even keep my eyes open. It's like they've been sown shut. Am I still...

The clatter of his empty soup bowl, joining other dirty dishes, snapped Alex out of his worried state. He rubbed the paste from his eyes to see again and stretched to muster enough energy to walk, not crawl, out the kitchen.

The shining bulb midway down the corridor flashed

and popped as Alex passed beneath it. He no longer saw or heard the soles of his shoes against the linoleum tiles. But he felt the movement of his hands in front of his face as they cleared a path through steamy air as thick as cobwebs until his finger tips brushed velvet.

City lights stung sleepy eyes as Alex pulled the curtain and squinted at the glass doors for the forbidden balcony. Beyond the black iron railings was Plaça Urquinaona, where street lamps were crowned with white halos and skeletal trees moved with a strong breeze.

Alex wondered what had possessed the last resident of the flat to throw firecrackers at the people below. Drunken stupidity? Maniacal euphoria? A desperate need to have his pleas heard above the bustle of the square? Every flat in Spain had a draught, even on calm days, except this one.

Alex shuddered at the thought. He looked over his shoulder at his flatmate's office. No light beamed from a projector to illuminate the glass door. Nor did the hum of fans seep from the hole where the doorknob should be. It couldn't be. Was that a growl? Alex listened. Silence. He decided his groggy state had begun to affect his auditory processing, introducing noises he had dreamed into his consciousness.

He returned to his bedroom, took three steps and stopped at the foot of his bed. The black curtain was pulled open, which he didn't remember doing. A chill ran from his sweaty neck to his damp tailbone as he stared at a lean man, in a doctor's smock, hovering over the recliner.

"*Oyé*," Alex shouted to get his visitor's attention.

No response, no movement.

"Who are you?"

The man turned to reveal pointy features and dripping skin. His black mustache was so thin and straight that it seemed to have been drawn with the same eyeliner pencil he used for the eyebrows on a completely hairless head. He stepped aside and waved his slender brass hand at a woman whose beauty made her levitate and the recliner beneath her spin.

"Isn't she lovely?" a man with a sinister smile asked. "Haven't you dreamed of having a woman like this at your finger tips, Alex?"

The woman dropped to the ground and landed on all fours. She flipped back her hair to reveal hound dog eyes and howled.

Alex fell out of the chair, his hands landing on the gummy kitchen floor. His ears perked as he listened for a woman or an animal. He heard the spitting of lentil soup that had been boiling too long and the steady drip of a leaky faucet, hitting a stack of dirty dishes in the sink. Still on his hands and knees, his eyes focused on the flowered tiles. Where he remembered a circle, there was now a line. Where there was once a single brown and mustard flower, there was now the word, "DIE," scrawled in the grime.

Alex jumped to his feet and looked at the kitchen counter. He gasped. A carving knife stuck out of his half-eaten apple. When? How? Why? He stumbled back, hands on his head, still trying to figure out what it all meant.

"Leave!" a voice hissed.

A slam shook the flat. Alex sprinted past the stained-glass rendition of Saint George. He jumped down the stone stairs, slamming into a landing's wall to break his fall. Dorothy had become an Irish Bar regular since the arrival of an Argentinean bartender. Alex flung open the orange door in search of her company and a drink to calm his rattling bones.

"You look like you've seen a ghost," Dorothy said.

"I think I have." Alex snatched the brown bottle she held to her lips, chugging the beer inside. He wiped his mouth and qualified his statement, "At least heard."

"Really!" Dorothy leapt off her stool and circled her finger in the air to motion the bartender for another round. "Oh. My. God. LOVE. Ghosts. Did the haunted tours in London and Prague."

Alex had been raised in a family of mathematicians, happiness and sadness weren't quantifiable, so they didn't exist. Same went for God or any other super natural being.

"What happened?" Dorothy asked, handing him a shot of tequila.

Alex winced after downing the liquor and pulled the lime from his clenched teeth. "I told you about the dog, right?"

He guzzled a lukewarm beer as a chaser. Dorothy nodded from him to continue and lit a cigarette. Alex snatched it from her hand and puffed away while he detailed his disturbing night.

"And you're sure your flatmate's not home?" Dorothy inquired. "Maybe it was some kind of prank."

"He said he was going away." Alex stubbed out the half-smoked cigarette. His insides felt too knotted to smoke or drink anymore. "Besides, I was in the kitchen the whole time. Why didn't I hear any footsteps?"

"Hmm... that is strange." Dorothy lit a fresh cigarette to ponder the events. She exhaled and delivered her opinion, "There must be a logical explanation," staring at Alex's face, which twitched, as he searched for his own rationale behind the terrifying ordeal.

Dorothy's baby blue eyes were sober and vivid. She slammed her full bottle down on the counter, snapping him out of his deep thoughts.

"Got an idea," she announced. "I'll stay the night with you."

"*¿Qué?*" Alex spoke his mother tongue, too shocked to communicate in English.

"It'll be fun." Dorothy had the type of grin that gave men the wrong idea.

"Are you crazy?" Alex was still startled by her offer to stay with him, but able to communicate in a foreign language again.

"Come on." Dorothy punched him in the arm. "Don't be a scaredy cat."

"I don't know..."

"You have to go back and get your stuff anyway." She patted her purse. "Don't worry, I've got pepper spray to protect us."

"What?" Alex was stunned, but not enough to forget his English. "How do you have pepper spray? It's illegal here."

"My mom brought me some cans the last time she came to visit. She didn't think Spanish customs would let her bring my gun."

"Why would you ever need a gun here? This is Catalunya, not Texas. "

Dorothy went on an unlady-like, foul mouthed tirade about the thieves who had snatched her purse at knife point in *El Born*. "Not getting robbed by those sons-of-bitches ever again," she declared. "Are we going fucking ghost-hunting tonight or what?"

Alex had hoped she had forgotten about her desire to stay at his possibly haunted flat after her rant. He wanted to tell Dorothy if evil spirits did exist, pepper spray was as useful as soda water. He would've then invited her to a five-star hotel to spend the night together before retrieving his clothes and laptop in the morning. Alex didn't want to get laughed at or have his offer politely rejected so he nodded in agreement and basked in the warm glow of a pleased smile as he paid their tab.

The air seemed denser inside number four Urquinaona. The stained-glass of the divider was the same shade of black as the wood in the lobby, thanks to a dormant chandelier. The light from the elevator shaft flickered and dimmed, projecting moving shadows on the dusty window of an empty doorman's booth.

Alex and Dorothy hurried into the tight confines of the elevator and shut all three doors. Her perfume triggered pictures usually reserved for erotic dreams when he closed his eyes and breathed. The wooden box slamming to a stop brought him back to the claustrophobic reality. He opened and stepped through the first of many doors again, including the red leather one, which lead to the entryway.

The stained-glass image of Saint George, standing above the vanquished dragon, was shrouded in black and gray. Alex had never wanted to be a knight, a saint or a mythical beast. He ran from bullies and never wasted his intellect on devising plans for revenge, choosing instead to lose himself in an infinite stream of binary numbers, as he played God and created virtual worlds from nothingness.

"We shouldn't do this, Dorothy," he said, unwilling to turn around and face his friend.

She put a soft palm on his hand and inserted the key he held into the lock. "Ghosts can't hurt you," she told him, "I promise. Poltergeists are a different story."

"How do you know?"

"Told you—I'm a total ghost-freak. Think I've seen every documentary on the Internet." Dorothy forced Alex's wrist to turn the key. The lock clicked and the door opened to the grating sound of metal on metal as they entered the dark flat.

Alex flipped the kitchen light switch and rubbed his fingers together to clean off grime. The florescent tubes in the ceiling cackled and buzzed. A bright light hit his eyes, which he rubbed and blinked, to make sure what he saw was real.

Water plopped into an empty steel sink. The glistening stove was free of soup pans while the counter gleamed. There was no apple or knife. Alex scratched his shaggy head. The floral tiles were back to the same random places he remembered and the white walls looked like the "after" picture in a *Don Limpio* commercial. Except for the area around the light switch. It had either been overlooked, as often was the case, or purposefully left untouched, to highlight someone's recent house work and their passive-aggressive streak.

"How long were we down stairs?" Alex asked, still trying to process the kitchen's immaculate transformation.

Dorothy looked at the clock on the microwave near the sparkling stove. "Maybe twenty minutes."

Alex raised his nose in the air. "Do you smell soap or detergent?"

Dorothy mimicked his actions and shook her head.

"This doesn't make sense." Alex's voice cracked as doubt crept in. "Everything I told you downstairs was true." He turned to the open kitchen door and cupped his mouth. "Sergi," he screamed. "Are you here?"

The only noise came from the sparking overhead light.

"I believe you," Dorothy said, taking Alex by the hand into the corridor. "No one could've made that story up."

The bulb midway down remained dark, even after Alex flipped the switch on the wall, repeatedly, to the point of obsessive compulsive. He called for his flatmate again. The kitchen door slammed, shutting out the light he had left on.

Dorothy' grip on his hand tightened. She jumped. "Must be the wind," she whispered, with a slight shudder.

Alex searched the splotchy darkness for her bright teeth and eyes. "Did you feel a draught?"

"No. It's actually quite stuffy and warm."

Alex yanked his hand from Dorothy's long fingers. "Exactly! Let's go back to the bar."

"Stop being such a coward, Alex."

He listened to his friend huff and stomp away before turning to hear the front door swing open.

"Leave her with me," a familiar voice hissed.

"Dorothy," Alex yelped, running down the corridor.

"What?" she snapped, drawing the curtain to the forbidden balcony.

"Didn't you hear something?"

The city lights outside highlighted her defined American features, revealing the suspicious glint in her eye. "Just you."

Alex looked at his flatmate's door that glowed and hummed. He knocked and shouted, "Sergi. Did you clean the kitchen?"

He waited for a response.

"Wow," Dorothy said, opening the door to Alex's

room. "It is big and luminous. Look at that view! I can see the blinking lights of the planes, lining up to land above Montjuïc."

Alex was surprised by her florid language. He stepped on the switch to the floor lamp by his bed. A spark and a pop and the bulb went dead. "*Coño*," he always cursed in Spanish.

"It's alright," Dorothy told him. "We have more than enough light if we leave the curtain open. Do you have something I can wear?"

Alex marched to a large closet and took out a clean pair of sweatpants and a t-shirt. "Here you go," he grunted, throwing them onto the bed.

"Thanks. Going to the bathroom to change."

Alex didn't hear Dorothy's comment. His mind span so fast, it hummed like an overworked fan. He went to the recliner to lose himself in the familiar view outside his window. The doctor's mustachioed visage flashed in the glass that rattled from a blast of wind.

Alex stumbled back. He turned around to stop from falling on his ass and his left thigh slammed into the corner of the desk.

"*¡Coño!*" he belted Spain's favorite curse word again.

"Are you okay, Alex?" Dorothy asked, running into his room. "You're whiter than milk."

"Not really." He spoke through gritted teeth as he applied pressure to the indentation in his leg. "Look, Dorothy..."

"Alex, don't say anything." She nodded at the bed. "Let's just lie down and see what happens. At least we have each other if anything gets too crazy."

He stared at Dorothy, standing in his bedroom, in his clothes. A dream of his had come true, although the scenes which made him stir were still part of his imagination. "But aren't you worried I might try something?"

"You, Alex?" Dorothy laughed. "You're too nice. Besides, I'm a light sleeper."

He thought how dreams were famous for being non-linear, but reality was just as herky-jerky. They climbed into his bed, just as his subconscious had pictured many times, but fully clothed now, instead of buck-naked. Perhaps more fantasies were to transform into a reality that ran in reverse order to what he had seen when he slept? Might they fall asleep in each other's arms and wake up to a kiss?

Alex felt Dorothy's body-heat under the blanket as the thickening crust beneath his eyelids sealed in the darkness. He wondered how close the sensation of sleep was to death as breaths faded, taking with them basic concepts, like space, time and self-awareness.

A flip of a light switch sparked the coils of what had been a dead light bulb. The curved glass shell plugged into the ceiling captured Alex's reflection as he got up and strode to the other side of the bed where Dorothy slept on her back, spread out like a star.

He licked his lips. The pencil he had drawn his mustache with tasted sweet. He snapped off a latex glove to unveil a slender brass hand that moved with the fluidity of muscle tissue, ligaments and bone. His cold fingers stroked Dorothy's smooth cheek, down to her neck and the collar of his t-shirt, which rose and sunk with her chest.

Alex clenched the cotton fabric and readied to rip. A growl rose in volume to rattle the closet doors. He span around, still gripping the t-shirt, to see a snarling Yorkshire terrier at the foot of the bed. His brass hand let go of Dorothy. A smile curled his pencil mustache as he imagined himself the next great Asturian striker with the last name, Villa. The far closet was a goal. The animal, the football. The lap dog's claws scratched the slick tiles as it tried to gain traction. Alex took two long strides and planted his left foot. The snarling dog sprang into the air. Alex swung his leg back to deliver a devastating right boot to the puny canine that sank small teeth into his exposed left thigh.

"*¡Coño!*" Alex jolted awake, as if electric paddles on his chest had shocked him back to life. He clutched where the dog had bitten him, expecting blood, and felt the tender bruising, from his run-in with the desk. Dorothy continued to sleep curled up, her knees bent and touching. So much for being a light sleeper, Alex thought, as his mind returned the bizarre dream.

Was it him or the flat? He hadn't been with a girl in over a year. Maybe his pent-up sexual frustration was manifesting in peculiar visions? It couldn't be that. Alejandro Villa García was a geek who hadn't invented anything revolutionary yet. He was used to going long periods without sex. It had to be the flat and the key was Sergi.

Alex grabbed the Spanish-English Dictionary on his desk to prop open his door. He returned to the bright kitchen and ransacked the drawers in search of some tools. Once he accomplished his objective, he dragged a breakfast table into the door frame on his way out. No more slams, no more people entering without me knowing, he decided.

At Sergi's office, Alex stared at a hole for a doorknob. He worried about kicking the glass. Would it shatter and slice my leg? He jabbed a long flathead screwdriver between the door and jam. He pushed; he pried. The wood started to splinter. He took the hammer and wailed on the screwdriver's handle.

"What's with all the noise?" Dorothy yawned, stretching her arms and neck.

"Getting to the bottom of this," Alex declared, with a final swing of the hammer.

Sergi's office door cracked open, unleashing a trapped cloud of mephitic gas. Alex fell on his haunches. He grabbed his mouth and squeezed his nose to stop any more particles of stale vomit and booze from reaching his pickled brain. The overhead projector inside the room beamed a streaming code on a black screen. The red letters and symbols were unlike any computer script or language Alex had ever studied.

"Looks like someone else was here." Dorothy's voice squeaked as she pinched her nose and pointed an elbow at a desk with two empty glasses and a half-drunk bottle of whiskey.

Alex pushed himself to his feet while sipping air to breathe. He didn't think his flatmate was capable of forming a friendship with another human being.

Dorothy took a book from the shelf and read the back cover. "My Catalan's not all that great," she admitted, still pinching her button nose, "but think this is about magic and spells. Maybe your flatmate is a Satanist?"

"This is insane," Alex yelled, no longer able to stand the putrid stench of the office. He stormed back to his room and threw open a closet.

"Alex," Dorothy said his name with the tone of a strict

mother. She picked up the dictionary and carried it to his desk. "It's almost five in the morning. There's no point in leaving now. Why don't we Google this place and see what we can find out?"

Alex threw a large suitcase onto his bed. "Go ahead," he told her. "I'm getting out of here," dumping shirts, sweaters and slacks, all still on hangers, into his luggage.

"Let's see." Dorothy sat at his desk and typed in the address. "Nothing but listings for apartment and hotel rentals. What else do we know?"

"There was a doctor who lived here." Alex crammed more clothes on hangers into his suitcase. "Maybe he has something to do with it."

"What makes you say that?"

He didn't need to face Dorothy to feel her eyes on his back. He kept it vague, "Some strange dreams I've been having," zipping up his biggest piece of luggage.

"You know his name?" Dorothy prodded.

"No." Alex dragged the heavy suitcase off the bed and heard his bedroom door slam. Vibrations ran up his legs to his fingers and he let go of a plastic handle as he focused on Sergi in the umbra of the bedroom's entrance, a glistening carving knife in his hand.

"What were you thinking, breaking into my office?" he hissed.

"I'm leaving." Alex decided an armed man didn't deserve an answer to his actual question or two weeks notice.

"No you aren't." Sergi stepped from the darkness into the soft light of the room. "You promised to stay one month."

Tiny dust-bunnies scurried under the bed Alex had never gotten around to moving.

"What the fuck, man?" He gripped a plastic handle, wishing he had the strength to wield the heavy luggage like a war hammer. "Thought you were out of town. Have you been sleeping in the interior room all this time? Did you stick a knife in my apple and clean the kitchen?"

"Do not accuse me of such things." Sergi stabbed the air with the long blade.

Alex moved behind his upright bag for a shield. "If you didn't, then who did? "

"Our special friend." Sergi wore a familiar sinister smile, one which Alex had felt brighten his mood in his most recent dreams. "Your room used to be his private office."

"What the hell are you talking about? I thought only you and I lived here."

"Come on, Alex. Don't tell me you haven't seen him, felt him, been him."

"Are you crazy?" Dorothy shouted as she stood by the desk.

Sergi spun around and pointed the knife at her. "You! Don't move."

"You can't stop us from leaving." Alex stepped from behind his suitcase.

Sergi wagged the blade at him. "Yes I can. And I will."

If only he didn't have the weapon, Alex knew he could take down the hunched psychopath. "Why are you doing this?"

"As long as I bring the doctor someone once a month to... let's say, 'play with', I can stay here rent free." Sergi explained the doctor's ghost, as his living predecessor had done, preferred women to men, but he had failed to convince any females to stay lately.

Both sides of a sagging face lifted from a smile when

Sergi nodded to Dorothy. "Little did I know you'd bring her to me."

"And the dog?" Alex asked.

Sergi's raving eyes calmed. "It belonged to the doctor's last patient." His voice was almost wistful as he spoke. "It started barking and woke up the owner. It was the only time the doctor ever killed anything, but the damage had already been done. He had been caught and went to prison where he died from prostrate cancer."

The lunatic's story was too much for Alex. "You're saying—you made a deal with a ghost to stay here?"

Sergi shrugged and deadpanned, "How else can a person afford to live in Barcelona?"

The sentence hung in the air like a bad punch line. Alex watched his flatmate blink and the madness return to the non paralyzed side of his face. "You're certifiably insane."

"Am I?" Sergi's dark one-eyed glare latched onto Alex's squint. "Or are you the crazy one?"

The two of them locked in a high-noon stare, Dorothy seized the moment. She snatched the Spanish-English Dictionary on the desk, flinging the book like a discus at Sergi who took a menacing first step toward Alex.

A loud smack. Both of them jumped back. Alex was the first to look up from the dictionary at their feet. But Sergi slashed at the air with his knife, stopping the man from Asturias from taking a second step.

"Easy there," Alex said, retreating behind his suitcase again.

Both of Sergi's eyes narrowed into blazing slits as he turned his attention to Dorothy. "You've asked for it now, bitch."

A steady hiss punctuated his declaration. Dorothy

leapt onto Alex's bed, her index finger on the nozzle of a palm-sized can. She extended her arm to narrow the distance between the pepper spray and Sergi's eyes until he slapped his face and collapsed.

The ding of a knife bouncing off the hard tiles chimed in Dorothy's ears. She stopped pressing the nozzle and jumped off the bed. She snatched Alex's hand, dragging him down the long corridor, away from the toxic fumes and Sergi's wailing.

"You can stay at my place," Dorothy told him, as they dashed out the flat and down the stairs. "Don't worry. I won't pull a knife on you, unless you don't do the dishes."

"Actually, Dorothy." Alex huffed dusty air, as they stood under the lobby chandelier and panted to catch their breaths. "Think I'm gonna stay at the hostel next door and wait for the ambulance to arrive before getting my stuff." It was a lie. He was going to put Dorothy in a taxi and then wait at a bar around to corner. He didn't know where he was going to go after he collected his belongings. Maybe back to Asturias, where the people were warmer, despite the gloomier weather. Maybe he'd give Barcelona one more month because he liked its cosmopolitan atmosphere. Wherever he went, Alex wouldn't repeat the mistake of living with a hottie who only wanted to be friends. That was a bigger nightmare than sharing a flat with a horny ghost.

The Sound of Barcelona

Night has traditionally been the time of quiet and dreams. In Barcelona, garbage trucks collect the trash under glowing street lamps. Tricked-out scooters rev down both well-lit avenues and dark alleys. Loud drunks stumble out of closing bars, within shouting distance of your window.

Then morning arrives. Monday through Friday, it's the blare of an alarm clock an hour or so before work. On Saturday, it's the loud racket from either the flat next door, above or below, at eight o'clock in the morning.

"It's the weekend for fuck's sake," you scream in Spanish. "Do you have no sense of common courtesy?"

A loud thump signals a bored hole in some wall, where exactly you still do not know. There's the wheeze of a spinning drill bit before the work stops. One, one thousand... two, one thousand... three seconds of quiet until the hammering and sawing commences.

You sit up on a bouncy mattress and rub out the sleep which gums up eyes. The neighbor stops working long enough for the bed to settle. A minute passes and silence continues to reign. Whatever was so urgent that it couldn't wait until afternoon, or even ten o'clock, has now been put on hold, with construction set for tomorrow, Sunday, at the same hour.

The sputtering, banging and scraping still echo in your head, though, even when you massage your temples and hum, "Om," in search of inner peace.

Strident neighbors are an inescapable part of Spanish life, no matter if you live in Catalunya, La Rioja or León, so it makes no sense getting worked up over the rude awakening. Fits and starts with meandering lulls, meanwhile, is the rhythm of the country from the simplest task, like hanging a picture on a wall, to the most complex, like trying to get a good night's rest.

You grab a cellphone from the bedside table to check the time. It's too early to be awake with nothing to do, too loud between the ears to fall back asleep.

Nobody lounges in the privacy of their own homes in Barcelona, or in Cádiz or Oviedo, either. People might host a dinner party, but not one that runs too late, lest the neighbors complain to the police about not being able to sleep because of the noise. Gotta wake up early and work on that cabinet, after all.

To relax, people head somewhere public, like the beach, a park, the tables outside a bar, maybe a bench along the perimeter of a square. Much depends on the weather. Is it too muggy? Damp from the million drops of an April rain? Blustery from the northern *Tramuntana* wind? The good news is, except for Spring and September, the sky is often sunny and calm, even if the sea is too cold to swim in.

At the elevator outside your flat, an orange light glows by the call buttons. One of the neighbors is getting on or off the lift. Another neighbor plays the music of Queen at a volume that shakes the elevator shaft. He sings along, out of tune, but at an octave higher than the band. The stone walls do funny things to the acoustics. The noise level remains the same, even as you descend smooth stone stairs carved by a drunken mason who used 19th century tools and ended all of his measurements, "more or less."

Two floors down, a *White Pages*, props open the exterior elevator door. No one is around so you kick the thick book away with your heel and enter a space the size of a changing room.

A split second of silence as the CD shifts to a new track. The crooning neighbor collects his breath.

"What are you doing?" a woman shrieks in Spanish, flinging open the exterior door. The interior one stops sliding and retreats back into its recess.

You dream in her native language, which has none of the formalities, nuances or pleasantries of English. There is no instinctive need to apologize or explain your behavior. "*Yo bajo*," you growl, which means: *I'm going down*.

"You can't," she tells you.

"Why not?"

"My children and I are going shopping. Just five more minutes. Let me explain..."

Kids rank right up there with skunks on your list of least favorite things. Freddy Mercury and the neighbor listening to him are both wailing about wanting to ride a bicycle, leaving little auditory capacity to also listen to the woman's story. You try to pull the door, but long leathery fingers have a tight hold on the thin metal edge. "Let go," you hiss.

The black haired woman shakes her head, squinting her equally black eyes in defiance. Her fingers clenching the door begin to strain and tremble. Her grip loosens. "Yank it shut!" screams your inner voice. The exterior door slams and you pull the handle, preventing it from budging. The woman curses and bangs the window as the interior door slides to a close. Your Spanish chip is off, turning insults and damnations into gibberish. Metal touches skin and you let go of the exterior door, as the tinny elevator heads down to the song, *Bohemian Rhapsody*.

Outside, the pavement is free of metal plates, yellow barriers and jack-hammering construction workers for the first time in two years. Locals sit on shaded benches in the square across the street, legs crossed, immersed in newspapers, as a flock of escaped parakeets chirp in the powder blue sky.

A noisome stench sticks in the nose. You hold your breath, sidestepping a pile of dog shit on the pavement. There is no time to wonder why the people here don't pick up after their animals. An impeccably dressed elderly lady is heading straight at you.

Her hair is permed and dyed red while thick glasses magnify unblinking eyes of a determined face. She pushes a *carito*, a shopping cart consisting of a canvass bag mounted to the front of a walker. Knees and shins are her favorite thing to take out. Veering left doesn't avoid possible impact. The old lady steers her fully loaded *carito* with youthful dexterity and mirrors movements. The stone wall of a building brushes your shoulder. The entire pavement is there to pass, but the fake red-head still hugs the same wall as you as she closes in, wild-eyed and frothing, her tote-bag on wheels battering ram, ready to inflict maximum damage.

Her musty fragrance tickles your nose; you jump out of the way. A sneeze erupts and the world goes black when your eyes shut to stop from exploding out of their sockets.

As with not cleaning up after their dogs, there is no time to think about why the Spanish and Catalans like to play the game, "Chicken," but on foot, instead of in American muscle cars. A man has stopped, leaving less than a second until slamming into his back. You drop a spin move, like a football player shedding his marker on a corner kick, to avoid the collision as he strikes a lighter.

A deep breath to calm down from the sudden burst of energy. The couple ahead strides hand-in-hand. An opening appears to their left. They move in unison to stop you from passing. Some space appears between them and a high-strung woman who smokes and pushes a baby stroller. Again, the couple prevents you from overtaking them. Sometimes, its seems, the locals have a sixth sense that detects and feeds off other people's frustration.

Everyone stops at a red light. Across the street is the famous Casa Batlló by Gaudí. The curved purple roof is the back and head of a dragon. The cross-shaped chimney, the hilt of a sword. The bone-shaped windows, the skeletons of the victims devoured by the beast. The traffic light changes from red to green. Your focus shifts from the architectural rendition of the tale of *Sant Jordi* to a bus full of passengers that runs a red light.

A scooter screeches to a stop and you jump ahead of the other pedestrians. The Spanish and Catalans, like other Mediterranean people, are coffee, not tea, drinkers. At home, unless there's an expensive espresso machine, it's usually instant, but never drip. For a proper cup of java, everyone heads to the neighborhood bar, but at different times, because it always empty when you get there.

You take a seat at an aluminum trimmed counter and

nod at the sole employee. He makes eye contact. He finishes giving a single glass a thorough cleaning. He then lifts the snifter-shaped chalice into the light to inspect his work before setting it in the freezer under the sink.

You cough to clear your throat and say, "*Hola.*"

He acknowledges the salutation with a quick glance over his shoulder on his way to count a full box of potato chips before checking the cash register tape.

You shout, "Excuse me," in Spanish.

He straightens the plates of chopped squid, potato omelet and anchovies marinating in vinegar, displayed under a glass case.

"What do you want?" He saunters over to take your order.

"*Un cortado,*" which is a shot of espresso topped with milk.

He grunts and leaves.

A deep hack and cackling cough announces the arrival of a second customer. A man with slicked back gray hair puffs on a pungent Ducado cigarette and wears three-day-old stubble on a weathered brown face. The bar is empty, but he sits next to you, a thick cloud of tobacco smoke blowing from his large nose.

"*Hombre,* pour me a *carajillo,*" he demands.

The bartender delivers your coffee in a large shot glass that burns to touch. He treats the new customer with the same warmth as you. Bangs ring out as he smacks the brewing spout against the wall and readies the espresso machine. He then grabs a bottle of brandy from a shelf to complete the smoking man's order.

"All politicians are sons of whores," his husky voice declares, as his spiked coffee arrives.

You agree—we, the people, are mostly good; our leaders, however, are mostly sociopaths—but adhere to the philosophy that religious and political discussions don't make good small talk. The swirl in milky coffee is the sole focus of your attention as you stir in a pack of sugar.

The man taps your arm. His angular features have the lines and character of an epic life, but his blank expression indicates an almost child-like confusion at your unwillingness to engage in conversation.

"Where *jou* from?" he shouts in English, because like most locals, he thinks the louder he speaks, the better you understand.

You wrap a napkin around the hot glass and drink the shot of espresso with milk and sugar. "America," you mutter, hoping to escape the lecture on the US's imperialistic, oil driven foreign policy, which usually follows the announcement.

"America," the man repeats, waving his hand, as if to say—*get out of here, you liar.* "I was there many years ago."

"Did you like it?"

"No." His face twists with disgust and he shudders. "The cities are ugly and the food was terrible. Why only you eat hamburgers?"

"We eat other things."

"When I was there," the man wags his tobacco stained finger in admonishment for daring to contradict him, "only hamburgers." He pulls out a cigarette pack. "You smoke?" offering one.

"No, thanks." You wave at the bartender and tick the air to signal for the check.

The man with slicked back gray hair presses to have a

chat. "You like Spain? "

His breath smells like watered down whiskey in a glass, which was later used as an ashtray.

"Some days." You count the exact change necessary before stepping back to get some air.

The man sticks close and continues his interrogation, "You like Spanish food? It's the best, no?"

It lacks spice and flavor, but the Spanish and Catalans take great offense should anyone ever speak ill their mighty gastronomy.

"You don't put ketchup on paella, do you?" The man cites the local urban myth attached to all Americans who visit Spain when there is no instant reply to his initial question.

You shake your head. "But I have made bacon out of *jamón iberico*," telling him another serious culinary *faux pas*. "And it was deeeelicious."

He clutches his chest; eyeballs roll in the direction of bushy eyebrows. You take advantage of the near heart-attack and run outside to gulp exhaust fumes and dust as you stand in the middle of a pavement full of people eager to play "Pedestrian Chicken."

The paradox of becoming a transplant. You complain about the locals, yet you're becoming more like them. It's not just losing the ability to be civil toward your neighbors, or using 'boy' and 'girl' to describe people younger, your age, sometimes older. Thoughts, ideas and tasks pop up in fits, but there's no urge to start, let alone accomplish the chores or errands any time soon. *Tranquilo amigo*, your Spanish voice says. *Mañana.*

An advertisement at a bus stop hypes the cheap price of an all-in-one printer/scanner/fax at a local electronics store. Buying such an item has been a pending issue for a month. No one calls with an offer to meet for lunch or go to the beach, which usually happens at such moments.

Most computer and electronics stores are clustered near Ronda Sant Antoni. The metro is the fastest way to get there, but a wall of teenagers blocks the entrance. The bus might take longer, but at least it's above ground, offering views of Barcelona's stunning scenery.

At the enclosed bus stop, elderly ladies in ironed blouses and skirts squawk as they wait. The late morning sun sees you perspiring, but their aged madeup faces are free of a single bead of sweat. The long red bus arrives to a joyous, almost youthful, cackle as the women throw the occasional elbow and hip-check to be the first in line.

The old ladies funnel onto the bus, stop and search their bags for their tickets or the change to pay the driver. Everyone then takes the fewest steps possible before stopping. By the time the ticket machine beeps with your ticket, the front of the aisle is standing room only and the bus is chugging along to its next stop.

You lower your head and shoulder through the congestion. There is a free seat at the back, near a teenage girl who talks on her cellphone about her boyfriend, loud enough for the driver to understand her complaints. A serious looking young man, two rows in front, offers his detailed analysis of the new Woody Allen movie. His conversation partner checks her reflection in the window and tosses her hair.

Not being fluent in Spanish makes it easy to tune out the inane conversations, which take place in every country, and your mind jumps to the future, imagining a dark room and an unmade bed.

Inside the two-story electronics store, there are no signs above aisles. Monitors sit next to washers and dryers while televisions are paired with coffee machines. Employees appear and disappear in a flash and you give chase like a cat hunting a fly.

You finally corner a scrawny teenage boy with a mullet and say, "I'm looking for..."

"We don't have it."

"I haven't told you what yet."

"We still don't have it."

"It's that all-in-one printer advertised everywhere."

"I told you," the store clerk folds his arms across his bony chest, "we don't have such a thing. It doesn't even exist."

"How does it not exist?" you shout to make sure he understands the absurdity of his statement. "Your store is advertising it all over the fucking city."

He shrugs and repeats, "Look. I'm telling you—it doesn't exist, okay?"

After one month of thinking about the task, you finally do it and now this little shit denies his own company's sales campaign? "Do you have anything similar?" you ask, wishing you had the courage to pinch his big nose and twist.

"No," the clerk says. "Check another store," strutting away, as if he's just made a million euro commission.

You think about reporting the kid to his boss. Why bother? He'd just send his assistant to say the manager was busy right now. When people ask what you miss most about home, the answer is service. But when you go back to visit, you hate the fake smiles and chipper, "Hiya. How's your day?" before pitching the daily specials. One more paradox that comes from living abroad, it seems.

Hunger gurgles in your stomach; your eyes flick to the digital clock above the store's door. Most restaurants don't open for another half-an-hour. People talk about the Germans being regimented, but they ain't got nothing on the Spanish and Catalans when it comes to eating times. Two-to-four for lunch, nine-thirty to eleven for dinner. Feeling like trying their famed cuisine in between those set hours? Not happening, my friend. But there are bars with *bocadillos*, which are sandwiches with one slice of meat or cheese on French bread hard enough to scrape the roof of the mouth.

There's a twenty minute wait for the next bus home. It's a half hour walk uphill to get there so the metro makes the most sense, in terms of time and minimal physical effort.

A flood of people hurry out of the underground station, up the stairs. Among the crowd is a man with a sour face hellbent on playing Barcelona's favorite game, "Pedestrian Chicken." He isn't elderly. You grab the banister as you barrel down the steps. He doesn't give way. You puff out your chest to remind him who has leverage. A defeated grunt blows in your ear when he circles around.

It's a short-lived victory. Frantic passengers stampede from both the entrance and the exit doors. You wade through the onrushing crowd and step into the station. The aim now is to make it to the row of three turnstiles without touching a person. You weave through commuters, like a midfielder from Barcelona Football Club, juking the oncoming waves of people, spinning around anyone who sticks out a foot.

Mission successful. A man tries to make his stripped ticket work at the first turnstile, repeatedly, to the grumbling of those who line up behind him. More people queue to pass through the third turnstile, leaving the middle one clear. Don't ask, "Why?" Run before anyone notices.

The station vibrates; the dark tunnel lights up. You pick up speed and watch commuters disappear as time skips ahead to the near future.

Doors close on your nose. The train rumbles and leaves. The clock hanging from the ceiling says, *Proper Tren: 10:00min.* Piping hot steam fills the air in like gas and you melt.

The worst case scenario vanishes and your thoughts return to the present situation. In front of you, women stand, side-by-side, midway down the slow moving escalator. After them it's a clear shot down to the platform and the arriving train.

The women pause their conversation, look up at you and then back down the mechanical steps.

They continue talking.

"Excuse me, ma'am," you say in formal Spanish, giving one lady a light tap on the shoulder.

She looks perplexed, borderline annoyed, as she moves to let you pass. "Can you believe him?" she asks her friend, loud enough for you to hear. "He should have left earlier so he wouldn't have to rush."

The train doors open just as your foot steps on the platform. Scrums break out as riders storm in, pushing back those trying to get out. All the action takes place at the first and last carriages, near the stairs and escalators. In the middle of the train, a solitary, bald man politely waits for the people to get off.

He enters, turns and stops. His forearms are perched on his belly by the time you arrive. He shows no intention of budging. The train beeps and powers to a start. You lower your shoulder and charge as the doors slide close, nipping your heels.

The man curses at you under his breath and his small brown eyes narrow in anger. The carriage jerks and swerves as it races down a tunnel. He grabs a rail near the door while you stumble into a seat where the woman across gawks, as if your mugshot has been on the news. Mothers in most countries teach their children not to stare because it's rude. In Barcelona and the rest of Spain, it's the norm, along with poor service, strident neighbors and the love of playing, "Pedestrian Chicken."

A man with a white-painted face pops up with the suddenness of an apparition and whips out a life-sized puppet from a black duffel bag. He flips the switch to an old dusty radio. Fiddles and a Latin beat blast from the speakers. The puppet of a skeleton in a tuxedo mouths the nonsensical lyrics and dances down the aisle to the rhythmic music.

Kids on chairs and leaning against doors start clapping and shouting, "*Olé, olé, olé! Ooooooléeeeeeeee!*" at the impromptu performance.

The applause shakes the carriage's windows and seats. The music fades; the skeleton puppet vanishes into the black bag. Commuters reach into their purses and wallets for loose change as the train grinds to a stop. Those leaving give the performer coins and wait by the opening doors. In the middle of them stands the bald portly man, arms folded across his chest, unmoved by the struggle of the passengers, who battle to get on and off.

The next stop is yours. University students block the platform as they congregate and debate what to do next.

A metal bench provides an unconventional way around the congestion. You hop on the wide plank to pass the group, jumping down behind a middle-aged man, who manages the complex feat of walking and reading a book, at the same time.

Rubber tugs your skin as you lean on a handrail and let the escalator take you up. Certain aspects of life in Barcelona — the incivility of the people, the fits and starts to the day, an inability to accomplish the simplest task — pluck at the fraying threads binding your patience.

A girl on the escalator going down smiles, as if to say, *Tranquilo amigo, no pasa nada.* Life's not that bad. You're not stuck in traffic. A monthly ticket for the public transit costs less than a tank of gas. At least no one has asked, what you've done with your life or if you have a five year plan, just where you're from and whether you like the local food.

The rumble of the next train drowns out the sound of a cellphone hitting the ground, when you take out the ticket to pass through turnstiles before continuing up a steep set of stairs.

At street level the sun shines down on a mustachioed man in a white van. He lays on the horn, leans out the window and shouts at the top of his lungs, "I shit on your whore of a mother! Fuck! Come on, cunt! I'm in a goddamn hurry."

It's not clear who he's yelling at. It could be the car in front, the red traffic light or Gaudí's ghost. But, he's not alone. The street erupts into an cacophony of long, angry honks and shouts. But the only noise you only hear is a twang, as the last strings binding your patience snap, not into violence, but the phrase: "I've had it with this fucking place."

You feel a tap on your shoulder and turn to see a girl, a few years younger than you. She has an easy smile and holds out your cellphone with its shell. The locals might not give an centimeter of space on the metro or in an empty bar, but they'll hunt a person down to return something they've dropped, as if admittance into heaven depended on it.

"This is yours," she speaks in Spanish, but her blond hair and pale skin make her seem Northern European.

"Oh, *gracias*," you mutter, trying to recognize her accent. "Where are you from?"

"My father is from here and my mother is Galician." She squints and studies your face. "You look frazzled. Are you lost?"

You shake your head. "Just wandering around, looking for a place to eat."

"Are you visiting?"

"No. I live around here. I'm the *guiri* who sits at the table during a neighborhood fiesta."

She laughs. "Really?" her voice cracking with surprise. "How long have you been in Barcelona?"

"Almost a decade."

She raises her shoulders and nods in that very Spanish way, impressed by your longevity. "Meeting some friends for lunch," she says, brushing your arm, as all local women do when they speak. It's the touchy, feely Latin blood, nothing flirtatious. "Do you want to join us?"

If you had to sum up the majority of Spanish and Catalans in two words, it'd be hospitable and non-cynical, which in turn has made you more friendly and open to chance encounters. "Um, sure..." you shrug as they do, "why not? Always better to eat with pleasant looking company, right?"

She smiles at the compliment and leads the way.

"Here we are." She stops at a wrought-iron door. The black bars are bent into the outline of a vase with flowers. You've passed the building before but never entered. The girl buzzes and two seconds later, a longer buzz unlocks the ornate door.

Inside a sunny entryway, you look up to see a dirty glass roof atop five imposing stories and no elevator.

"Come on." The girl waves for you to follow as she starts up the first flight of short and worn steps. "It's only on the third floor."

The low ceiling of the shadowy *entresuelo* (between floors) forces you to duck at small doors of flats seemingly built for hobbits, not humans. The next set of steps leads to *la planta principal* (principal floor), with normal sized doors and no ceiling, bringing back the light from the dirty glass roof. Next is *la planta primera* (the first floor). The sputtering, spinning and wheezing of a drill seeps from a door-jam. The girl sees the twitchy look of agitation on your face and says, "Don't worry, just two more flights."

You fake a smile and continue up the stairs.

The restaurant, like many places in Barcelona, is a converted flat. Card-tables and folding chairs line walls decorated with local art. The nidor of fried fish, eggs and potatoes wafts from the kitchen, up your nose, the food flavored air aggravating the hunger in an empty belly.

At the end of the hall, glass-doors open onto an oasis of green space amid the surrounding stone buildings with wrought-iron balconies.

"*Hola*," the girl says to a middle-aged man behind a

makeshift bar.

"Hello, beautiful," he replies, never looking up from washing a glass to see if the adjective applies.

The two of you stroll past locals who sit at plastic patio tables. The volume of chatter and laughter shakes the air as birds sing in the branches of the trees, shading the cement.

A group stands from their chairs at three round tables, put together near a wall, and motion to join them. Everyone gives a quick peck on each cheek for introductions before a skinny boy in a Vans t-shirt says, "Welcome," in Spanish.

You smile at their hospitality and say, "Thanks for having me."

He frowns and shakes his head. "We're Spanish and Catalans, not English. You don't have to say 'please' and 'thank you' all the time. It comes across as insincere. What do you want to drink—beer?"

You nod to avoid offending him again. The boy cups his hands to his mouth and belts at the waiter, "Hey, come here!"

A silver-haired man arrives, looking like he'd rather be at the customer side of a bar counter, drinking brandy and coffee. He scratches the side of his nose. "What do you want?"

"More beer," the boy in the Vans t-shirt orders.

The grumpy waiter says nothing. He heads towards the patio doors, ignoring the couple with empty glasses and dirty plates, who bark and wave to get his attention.

The boy in the Vans t-shirt looks at you and asks, "Where you from?"

"America."

"America!" The blond girl who brought you shrieks. "Who would ever want to go there? Australia is much better. They are much more welcoming to foreigners."

"Have you ever tried to go Australia?" The boy in the Vans t-shirt comes to the US's defense. "You need a visa and the immigration officers don't speak any Spanish!"

"What the hell are you saying?" the girl retorts. "At least they don't have Bush."

"But he's not the president anymore." The boy's voice rises with patriotic pride, as if he is speaking about his own country. "Now they have Obama!"

A man in a Ramones t-shirt taps your shoulder. You turn away from the heated discussion about which country is more open, America or Australia, being waged by two *Barceloneses*, and nod.

"I went to Boston once." His wide eyes and bobbing head suggest that should mean something. It's not just the Spanish and Catalans, but Europeans in general, seem to think Americans have been to every major city in the US, not realizing the vast distance between them. The only thing you know about Boston is that it celebrates its Irish heritage three hundred years after the original immigrants crossed the Atlantic, unlike Barcelona, which has spent the last three decades trying to erase its centuries of Spanishness.

"Did you like it?" you ask, trying not to think about the region's one big negative: the small, vocal *Cataloonie* segment who see a conspiracy in everything and always shout about the greatness of the Middle Ages and the horror of life under Franco, as if those were the only two periods in Spain's history and nothing has changed.

"Yes. I love American music." The man in the Ramones t-shirt adjusts his nerdy glasses and claims REM (pronounced as in the type of sleep) and *Ooh-Dos* (U2) as his favorite bands. He states an emphatic hate of heavy metal and rap. He doesn't mention punk or *Los Ramonés*. "Do you know Spain very well?" he asks, once done sharing his unsolicited musical opinions.

You tell him about different places visited as the waiter arrives with brown bottles. "Haven't been to Madrid yet," you add, sipping cold beer.

"Why not?" Your conversation partner seems shocked and a little offended. "Madrid is a lot of fun. Do you like it here?"

"Where?" You need clarification. "Barcelona or Spain?"

The man in the Ramones t-shirt says, "Both."

Like most simple questions in life, the answer is long-winded and meandering. The truth is—feelings change, depending on that fickle aspect of our personality which governs our mood. "Prefer it to home right now," you say, not knowing where your gypsy spirit will lead in the future.

The bald man in glasses chuckles at the vagueness of the reply, but offers no follow-up question. "We like to party, no?"

It's your turn to chuckle. "Yes, you all do," you tell him, thinking of all the fiestas, from national holidays, like October 12th when Columbus set sail for the new world, to city only parties, like *La Merced*, honoring Barcelona's designated virgin, to regional celebrations, such as *La Diada* on September 11th, to the most epic of fiestas, *Sant Joan* [Ju-on], which kicks off summer at the end of June, with nonstop firecrackers and bonfires in intersections.

"How do you know everybody?" you ask, coming out of your wayward memories.

"We all went to high-school together," the man rubs

the patches of black stubble on a brown crown, "some of us since elementary school."

The only way you know friends from childhood is thanks to Facebook.

"We meet here every other Saturday," the man speaks when there's a pause in conversation. "I like this place."

The grumpy waiter returns with a stack of plastic plates which he drops at the edge of the table.

"You like Spanish food?" the studious looking man in the Ramones t-shirt asks.

The truth is you do, but it's not your favorite.

"It's better than American food, no?" he presses for an answer.

Everything has to be a competition with the Spanish, Catalans included. "It depends," you say, trying to relay the question is more nuanced than good or bad. "You eat a lot of fried food."

"Yes." His large brown eyes behind black-rimmed glasses don't blink. "But we use oil and not butter. But enough talk. Now is time to eat."

A new waiter brings a fold-out table that supports a massive round pan full of yellow rice topped with unpeeled seafood. The grouchy waiter comes back with dishes of more local delicacies.

"*Bon profit*," he says in Catalan, as everyone does in Barcelona, even native Spanish speakers.

"Eat, eat." The man in the Ramones t-shirt says, handing you an empty plate. "Do you know the secret of a good paella?"

You shake your head to admit ignorance and load a plastic dish with sliced blood sausage, cured ham and white cheese. The topic of conversation in unappealing. Your fingers have the dexterity of a toddler and can't peel the jumbo shrimps, baby lobsters and crayfish, without getting more fish juice on your hands and chin, than meat in your stomach.

"Patience with the rice." The man in glasses hands you a plate of paella he has prepared and says the famous Catalan phrase, "Eat well, shit hard."

Lunch starts with *Pa amb tomàquet,* a local version of Bruschetta served with almost all meals. The toasted bread sops up the stomach acids while the fresh tomato rubbed on top moistens the palate, with a bite of garlic and extra virgin olive oil.

You pick at the paella, avoiding the bug-eyed and clawed sea-insects. The man in the Ramones t-shirt was right about the rice, soft and sticky, without the slightest crunch or sogginess, a mouthful bringing the salty flavors of the sea and a visceral memory, of last weekend at a beach bar with dear friends who would have only met in Barcelona.

Most of the lunch conversation takes place in rapid fire Spanish, with a sprinkling of Catalan. Conversing in a foreign language makes it easy to lose track of the shifting topics, people and locations. Your capricious mind wanders to the serendipitous twists life in Catalunya brings. A satisfied smile lifts your face and spirits before you sigh, with contentment, and sink into the plastic chair.

An hour later, the round paella pan is empty save for a few kernels of rice and the peeled shells of seafood. The plates are gone and languor sets in as blood flows to a stuffed stomach.

A picture of an unmade double bed, with two pillows, takes shape in your mind. The time after lunch, especially on the weekends, is the one moment during the day when neighbors hold off on home improvements and Barcelona falls quiet, although not silent.

"That was good, no?" the blond girl who brought you asks, her argument about Australia versus America long over.

Your heavy head nods with slow blinks. "Thanks for inviting me."

"Enough with the please and thank you." She, too, it seems, has no tolerance for politeness.

You need to move before you pass out face first on the plastic table and stand on wobbly knees. The group of strangers, most of whom you haven't exchanged more than pecks on the cheeks with, look up and smile, as if you are the one who has made their lunch complete.

"Thanks for having me." What else are you supposed to say when you're grateful? "How much do I owe?"

You count off a couple of €5 bills that you pull from the wallet, carried in the front pocket, to keep cash safe from thieves.

The man in the Ramones t-shirt says, "Don't worry," throwing an arm around your shoulder. "It's on us."

"That's very kind." You toss money on the table, wanting to chip in your fair share. Lunch with the locals has changed the direction of the day and not for the first time. You owe the good people of Barcelona more than what you have in your bank account.

The man in the Ramones t-shirt and black glasses stuffs the cash back in your hand. "Please, don't worry," he says. "Just remember that not all Catalans are cheap."

"And just remember," you tell him, "Not all Americans like butter."

Other Books on Barcelona

A Short Cut to Paradise, Peter Bush

Barça: A People's Passion, Jimmy Burns

Barcelona Calling: A Novel, Jane Kirkpatrick

Barcelona Noir, Adriana Lopez, Carmen Ospina, Archy Obejas

Barcelona, Robert Hughes

Cathedral by the Sea, Ildefonso Falcones

Dead Man in Barcelona, Michael Pearce

From Barcelona, with Love, Elizabeth Adler

Homage to Barcelona, Colm Tóibín

Homage to Catalonia, George Orwell

Home to Barcelona: A Foreigner's Story, Richard Manchester

My Christina and Other Stories, Mercè Rodoreda

The Angel's Game, Carlos Ruiz Zafón

The Colour of a Dog Running Away, Richard Gwyn

The Secret Shofar of Barcelona, Douglas Chayka

The Shadow of the Wind, Carlos Ruiz Zafón

About Jeremy Holland

Jeremy Holland was born near Los Angeles, California, but spent his formative years in the Philippines, Saudi Arabia and England before returning to the US as a teenager.

After attending high-school, he like many others at his age, searched for what he wanted to do, including a stint with a brokerage firm in Silicon Valley and as a paid intern for Republican fundraising group near Washington DC. He then tended at a bar while going to community college before enrolling at liberal arts Occidental College in Eagle Rock California, to study Diplomacy & World Affairs.

Attracted more to the seedy side of nearby Hollywood than the causes of ethnic conflicts, Jeremy dropped out of university and began a succession of jobs in technology. Working in a cubicle only intensified his desire to follow his gypsy nature and seek out new adventures in exotic lands. A trip to Barcelona cemented his decision to leave his family and friends. He had found his calling. He wanted to follow in the footsteps of Hemingway, Orwell and others, move to Spain and become a writer.

In 2002, Jeremy returned to Barcelona with a blanket, a laptop and just enough knowledge of the local language to order a beer. Eight years later, he dreamed in Spanish with a sprinkling of Catalan and published *From Barcelona Vol. 1*. This edition expands on those short stories and offers a few more tales that peek at a life not found in the guidebooks.

Jeremy now lives in Alkmaar, the Netherlands, with his wife, their young daughter and cat who flees from the sunlight. To read more about his life in the Dutch cheese country visit his blog www.hollandfromholland.com. For more about Barcelona, visit www.frombarcelona.com.

BITTEN BY SPAIN

THE MURCIAN COUNTRYSIDE
— A BAPTISM BY FIRE

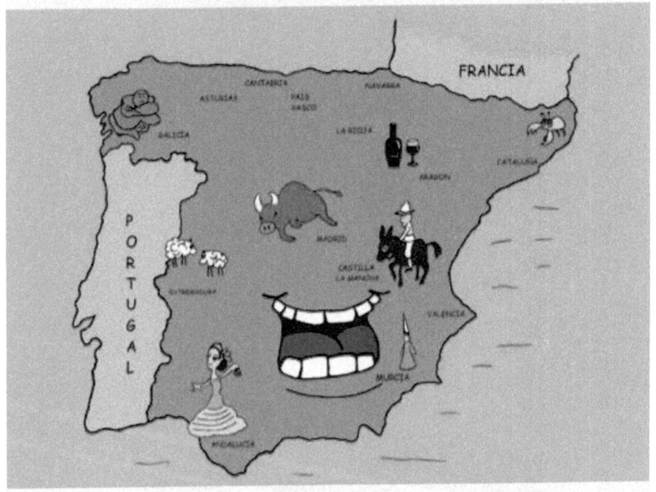

DEBORAH FLETCHER

… had me chuckling from the first page till the last"

Vanessa Rocchetta, Expatica.com

How to Buy
SPANISH PROPERTY
and Move to
SPAIN
SAFELY
NICK SNELLING

Matthew Hirtes

Going Local in
Gran Canaria

how to turn a holiday
destination into a home

The Thinking Tank

JAE DE WYLDE

'Sensitively written and delicately observed, an enthralling and suspenseful book that is literary but never difficult'
Leslie Ann Kesher, author, To The Manor Drawn

expat
bookshop.com
books by people living abroad
for people living abroad